BEFORE BETHLEHEM

A Novel

BY JAMES J. FLERLAGE

Published in the United States by DreamScapes Publishing Ltd., Cincinnati, Ohio.

ISBN: 0989828107
ISBN 13: 9780989828109

Library of Congress Control Number: 2013947520
DreamScapes Publishing Ltd, Terrace Park, OH

Website: www.beforebethlehem.com.

To schedule the author for a speaking engagement, public appearance, video conference, or teleconference, please contact DreamScapes Publishing Ltd. at www.beforebethlehem.com.

DREAMSCAPES
PUBLISHING

PROLOGUE

THE LOST LETTER OF JAMES THE JUST CIRCA 69 AD

Jerusalem is under siege.

Three days ago an army of Zealots numbering at least two thousand stormed the gates and attacked the city. Many friends and fellow rabbis are dead. My family and several others escaped to secret catacombs buried beneath the Temple. We're trapped like ants in these ancient tunnels of stone, but we're safe...for now.

Every passing day brings fear and uncertainty. The constant darkness adds to our misery. Yesterday we discovered a large store of candles, oil, lamps, and fire boards. Today one of the rabbis found a small enclave filled with large stone jars containing provisions, water, papyrus, ink, clothing, blankets, and scrolls that appear to be writings from our ancestors. The catacombs have no sewers or drainage, and the stench from human waste is unbearable. I fear that sickness and disease will kill us long before hunger or thirst.

My sons and I crouch over a long flat rock on which I draft the first of my letters. My oldest son, Joseph, holds the candle by which I write. He is named after my father, Joseph bar Jacob, the guardian of my half brother, Jesus. My younger son, Simon, keeps the papyrus stretched out flat so that I may write these words legibly. He is named after my oldest brother, Simon bar Joseph, who risked his life to shelter our family in Bethlehem, the year Jesus was born.

For decades I recorded the events our family witnessed throughout Galilee, Egypt, Samaria, and Judea. With the prospect of death before me, I have bundled these writings, each with its own letter. This scroll contains the story of one of the most painful periods in our family's history—the year leading up to the birth of Jesus. I was fifteen, old enough to be considered a man yet young enough to be in the care of my father. I have written down my family's sufferings as I saw them through the eyes of my youth.

The year before my brother died, he taught us with simple stories, and we remembered them. My stories shall be simple too.

—James bar Joseph

CHAPTER ONE

Around midday I heard the long high-pitched sounds of trumpets. The Sanhedrin, the Jewish high court, had condemned a young woman to death for the sin of adultery. At the sound of magnificent silver instruments, local merchants, artisans, moneylenders, Jews, and Roman officials trickled out from their homes and businesses onto the streets of Sepphoris to join the slow procession to the execution site.

I carried a pitcher of water to where my brother Jude, my uncle Clopas, and my cousin Simeon were mending a stone wall in the courtyard of a prominent merchant's home. Clopas shook the wet gray mortar from his hands and wiped them on a long piece of cloth tied around his brown leather belt. Father was repairing a joist on the second floor of the house. I heard the old wooden ladder creak as he climbed down. He came out to the courtyard, lifted the tattered hood of his tunic over his slightly balding head, and spoke gently through his thick beard.

"James," he called out, "you will come with us today."

Uncle took the pitcher from my hands and lifted it to his lips. After several gulps he passed the pitcher to Jude and wiped his mouth with his tunic sleeve.

"The boy is too young, Joseph," Uncle protested. "And we're behind in our work. If *you* want to go, then go."

Father walked over to where I stood. He looked down at me, stared into my young face, and ran his fingers through my black curly hair. His dark eyes twinkled like stars. He spoke softly and with certainty. "He is of age, Clopas. All the boys are of age. They've already seen the Roman crosses."

"But this is different," Uncle insisted. "The boys didn't have to witness the torture."

"Isn't the sight of a crucified man brutal enough?" Father asked.

Uncle frowned. "There is *no* reason for us to be there," he protested.

Two weeks earlier Roman soldiers had crucified more than a hundred Zealots associated with a minor uprising west of the city. The soldiers left the bodies to hang along the main road for all to see.

"Why are we shielding the boys from an execution conducted by our own people?" Father asked.

"We're not shielding them," Uncle mumbled. "They will see these things soon enough."

Father looked at us, staring straight into our hearts. I'm certain he caught glimpses of fear and uncertainty churning inside us like a flat wooden paddle in a bucket of warm goat's cream. I know Uncle hoped that Father would agree with him, but since Father was the older brother, the final decision remained his.

Father spoke to Uncle in a low, firm voice. "You and I know what is going to happen here today. The peace we long for will never be in our lifetime. If our sons do not see the things we have seen, how can *they* hope for change? If we are not here to teach them peace, who will?"

"If you take James, then you have to take Jude and Simeon too. And if you take Simeon, then *I* have to go. Frankly I'd rather we stay here and continue working."

My uncle rapidly stroked his thick brown beard, which was grayed by mortar dust. He closed his aging eyes and dropped his head to the ground. His lips formed a slight frown as he continued to talk. "I have witnessed enough violence in my lifetime to invite a thousand nightmares, Joseph. How can we *not* protect them from this?"

Father ran his hand through his hair. "Is not the terror brought about by our own people as frightening as Herod's?"

Uncle opened and closed his sore, wrinkly hands. He threw the mortar trowel onto the ground in disgust and placed his hands on his hips. He lifted his head, opened his eyes, and with a slow movement of his hand, motioned for Simeon, Jude, and me to join them.

We walked across two residential streets made of gray stone pavers to Decumanus, a street that ran east to west and served as one of the main Roman roads through Sepphoris. Decumanus ended at the eastern gates, where six hundred armed Roman soldiers stood guard. The Romans controlled Sepphoris, and because a Jewish court passed down the sentence, the soldiers forced the Sanhedrin to perform executions outside its protective walls.

The procession continued until the crowd was a mile outside the city. I was tired from our work. My steps were unsure, and I wobbled under the blistering August sun. My filthy tunic absorbed the sweat from my body like a sponge. The dust from the streets, whisked away by the strong gusts from the highland winds, matted against the damp wool cloth, clumping and drying before falling back to the earth as mud-hardened crumbs. I thought about the pitcher of water I had drawn the hour before and regretted not having taken a drink.

As we walked from one side of the city to the other, Sepphoris's Jewish upper class mingled with the lower classes. Roman citizens lined the streets, staring curiously at the crowd, while drunkards yelled profanities and merchants shouted about their wares. The noise settled like a fog on my ears, and I was relieved to see the gates ahead.

At the front of the procession was the condemned woman, surrounded by a contingent of priests, scribes, and elders. I looked at my father and saw that his lips were moving.

"Father, I can't hear you."

He looked at me then pointed to a row of thick, white stone columns that lined the street. "Do you see those children huddled together?"

The last two blocks of Decumanus contained the Lower Market, an area crowded with merchants who sold fruits, vegetables, livestock, cheap fabrics, and pottery. I glanced at one of the columns and saw four boys only slightly younger than me, along with two girls, in wasting human forms, barely covered in tattered tunics. One of the boys had his chest exposed; the round bones of his ribs pushed and stretched against the hungry insides of his thin brown skin.

"They're the *mamzers*, the silenced ones of Israel," my father mumbled. "Israel's unwanted children, marked by the sin of illegitimacy and cast out on the streets like rotten vegetables. They'll never see the inside of a synagogue, or learn to read or write or pray. I don't know how our people can treat them as inconvenient burdens, offering them up to the mouth of misfortune, like a mouse to a snake."

"Will they live, Father?"

He closed his eyes. "I pray for them, James."

As we passed by, Father tossed a denarius to the oldest boy, bowed his head, and kept praying.

Clopas looked at Father then at me. With a finger over his lips, he motioned for me to be silent. My head was full of questions, but I knew better than to disobey Uncle. I bowed my head in prayer and asked God to hear my father.

CHAPTER TWO

When we passed the city gates, the procession broke to the right to follow a Roman road that slithered around the aqueducts. A little ways off the road, a flat, oval-shaped limestone rock with the Star of David carved on its top protruded from the hillside. Some of the crowd dispersed around this stone; most split off and continued along the road, which curved to the left and down the hill.

To the right the hillside formed a natural cliff that dropped off twenty feet to the lower road. As the crowd made their way around the curve, my father and uncle took us to the edge of this cliff. The crowd looked up at us like sheep in wintertime, waiting for their masters to throw them grain, but the masters were about to throw them a human life. Father and I watched as a beautiful young woman was led to the execution stone. Clopas guessed the woman to be about sixteen—only a year older than me.

The hot August breezes blew against her thin homespun dress, outlining her girlish curves and tugging at her strands of long black hair. Tears wetted her pale face, causing the dust to form small trails around her high cheekbones. She shook with fear and anguish, as if violently shivering from cold, and her wrists were bloody from being tightly bound in rough horsehair cord.

A tall, thin man with short brown hair approached the priests. He pulled his arms inside his tunic and stood there, looking at the woman. A large older man, whom I later learned was the woman's husband, walked up behind the young man and jerked the top half of the tunic down to the man's waist. The young man let out a horrifying scream. Several of the women gasped, and my uncle turned his eyes away. Dozens of bloody crisscrossed lines covered the man's back, his mangled flesh oozing a yellow fluid from the ruptured scabs.

Father leaned down to whisper to me. "He received forty lashes for lying with the woman."

The young man walked over to the woman, knelt in front of her, and bound her ankles together with a piece of cheap twine. The woman groaned as the thin cord cut into her ankles. When he had finished, he stood and looked into her face, while a young scribe named Nicodemus read the Ten Commandments from the Torah. When the scribe was finished, the high priest, Rabbi Joazar ben Boethus, read the charges and announced the Sanhedrin's judgment.

While the priest spoke, my father looked at the small crowd gathered around us. The woman's parents and relatives, full of agony and grief, cried out for mercy. The mother, with a black headscarf matted to her tearstained face, collapsed in a pile of despair. Two young girls rushed to her side to hold her up.

My throat swelled at the sight of the mother's suffering. I had lost my own mother when I was eight, and at that moment, I missed her with all of my heart.

Father whispered again. "Someone will push this woman off the cliff. If she survives the fall, people will hurl stones from their hands and slingshots. When the woman is close to death, the priests may show her mercy by crushing her quickly." He pointed to a large a boulder next to the ceremonial stone.

Just as Father finished speaking, the priests and scribes moved toward the crowd, leaving the woman to stand alone.

"What are they doing now, Father?" I asked softly.

"She is unclean, so the priests will not touch her."

"What about the soldiers?"

"The Romans don't intervene in Jewish matters. They don't believe in our God and scoff at our rituals."

"Who will push her off the cliff?"

"The priests will force a sinner to carry out the judgment."

A short stocky man with a severely deformed face stepped forward from the crowd. As he walked toward the ceremonial stone, he glared at the scribes and priests with a crimson hatred. One of the young scribes tossed a bulging sack at him, which the man failed to catch. Several loaves of hard bread spilled onto the ground. The sinner bent over to pick up his payment and stuffed it into the sack. He picked up the sack, walked ten paces to the left of the woman, and set the sack on the dirt.

As the sinner approached the woman, she struggled against her restraints. She spat angry accusations at her lover and the Sanhedrin, but her words languished in hopelessness as the crowd watched the frivolous exchange between the scribe and the sinner.

Then I witnessed what Father calls *rachamim* or "mercy."

As the sinner turned around to walk toward the stone, he erupted into a run with his arms outstretched. He pushed the woman off the cliff without waiting for the command from the priests.

Father and Uncle gasped.

The woman's high-pitched scream drowned out the angry shouts and fiery protests from the priests and scribes. In his haste the executioner mistakenly pushed her off the cliff sideways. I heard sounds like twigs snapping in the wind as her body smashed into the ground. The crowd below threw small stones and pebbles at the woman's head and eyes. Her high-pitched shrieks became shallower as more stones struck her face and mouth. A gargled cry echoed up the canyon, but the crowd ignored her as they scrounged the earth for more stones. A handful of women covered the eyes of their small children and ushered them away.

The high priest stood over the scene, shaking his fists in rage. Robbed of his lengthy speeches and ceremonial duties, he sought to avenge his status by stoning the executioner. Uncle leaned over to Father and whispered, "He's gone." Father looked over his shoulder and nodded.

The crowd continued to throw stones while the uninterested high priest searched for justice as if it were a lost gem. He stomped among the crowd, shouting and cursing at our people. His threats were coated in venom; his words jabbed into us like a spider's fangs. A gathering of men shrugged and pointed to the trails that led up to and away from the city.

The high priest looked at the group of priests and scribes, who offered nothing more than empty stares. Nicodemus, the youngest scribe, pointed to the sack of hard bread that lay near the ceremonial stone. The high priest raised his hand in disgust, as if to say, "Leave it." When Nicodemus joined the bewildered holy men, the high priest motioned for them to congregate on the main road. Once all the priests and scribes were accounted for, the unceremonious Sanhedrin left the execution site.

Father began to pray. I was startled by what he said yet distracted by the loud moans that bubbled up the canyon walls. The woman was still alive, but nothing remained of her except a bloody pile of flesh. Over and over she called out to her mother, to her lover, and to God, for mercy. The woman's brothers heard her plea and pushed the massive boulder over the cliff.

CHAPTER THREE

The execution ceremony lasted two hours.

By the time we returned to our employer's house, it was time to clean up and return to Nazareth. I packed the last of the hammers and trowels in our cart, and we began the journey home. Uncle led the mule and cart through the streets, while my brother and cousin walked on either side to protect our tools from street thieves.

I walked behind with Father.

The trip home, which depended greatly on the weather and road conditions, would take a little more than an hour. During the summer we always had plenty of daylight to get us home. But in the winter, Father and Uncle would leave in late afternoon, in the safety of daylight, to protect us from the thieves and wild beasts that roamed the narrow trails at dark. We traveled in numbers for safety, and tonight four other families joined us. With the summer sun to our backs, we set out on the dusty trail that led to Nazareth.

We walked in silence through the gates and down the Roman switchbacks, but I knew Father would answer my questions once we were out of the city. We followed the old trail as it snaked around the rocky hills populated with cypress, olive, and palm trees. It was a clear day, so I could see across the valley. Uncle Clopas pointed out the bowl-shaped outline of Deborah's mountain. As we walked, Uncle recalled the great story of the

Naphtali tribe, their leader Barak, and how their army of ten thousand men defeated the Canaanites on that mountain.

The idea of God talking directly to one of our ancestors fascinated me. If he spoke to Deborah, could he speak to me? And if God ever spoke to me, how would I answer him?

Uncle told stories from the Torah with such enthusiasm that our whole caravan buzzed with talk. While the people around me were immersed in conversation, Father looked over at me and smiled. "James, do you think Barak was a hero?"

I nodded. "Yes, Father. I do."

"Why do you think that?"

"Because our ancestors won the battle and defeated the Canaanites."

Father grinned. "Is this truly your reason for making Barak your hero?"

Father always asked another question when he thought my answers were wrong.

I shrugged. "What do you think, Father?"

"I think Barak is a hero because he listened to God."

I thought about this for a moment. The wind passed through my hair like cool water, and I heard the crunching of the loose dirt and gravel beneath our sandals.

"Didn't Barak do what Deborah asked of him, Father?"

Father chuckled. "You're right, James. He did. But Barak also knew that God spoke not only *to* the prophet Deborah but also *through* her. Barak knew Deborah spoke on behalf of God, in the same way Moses and Elijah did. By following her commands, he was obeying God."

The idea was new to me, but I nodded in agreement. I hesitated for a moment before I asked my next question. "Father, may I ask you about the stoning?"

He cleared his throat and kicked a small rock out of his path. "You may."

"Why did they put that woman to death?"

He took a deep breath. "The law says that any husband who suspects his wife of lying with another man is expected to turn her over to the chief priests or he will be judged in the next life."

I had heard this law discussed at our synagogue in Nazareth but never understood its meaning. "But what if the husband falsely accuses his wife or his accusation is simply wrong?"

Father looked out toward the valley and slowed his pace. "Husbands are wrong about a lot of things, James. I have come to believe that parts of the law need to be changed. The law, as it is written, offers little protection for the woman."

His answer worried me. I was very close to my sister, Lydia, who cared for me after Mother died. She recently married and moved to Judea.

"Isn't my sister a child of God?"

Father smiled at me. "She is, James, and she is just as deserving of God's protection as either you or me."

I was pleased to hear this. "Father, if a woman takes another lover, why not put that man to death too?"

"In most cases the man *is* put to death. But certain interpretations of the law suggest that a man may confess against his lover as restitution for his sin. As part of his penance, he must endure forty lashings, but in doing so, he saves his own life."

The wind kicked up, filling my mouth with dust, and I spat on the ground. "This is all so confusing."

Using the sleeve of his tunic, Father wiped the sweat from his forehead. He spoke just loudly enough for me to hear. "It *is* confusing, James, and maybe now you understand why

I prayed all day. We don't always know if the man is telling the truth. We don't always know if the woman is guilty. The Sanhedrin may offer mercy to one but lack mercy for the other."

"If God made both man and woman, why not make laws that apply to both? Could some of the teachings in the Torah be wrong?"

As soon as I had spoken, I covered my mouth in shame. If my words flustered my father, he didn't show it. Instead he answered my question with another. "When Eve persuaded Adam to eat the fruit from the tree, did God spare Adam then banish Eve?"

"No, Father. He banished them both."

"Did God kill Adam and Eve?"

"No."

"Did God still watch over Adam and his family?"

"Yes."

At this Father said no more. We continued to walk for several minutes before he asked, "Do you have any more questions?"

I was scared to ask all the questions that were in my heart.

"Go on, James. You can ask me whatever you wish."

I cleared my throat and spoke softly. "Would God have put that woman to death today?"

Father looked at me with a gentle expression and a smile that reassured me. "You ask thoughtful questions, but I don't know what to say. No one knows the answer to that question. We can't know, nor claim to know, God's thoughts. What I do know is that when Abraham and Elijah asked God for mercy, mercy was shown. Even Noah and his family received mercy, as did Job, Jonah, and many other prophets."

"Is that why you were praying today? To ask God to show mercy on the woman?"

Father nodded. "I also asked him to show mercy on the young man, their families, all of us in the crowd, the priests and scribes, and the Romans. By taking part in her condemnation—by either doing something or doing nothing—we are all connected to this woman's death. God's people failed to show mercy today, and I hope he forgives us."

The sun cast long shadows on the ground. We could see Nazareth ahead of us, and our pace quickened. In twenty minutes we would arrive home, unload our cart, and sit by the fire to share our evening meal as a family.

I thought about the young woman put to death and the confusing words from my father's lips. My thoughts drifted to her weeping mother, her sisters, and the poor brothers who had to take their sister's life to end her suffering. Tonight, and for many, many nights to come, there would be an empty place by their fire.

Father saw me wipe my eyes and look away to the horizon and the blood-orange sunset. "What is it, James?"

"I feel sorry for the woman and her family. It made me think of Mother."

He walked toward me and put his arms around my shoulders.

CHAPTER FOUR

The gruesome images from the execution ceremony chased away my sleep like shepherds driving wolves from their flocks. And though we were all tired from a fitful night of rest, the ceremony had delayed our work.

My brother and I grumbled when Father woke us. We dressed and went outside to help him pack for the day. The Galilean valley was quiet and still, the warm summer air reminding us that we were in the middle of the dry season. It was still dark when Uncle Clopas and Simeon arrived. Uncle hitched the mule, while my weary brother and cousin loaded our cart with tools, water, and materials. Father had forgotten to pack our midday meal and sent me into the house to find the leather bag he had filled the night before. By the time I found it, the caravan already was moving toward Sepphoris, and I had to run to catch up with the others.

The city stood on a hill, four miles northwest of Nazareth. Travelers had to walk up the trails that led to the city, but the trails eventually became colonnaded roads used to move the Roman military. Its citizens, both Roman and Jew, provided more than enough work for families who made their living as builders, carpenters, and masons. As our group trudged up the main road, we watched dawn's pink and purple hues become the red-orange welcome of the rising sun. The buildings in Sepphoris were made of white limestone and shone like sparkles on the water.

We reached our employer's home just after dawn and unloaded the cart. To ease the growling in our stomachs, Father passed around a breakfast of brown dates and hard cheese. When we finished eating, we sipped water from sheepskin pouches and prepared for the day's work.

Our first job was to mix clay, straw, and slaked lime into a thick paste we used as mortar. Jude, Simeon, and I stirred the mixture while Father and Uncle gathered red sun-cured bricks to construct the courtyard wall. Father slathered mortar onto the wall while Uncle stacked the bricks. Throughout the morning, Jude and Simeon mixed mortar while I fetched bricks from the pile.

Two hours into our work, we heard hoof beats. Jude pointed to a cloud of dust several streets away. The sound grew louder as the mounted riders approached. Iron horseshoes pounded against the beige Roman pavers. The thunderous rhythm echoed off the white limestone buildings, creating the illusion that the entire Praetorian Guard was approaching. My heart thumped like a mallet against my chest as I watched more than thirty riders cluster together on the street near our employer's home. The men, dressed in scarlet tunics covered in black chainmail armor, wore bronze helmets and brown leather belts, with long swords sheathed in bronze scabbards fastened to the left sides of their belts.

Our employer, Marcus, was a short, plump, balding man in his late thirties who earned a successful living as a spice merchant. He waddled into the courtyard like a duck. The midmorning sun glared off his smooth head, and the cool morning breeze made his thin wool tunic flutter like a curtain. His thin mustache was upturned; his brown teeth showed signs of rot; and the pungent stink of his perspiration preceded him like the warning stench of a skunk. The sleep tunic stuck to his front, revealing a round, kettle-like belly. He rubbed his eyes and waddled closer to the courtyard wall, his stubby legs moving as fast as they could, his hips and backside jiggling with what Father called "his winter stores."

The riders came to a halt on the street that ran alongside the four-foot-high wall. A man with black curly hair and a gold crescent crown shaped like an olive branch guided a magnificent white horse to a section of the wall we had completed the previous day. He was dressed in a scarlet tunic and a deep-purple cape. The cape, covered with leaf patterns made of gold thread, hung from his neck, secured by a gold bird-shaped clasp. Like the other men, he wore tan breeches and sandals made of brown leather. His enormous horse was draped with a blood-red blanket, and he controlled the beast with reins made from pitch-black leather.

The Roman dismounted and headed toward Marcus, who was still rubbing his squinty eyes. The soldier approached the wall slowly, trading stares with my father and uncle. My brother, cousin, and I glanced fearfully at one another. Father was more than forty years old, but the Roman's smooth olive skin and soft facial features made him appear twenty years younger. He was of medium build and height and walked with such confidence that I thought he owned the city.

Placing both hands on the top of the wall, he leapt over it then stood in the courtyard with his hand on the gold hilt of his sword. Thin black brows lined the top of his face, and his glowing eyes shone like the silvery skin of an asp. There was something wild, something uncontrollable about his stare. It struck fear so far inside me that my hands quivered. I kept them at my side and struggled to remain still. The merchant knelt on one knee before the Roman and looked down at the ground. "My lord," he said softly.

With a booming voice, the leader ordered him to rise then turned around to look at my father and uncle. "Which one of these is the craftsman you employ?"

I held my breath as Marcus pointed at Father. "That's him."

The Roman walked over to Father and Uncle. Neither knelt before him but instead looked away to the horizon.

"Jews," the Roman snorted. Laughter erupted from the men on the horses, startling me. The leader quickly turned his head in my direction, as if I'd committed a serious offense. "Who is this boy?" he asked.

"He is my son," said Father. "His name is James."

"Your son?" the Roman huffed. "Are you sure he's not a slave? I have need of slaves in my work camps in Tiberias."

The men on their horses laughed. My insides quaked, and I almost vomited.

"He is my son. His name is James," Father repeated. "He is registered in the tax rolls in Bethlehem of Judea, along with the names of my deceased wife and the rest of our surviving children."

The Roman glanced at my brother and cousin and stepped in front of Uncle. "Who are you?"

"Clopas bar Heli," Uncle replied.

"A son of David!" shouted the Roman leader sarcastically. The soldiers on their mounts responded with laughter. The Roman took two steps to the right and stood nose to nose with Father. His voice deepened to a wolf-like snarl. "Then who are *you*?" The Roman leaned in toward him, but Father stared straight ahead. "*Speak!*"

Father licked his lips to moisten them. "I am Clopas's half brother, Joseph bar Jacob. My father died when I was young. My mother was taken in marriage by my uncle, Heli."

The Roman crossed his hands behind his back. "Then I presume your deceased father is Jacob bar Matthan?"

Father stopped staring at the horizon and looked directly into Roman's face. "He is," he replied confidently.

The Roman paced slowly. "I have knowledge of those on the tax rolls in Bethlehem. I have studied your Torah. I know all about your warriors, your prophets, your laws." Then he spoke in a sinister whisper just loud enough for those in the courtyard to hear. "And I know *who* belongs to the line of David."

While the Roman continued to speak, Father closed his eyes as if in prayer.

"I have read about this God of Abraham," the Roman said. "I am baffled by how you can believe in a god that continues to allow your kingdoms to be destroyed. Have you people gone mad?"

Another loud roar of laughter came from the mounted soldiers. Father and Uncle looked from left to right, as if counting the men and our odds of surviving a confrontation. Uncle returned his gaze to the courtyard wall. Father looked the Roman in the eye but ignored the comment. I couldn't understand why Father and Uncle would let this man say these things. Rage filled my heart, but at the same time, I felt scared and helpless.

When the Roman leader realized he could not provoke my father or uncle, he resumed his questioning. "Your reputation, Joseph bar Jacob, precedes you. Do you know this?"

"I do not," Father replied.

This of course was not true. Father and Uncle were known as two of the best craftsmen in all of Galilee.

"The great people of Sepphoris speak boldly about your skills as a carpenter and mason. Your master, Marcus, is quite pleased with your work and has told many in Sepphoris that he employs the best journeymen in Galilee. Some say that you build the finest structures in the region."

"I am humbled," said Father.

The Roman stopped pacing to look at him. "I understand you have other skills too, Joseph bar Jacob."

Father gave the man a slow nod. "I am also a metalworker."

"So you make swords and hilts!" shouted the Roman.

"I make wheeled carts, iron-tipped ploughs, yokes, horse-shoes, and furniture," said Father. "I have never made a sword, nor do I wish to learn how."

"Where do you live?"

"Nazareth."

"Are all of these boys your offspring?"

My father pursed his lips, stretched his neck, and leaned his head to one side. "Two of these boys belong to me, the other one to Clopas."

"Do you have any other sons, Joseph bar Jacob?"

"I have four grown children, two sons and two daughters. All are married. Some live in Galilee. Others live in Judea."

The Roman seemed satisfied with Father's answer. "You are telling the truth, Joseph bar Jacob."

"I have no reason to lie," said Father.

"And what do you do in Nazareth when you are not working in Sepphoris?"

"I farm, and I raise livestock."

"You own land?"

"I inherited a small plot of land from my father when he died."

The Roman lifted his head, surprised yet satisfied. "Joseph bar Jacob, will you seek the throne of Israel?" he shouted.

Some of the men on their mounts were archers. At this question ten of them knocked their arrows and raised their bows. Uncle looked at Father. He suffered from tremors, particularly when nervous or agitated, and the shaking in his hands was now visible. Marcus held his breath. Father cleared his throat and swallowed. His chest rose as he took in a long breath and, with a deep voice, made a declaration for all to hear.

"I am a journeyman. I am a widower. I work with my hands and labor with my back. I use my head for the Torah and my belt for my children!"

To hear this statement shocked me. Father never struck any of his children, in either the days before or after my mother's death. But the soldiers and the Roman leader laughed yet again when they heard this remark.

I looked over at Marcus and saw relief on his face. With a smug grin, the Roman leader nodded his approval of my father's confident response.

"Look around you, Joseph bar Jacob! I am rebuilding the city your ancestors destroyed! Twelve thousand people call Sepphoris home. We are a thriving city once more, known for trade, learning, and prosperity. We are a city of peace. But Sepphoris is merely a grand experiment. My plan is to move the entire provincial government from Sepphoris to Tiberias. The building program there is already five times the magnitude of the effort found here."

Such a building effort also required five times the amount in taxes. By the time my father finished his project for Marcus, he stood to lose more than half his earnings to taxes. While the Roman leader pontificated on all of his grand plans for Tiberias, Father remained unusually calm.

"Joseph bar Jacob, you are undoubtedly one of the most skilled tradesmen in Galilee. You have a reputation for quality and fairness that extends far beyond the province. Therefore I command you and your family to assist your Jewish brethren in building the finest synagogue in all the land. You are to report to the local authorities in Tiberias in four weeks. There you will receive your instructions and your wages."

I saw my father's eyes bulge, but his lips did not move. My uncle avoided the stares of the armed soldiers and tried to hide his tremors.

The Roman leader raised his voice once more. "Not only will I keep your hands and mind occupied, Joseph bar Jacob, but I also will keep my eye on these sons of David!"

More laughter came from the mounted soldiers, but the archers appeared ready to release their arrows. Father lowered his head and spoke meekly. "To work that far away creates a hardship on my family. I am a widower with children at home—"

"If you don't report to the Jewish authorities within four weeks, I will assume you have the political aspirations of your ancestors," the leader hissed.

Father spoke quietly but firmly. "I do not have political aspirations."

"Then you will report to Tiberias!" shouted the Roman.

Father, keenly aware that we were within ten feet of death, acknowledged the Roman with a quick nod. The Roman grinned, walked over to our employer, and handed him a small red bag, cinched at the top with gold yarn. Marcus opened it and pulled out a handful of gold and silver coins with the imprint of Caesar Augustus. I heard the bag clink as he kneaded it in his hand.

"For your trouble, Marcus," said the Roman leader. "If your workers cannot finish the job in four weeks, hire someone else."

The man nodded and knelt before the leader. The Roman ordered him to his feet then walked toward the wall and leapt over it. He mounted his enormous steed, glared at my father once more, and led his cohorts east toward Decumanus, in the direction of Tiberias.

Everyone in the courtyard stood motionless until the sounds of thundering hooves faded away.

CHAPTER FIVE

After the Romans left, we worked for the next three hours in silence then took our midday break. We reclined under the shade of a small cedar tree, at the far corner of the courtyard. I ran to our cart, which was parked in front of the house, and fetched the leather satchel of food. Before the meal we washed our hands using water stored in large clay jars near the house. Father prayed over the food then distributed the bread and salted fish. When each had eaten his share, Uncle Clopas passed around a leather bag of almonds mixed with dried grapes.

During our midday break, Uncle Clopas usually tested our knowledge of the Torah or building measurements or bartering practices. Father would question us about farming, such as which tools to use for certain jobs, when to plant our fields, how long to let grapes ferment, or the safest methods for collecting honey from wild bees. But today we ate in silence. Father and Uncle seemed cold, distant, and worried.

After passing around the almonds, Uncle finally spoke. "How will we earn a living, Joseph?" he asked.

"We will manage," Father answered.

Uncle continued, "The Jews in Tiberias earn the minimum wage and work alongside slaves. We won't have time to adequately work our farms. It's far too dangerous for our sons. There are stories that young men are being sold as slaves and that the Romans are afflicted with strange and deadly illnesses. We'll be cannibalized by the Jewish authorities who continue to subject themselves to the whims of Herod!"

Like waves lapping at the shoreline, Uncle continued to list the perils of our situation. Finally Father interrupted him. "That's enough, Clopas. Our family has endured tough times before. We will make the best of this situation."

"Father…" I said softly.

Uncle and Father turned to me. "What is it, James?"

"Who was the Roman we met in the courtyard today?"

"Antipas!" cried our plump little employer in a high, squeaky voice. He had snuck up behind us and was listening to our conversation. Since it was mealtime, I was thankful we were upwind from the man. He rubbed his hands together nervously. "Today you met the great Herod Antipas! My friends will not believe he was here. You must all be my witnesses. The great Herod Antipas visited my home. My business will *thrive* because of this!"

The man shook his fists in the air, as if winning a game of dice. As he did, the "winter stores" under his arms, on his hips, and around his legs also shook. Uncle cracked an upturned smile at the sight of this funny little man and his perceived good fortune.

I spied Father writing the symbol for *shlama*, or "peace," in the dirt. He lifted his head and spoke sternly to the man. "Do you realize he came here today to destroy my family? Then he would have burned your home and crucified you as a traitor for consorting with Jewish insurrectionists."

The man opened his clenched his hands, scowled at Father, then pointed a finger at him. "I spoke highly of you, Joseph! His Excellence came here today to give you a magnificent job!"

Father let out a deep sigh. He ran his fingers over the dirt to erase the symbol, stood up, and clapped the dust from his hands. He walked over to Marcus and stood face to face with him. "Marcus, I don't wish to appear ungrateful, but have you not seen the crosses beyond the aqueducts?"

"Those men were rioters, thieves, and looters. They threatened peace. The city can't survive another rebellion. It would be lost forever, covered by the sands of time. The king restored order and a sense of community and peace. He even sanctioned the rebuilding of the synagogues." Marcus spoke rapidly, as if arguing in front of a court. "With all the rebuilding, there's plenty of work for everyone and money to be made. We have plenty of food and drink, plenty of stores to trade, a new theater, and two major Roman roads that lead in and out of the city. Can you not see the good that's around you? Even you are profiting from these times!"

Father bobbed his head in agreement. "I *am* profiting at this time, but the Romans tolerate the Jews in order to collect taxes and control our leaders. The soldiers come to our homes in Nazareth and take what they want without asking. The Romans gain peace only through violence and fear, not by man's own accord and good sense."

Marcus shook his head in disgust. "I don't understand, Joseph. How can today's actions impair either you or your family? What good can come from resisting?"

Father walked away from Marcus, as if saying, "I've had enough," and sat down with us.

Marcus started to waddle after Father, but Uncle Clopas stopped him. "The Romans are drowning in a cesspool of greed, Marcus. They're thirsty for power. We are a simple, peaceful family with no such interest, yet Herod always will be infected with suspicion because we are of Davidic descent. His thoughts are haunted by the stories of King David, his ascent to power, and our people's hope that a messiah will one day come to rule over all of Israel."

"But are you *really* of the lineage of David?" Marcus asked.

Uncle nodded. Father spoke from his resting place under the cedar tree. "We are descendants from a line of very powerful Davidic kings, specifically Solomon. The messiah is supposed to come from my family's line. I would not be surprised if this generation of Herodians tries to kill off the descendants of David to preserve their kingdoms."

Marcus laid a hand against his plump cheek as he thought about what my father had said. "I can't see how this could be, Joseph."

Father shrugged. "Sending my family off to Tiberias to work for slaves' wages could impoverish our family so that we all go hungry. Antipas also will be able to keep an eye on everything we say or do. While we are away working, he might try to kill our families."

"Or us," said Uncle.

Marcus's eyes grew wide. Several seconds passed before he spoke. "What will you do?"

"I don't know," replied Uncle.

Marcus reached for the bag of silver and gold that he had tied to his belt. Through the leather bag, he rubbed at the coins, making them clink. Sadness covered his face like a dark shadow. His eyes fell to the ground as he folded his thick fingers together. He swallowed hard and stammered as the words tumbled from his lips. "Prince Antipas was in the Upper Market yesterday. His men purchased a cart, one Joseph had made."

The wind kicked up, and Father turned his ear to Marcus to hear him better.

"The man who sold them the cart also purchases spices from me. The Roman guards were impressed with the workmanship of the cart, said it was the sturdiest they'd ever seen. Prince Antipas had one of his guards inquire about the maker, and I told them the maker was doing building work for me. The guards asked me if I could make an introduction. In exchange they offered an honorarium that they would pay upon meeting you."

I looked over at Father, who was sitting cross-legged on the ground. He dropped his head sorrowfully and lifted his hands to his head. Clopas's face became red with anger.

"I'm so sorry, Joseph," said Marcus. He looked up at my uncle. "I'm sorry, Clopas. What can I do to fix this?"

Father rubbed his forehead with his thumb and forefinger. It was the same gesture he used when someone in synagogue argued a point with which he did not agree. A slight breeze tugged at strands of his long hair. He looked up a Clopas, then over at me, and smiled. He stood, brushed the dust from his tunic, and walked over to Marcus. He offered an outstretched hand as a sign of peace.

"There is nothing you can do, my friend. We'll need to find a way out of this mess ourselves. I know you were only trying to help, but it is probably best if you do not interfere any more."

Marcus rubbed a hand over his face. His eyes became moist, and his voice quavered. "What will happen to you and your family, Joseph?"

Father leaned over and picked up a trowel. "I'll go to work with my family in Tiberias. Our farm will suffer, but we will manage. The Jewish authorities there may be reasonable. I might even try to negotiate a higher wage, living expenses, or a shorter contract term. If there is one thing our father taught Clopas and me, it is how to negotiate."

Marcus lifted his hand as if he were about to speak, but a loud yell from the street interrupted him.

"Joseph bar Jacob!"

Father turned to see a young man in a ceremonial white tunic and blue robe. I recognized him as Nicodemus, the young scribe we saw at the execution ceremony.

"Shall I let him in?" Marcus asked.

Father winced. "Why stop with this man? You've let in everyone else."

Marcus waddled to the courtyard door and opened it. Nicodemus acknowledged him with a nod and strode briskly to where my father and uncle stood.

"Joseph, your presence is required at the synagogue for a meeting with Rabbi Boethus. You are to come at once. The matter is urgent."

CHAPTER SIX

Father threw his trowel onto the ground and put his hand on his hips. "I'm not going anywhere, Nicodemus. Tell the rabbi I'm behind on my work. I simply can't meet him today."

"Can you meet him tomorrow?"

Father walked away from Nicodemus and began collecting more bricks. Clopas followed behind him.

"You can't ignore me or Joazar forever, Joseph."

Rabbi Joazar ben Boethus, head of the Boethusian family and member of the Sanhedrin, was loathed by our Jewish community in Nazareth for being a Roman sympathizer. He supported both the Roman census and taxation, and used Jewish law when it was politically and personally convenient.

Holding a brick in his hand, Father turned around. "You're right. I can't ignore either of you." The corner of his mouth twitched, and he wrinkled his nose in disdain. "The Sanhedrin didn't have to condemn that young girl to death yesterday. Joazar could have stopped the execution. We both know this."

Marcus stood there fidgeting with his hands. As a merchant he was a skilled negotiator and accustomed to conflict. "Was the young girl innocent, Joseph?" he interrupted.

"She was caught in adultery!" protested Nicodemus. "There were witnesses!"

"Then the young man she was with also should have been stoned to death!" Father exclaimed. "Why was *he* not delivered up?"

Nicodemus crossed his arms. "You speak out of turn. I don't answer to *you*, Joseph."

"You will if you want me to see the rabbi," said Father.

Nicodemus looked at Marcus then at us boys. He deliberately lowered his voice, but we still could hear what he was saying. "The woman was seduced by the rabbi's nephew."

Marcus's jaw fell open. "And the nephew was spared but not the woman?"

Father and Uncle nodded. Nicodemus looked away in embarrassment.

"I will never understand you people," Marcus said with disgust. He pointed a finger at the scribe. "Whatever business this rabbi has with Joseph, he can take it elsewhere! He is busy here!"

"That's where we have a problem," said Nicodemus.

"What problem?" Uncle asked.

"You're working for a Roman."

Uncle walked over to Nicodemus. He was five inches taller than the scribe and towered over the man as he spoke. "Why should that concern you? We pay our Temple tax, our Roman tax, and our tithes, and we keep the Sabbath. What more do you want from us?"

Nicodemus tapped his fingers together. His dark-green eyes glared at us from under the deep-blue hood of his robe. He walked over to face my father. "The rabbi knows that Prince Antipas paid you a visit this morning."

"That doesn't surprise me," Father snorted.

"You're supposed to report to Tiberias in a month, Joseph. To disobey this order is punishable by death."

"We are well aware of this, and—" Uncle interjected.

"Hold your tongue, Clopas," snapped Nicodemus. "You may want to hear what I have to say."

Father looked at Clopas. Uncle shrugged his shoulders. We had much work left to do, and he knew that Father was physically tired and emotionally drained.

"Joazar possesses a tremendous amount of influence over the Jewish community at Tiberias. He may be able to suspend or even commute your work assignment, Joseph."

Father shook his head. "If Joazar has anything to do with this, then I don't want my family involved. Our lives are hard enough under the Romans, and I don't need to be embroiled in Roman and Jewish politics. I would be indebted to Joazar, and his debts are too difficult to repay."

"If you respond to his request, you'll be doing the rabbi a favor. *He* will be indebted to *you.*"

Father laughed. "Can you imagine a Sadducee indebted to a Pharisee?"

Nicodemus, who was also a Pharisee, tried not to grin. Uncle joined my father in laughter. Marcus just stood there, looking confused.

"If you accept the rabbi's request," Nicodemus said, "then you can't be in two places at once. You can't be in Tiberias *and* Jerusalem."

"Jerusalem?" My father sounded surprised. "What does Joazar need in Jerusalem that he can't get for himself? He is a Levite, is he not?"

"You'll need to come to the synagogue to find out," said Nicodemus.

Father dropped his head in defeat. I wanted to run over to him to offer him a hug and encouraging words, but I knew better than to meddle.

"Don't do this, Joseph," urged Uncle. "Joazar will find some way to cross you—"

"And I beg you," interrupted Nicodemus, "to ignore your brother. For the sake of your family and your livelihood, Joseph, please come with me. At least listen to what the rabbi requests of you."

Father leaned over and spoke quietly to Uncle. "Can you finish the work we started today?"

"I will try," Uncle replied.

Father walked up to Marcus. "You'll have to excuse me," he said.

"Take whatever time you need, Joseph." Marcus offered an outstretched hand, which Father took, and both men smiled.

Father motioned for me to come to him. "I will listen to what the rabbi has to say, but I want James to come with me."

Nicodemus stepped between Father and me. "That would not be a good idea."

Father spoke harshly. "My son is old enough to plough a furrow, herd sheep, get married, and fight in a war. He sits in our synagogue on the Sabbath, and during the week, he recites his lessons. Jude will marry soon and have a home of his own. At the very least, my actions will impact James. Whatever Joazar has to say, he'll have to say it to my son and me. There's more than just my own life at stake here."

Jude turned his head toward me, his cheeks flushed with envy. Simeon looked at me and grinned. Uncle motioned for me to join Father. As I walked over, I saw the reactions of the scribe and Marcus. Neither knew what to think of my father's assertions.

The scribe stared at me for what seemed like hours. Finally he motioned for us to follow him. "We need to go now, Joseph. The rabbi is waiting."

Chapter Seven

The morning's events were already more than my simple heart and mind could handle. And now I was walking with a scribe from the finest synagogue in Sepphoris. The three of us walked to Decumanus Street and headed west. We reached Cardo, the main north-south street, and walked north until we approached a small road that led to the synagogue that also served as Rabbi Joazar Boethus's home. The rabbi served a small wealthy congregation and as such was responsible for the most beautiful synagogue in Galilee.

I was already tired from a restless night of sleep. The worry and angst from today's events only added to my fatigue. Heat radiated off the stone streets, and the two-hundred-yard walk to the synagogue felt as if someone had caked my sandals in mortar. The scribe guided us through the Upper Market, where Marcus had boasted about my father. It was here where the wealthy could purchase expensive goods, such as rugs, jewelry, spices, and furniture, and inquire about tradesmen, physicians, rhetoricians, tutors, entertainers, and other professionals. I had been here many times, because this is where father often purchased lime, ash, and handmade tiles and glass for special projects.

A small crowd had gathered at the end of the market. One of the bystanders spoke to Father. "A slave stole a coin purse from an unsuspecting trader. As he tried to run off with the purse, he mistakenly turned down a street filled with Roman soldiers."

As we strode by the crowd, I heard a horrible yell then caught a glimpse of a long-handled sword being brought down on the slave's wrists. Blood spurted into crowd, inducing groans from the men and shrieks from the women and children. I looked for a reaction from either the scribe or Father but saw none. Father and Nicodemus seemed so painstakingly intent on ignoring the situation that it left my heart empty. Did this not matter because the man was a gentile? Did they think the slave deserved his punishment?

We approached the entrance to the synagogue from the south. Nicodemus opened a large stone door covered in a stained-glass mosaic that depicted the Ark of the Covenant. We followed him through a darkened corridor to a worship area that was the size of a courtyard and could comfortably hold more than forty men. The north and south walls were decorated with stone columns; the limestone floors were lined with ornate glass tiles and covered in two-foot-square mosaics that illustrated stories I knew from the Torah. There were pictures of Daniel's lions, Jonah's whale, Moses's staff and a serpent, vines of grapes, shocks of wheat, and a menorah. A lectern stood in the middle of the room, and to my right sat the Ark, where the Torah scrolls were kept.

Next to my mother, this synagogue was the most beautiful thing I ever had seen.

Nicodemus paused just long enough to allow me to view everything inside. He turned to Father and spoke. "Your son is lost in amazement. Is this why you wanted him to come along?"

Father looked at me and smiled. "James loves the Sabbath, listens closely at worship, and asks excellent questions. He appreciates the beauty in all things, and seeing a synagogue as grand as this will fill his heart and mind with wonder for many years."

The scribe looked at me and smiled. "Then it's good that he is here. Come. We'll converse with Rabbi Boethus in the courtyard."

If Father and the rabbi had business to transact, it never would have taken place in the synagogue, so we followed the scribe through another narrow hall until we reached the north end of the building. The scribe pushed on a door that led to a small patio with several small tables and chairs made for entertaining.

"Joseph bar Jacob," the rabbi called warmly. He approached my father, kissed him on the cheek, and offered a hug. He was dressed in a cloud-white tunic draped in a purple mantle and robes. He was a thin man of about sixty years. His white hair and beard were thinning, but the glare of his dark eyes was razor sharp. "I see you brought along one of your sons."

"This is James, my youngest. He still lives at home with me."

"The fine little farming community of Nazareth," said Rabbi Boethus. "How is Rabbi Ezra doing these days?"

The overly cheerful tone of the rabbi's voice made me wonder whether he had been saying his daily prayers in the wine cellar.

"He is doing quite well, Rabbi. I will tell him that you asked."

The rabbi motioned for us to sit at one of the little tables. Once we were seated, the scribe poured wine from a sky-blue glass pitcher into four matching goblets. After we all took a drink, the rabbi placed his goblet on the table and folded his hands.

"I understand that Herod Antipas visited you this morning."

Father set his goblet down and folded his hands like the rabbi. He grinned and simply nodded his head.

"You have been commissioned by the prince himself, have you not?"

"As you say," Father replied.

"Your business will suffer, Joseph."

"Yes, I know."

The rabbi looked at me. "How will this affect your family?"

"The prince expects Clopas and the three boys and me to report to Tiberias in a month. The wages in Tiberias are only a fraction of what we make in Sepphoris. The trip to Tiberias takes four to five hours. We will work all week and trudge home on Fridays to observe the Sabbath. After our travel expenses, tithes, and taxes, we'll have very little to show for our effort. The harvest also begins around this time. I don't how I'm going to manage it all."

The rabbi rested his chin on his hand. He was looking at Father, but I could tell he wasn't listening the way a man, or even a rabbi, should. Nicodemus, however, hung on to every word Father had to say.

"Our farms and homes will suffer from the lack of attention they need at this critical time of the year. We produce enough food to feed the widows and others less fortunate. If we're unable to contribute to the community stores, the whole village will suffer."

"Well, you're certainly a pious and charitable man, Joseph," the rabbi said in a patronizing voice. "We wouldn't want to deprive the needy of your generosity."

The scribe closed his eyes in embarrassment.

"I suppose you wouldn't," Father said quietly.

The rabbi took another drink from his goblet then spoke again. "I want you to do a favor for me, Joseph." Father lifted his head. "I want you to get married."

Father dropped his head in his hands and ran his fingers through his long, dusty hair. "Rabbi, I have no intention of getting married. I'm getting old. My son Jude will be married soon, and James is only a few years away."

The rabbi took another long sip from his wine goblet. "What if I could make Tiberias go away forever? What if you could continue to rebuild this city at a handsome profit, tend to your farm and children, and feed Nazareth's poor?"

Father pushed his wine goblet toward the center of the table.

"Rabbi, you have heard this man's case," protested Nicodemus. "It is the only fair and just thing to do. Absolve him from his duties in Tiberias."

Father lifted his hand, as if to say, "Enough."

"What do you want, Rabbi?" he asked.

"Your half brother's cousin, Rabbi Joachim, passed away two months ago. His wife, Anna, died the year before. He left behind a daughter who is now living with my family in Jerusalem. The girl is of marrying age, very beautiful, and a skilled seamstress and cook. She is also a virgin."

The rabbi repeated the five words again but more slowly. "She is also a virgin."

"I heard you the first time," Father said in a low voice.

Rabbi Boethus continued, "Joachim left a substantial dowry, one that includes land. There's also a purse full of gold and silver coins. You would have to meet me in Jerusalem and claim the young woman as your betrothed."

I never had been to Jerusalem. I fidgeted with excitement and took a small sip from my goblet in hopeful celebration.

"No," said Father. "I want nothing to do with this. I'm not using this woman as a bartering chip for a better life. My family and I will have to find another way." He stood up to leave.

My head turned fast, and my mouth opened slightly. I couldn't believe what I had heard. I was so lost in thought that I didn't stand up with him.

"Sit down, Joseph," pleaded Nicodemus. "You need to hear more of what the rabbi has to say."

Father sat down.

"Careful with your righteousness, Joseph," hissed the rabbi. "I hold the power to improve your life or ruin it."

Father gritted his teeth in anger, his eyes bloodshot. When a single drop trickled from the corner of his eye, I realized why he couldn't stand being in the presence of Rabbi Boethus. Father was a man who spoke with clarity and integrity. The rabbi, with his cunning ways and golden tongue, made conversations slippery, like olive oil on a wooden floor.

"But you don't know love," Father grunted. "I loved Salome. When she died I promised God I would dedicate my life to raising our children and caring for the poor. There is no proposition you could make that would be more worthy than what I have already offered. I have sacrificed my life, and now you threaten to take that away from me? How dare you!"

I was frightened by the way Father spoke to the rabbi and the look of disgust I saw in his eyes. Never in all my years had I seen him lose his temper. I knew he loved my mother, but at this moment, I felt just how much she meant to him. It was the first time I had seen him grieve in seven years. Father sat back in his chair and caressed his forehead with his fingertips. The scribe picked up Father's wine goblet and handed it to him. "Drink, Joseph. Take a moment to compose yourself."

We stared at Father, who did nothing more than look at the floor. He refused to make eye contact, even with me. Finally he spoke again, but the fire had faded from his voice. "I miss my wife. I loved her and only her. Having lived my life by the oath I made before God, I have also prepared myself for that day when I would die alone."

Nicodemus tapped Father's hand in compassion. There was a gentler look about his face. The rabbi, trapped by the compassion shown by the scribe, lowered his voice and changed his tone. "Joseph, I am sorry for your loss. Truly I am. But to keep your commitment to God, you must strongly consider this proposition. Go to Jerusalem and see this woman. See for yourself her beauty and vitality."

"And what do you get out of this, Joazar?" Father sneered.

To call a rabbi by his first name was not only improper but also insulting. It was as if Father were calling an asp from its burrow, or worse, picking up a scorpion by the tail. Even Nicodemus bristled at his assertiveness. The rabbi cast a sinister grin before answering, but Father stared him down with the weight of heaven and earth upon his shoulders.

"The Boethusian and Herodian families have a mutually agreeable relationship that helps us when dealing with the Romans. As you might assume, once Antipas becomes the king of Galilee and Judea, much privilege and power will be granted to me."

"And more control over Jerusalem and the Temple," Father grumbled.

"Perhaps," the rabbi concluded. He smiled disapprovingly at Father. "My dear brother, will you not consider my offer? Or can I count on you to stack stone blocks at my new synagogue in Tiberias?"

Nicodemus pulled his chair closer to Father. "Joseph, the young woman was offered to the Temple authorities as a gift to God. Joachim and Anna were old when they had her. It is

45

nothing short of a wonder that Anna lived through childbirth. The girl has been living in Jerusalem all this time, under the careful watch of the priests' wives."

Father stared at Nicodemus a moment before speaking. "Why did you choose *me*?"

Nicodemus rolled his head back and forth. He looked over at the rabbi, who gave him a nod of approval.

"You have a fine home, an excellent trade, and a reputable name," said the rabbi.

Father glared at him. "I don't know what your reason is for summoning me, but I will discover the meaning behind your actions."

The rabbi's words came fast and harsh. "Joseph, go to Jerusalem. If you marry the girl, I will see to it that your family doesn't have to work in Tiberias."

"I want our agreement in writing," Father demanded. "And if I choose to go and meet this woman, I want you to delay my report date by three months. I want time to harvest my crops and prepare my home and community for the coming winter."

Nicodemus nodded, as if favoring the proposal. "Then it is settled? You will go to Jerusalem?" he asked.

"Deliver the letter of agreement to my worksite today. I want it in my possession before I leave Sepphoris."

At that moment my heart leapt for joy. I couldn't believe we were going to Jerusalem.

The rabbi stood. Father stood. They gave each other the customary hug, but Nicodemus kissed Father on the cheek. Father's eyes darted between the two men. "Out of respect for her, and your request, may I ask her name?"

Rabbi Boethus cleared his throat and acted as if he did not hear my father.

Nicodemus turned nervously toward Father. "Mary," he whispered. "Her name is Mary."

Father inhaled a deep breath and let it out. He closed his eyes as if in prayer and waited for the rabbi to walk past him. Nicodemus walked up to Father and whispered something in his ear. Father opened his eyes and anxiously motioned for me to follow him.

I was frightened by this last part of the exchange. I was even more confused to see the rabbi walk in one direction while we walked in another. The scribe led us around the building, using a small footpath.

After walking about fifty yards, Nicodemus turned toward Father to speak. "When Joachim and Anna presented their child before the priests, everyone knew God had blessed them in ways we would never understand. It was the priests who insisted she be married to someone of the line of David."

Father leaned forward. "Why?"

Nicodemus stopped suddenly and leaned in to whisper to my father.

"Then my family is already in danger," Father said quietly. "She is a threat—a threat to King Herod and the entire Herodian family."

The scribe laid a hand on my father's shoulder. "Think of it this way, Joseph. In Tiberias you are within a spear's throw of Joazar and Antipas. If you go to Jerusalem, you'll have protection from the Temple authorities. You could also move away from Nazareth."

Father stroked his beard. "Is there any other way that Joazar can cross me or my family? If this is a trap to get me to leave Galilee, why not stay and fight?"

Nicodemus shook his head. "I don't believe this is a trap. But if there is trouble while you're gone, I will send word. I won't leave your family in danger if I can help it."

Father looked down at me. "What do you think?" Shocked by Father's call for counsel, I stumbled for words. He moved closer to me and looked into my eyes. "You are a man now, James. I want your opinion on this matter. It affects you too."

I had watched Father in his dealings with other men. When someone asked his opinion, he rarely answered right away. Sometimes he would ask for time to think and pray. In cases where a swift answer was necessary, he paused for a few seconds before responding. He used few words, spoke succinctly, and encouraged people to seek God in their quest for answers. In the end he always reminded the other person that he or she alone owned the decision.

I paused for a moment and, in the most confident voice I could muster, answered Father. "Our family has suffered greatly before, and things turned out all right. I would turn to God for guidance and protection, just like we always have. But this decision is yours. You should do what you think is right."

Nicodemus nodded his head and cracked a thin smile. "These are very wise and amazing words for such a young man."

Father's eyes became moist as he clasped a hand on my shoulder. "He takes after his mother."

CHAPTER EIGHT

F ather didn't speak during our walk back to the worksite. Lost in thought and deeply troubled, he seemed both anxious and sad. He was caught between two masters, Rome and Israel. Both had the power to take away his home, his livelihood, and even his life. If he defied Rome to serve Israel, he would be killed. If he defied Israel to serve Rome, both he and our family would be banished from our synagogue, or worse, killed by Zealots. After today's events I knew we were no longer insulated by the honesty of our trade or our simple lives in Nazareth.

When we entered the Upper Market, we passed the place where the slave had been punished for stealing. The only evidence of his punishment was a dark burgundy stain on the rock. I stopped for a moment and stared. There were no soldiers, priests, officials, or crowds of Jews or gentiles. Father walked up beside me. When I looked up at him, his warm sparkling eyes reappeared.

"What is it, James?"

"All that blood...all the screaming... The crowd was so large that not even a horse and cart could pass through the streets. Yet now there is nothing here to remind us of what happened."

"Why should there be? It is done."

My eyes began to water. "I know stealing is wrong, but it was horrible to see that man's hands cut off. How will he feed himself or work or put on his clothes or—"

"Put to memory the feelings you are having today."

I let out a long sigh and looked away to cry. My mind was like a jar overflowing with water. All I felt was fear. Father knelt to speak to me. He reached out and put his hand on my arm. "When we use violence as a currency to buy justice, it is like a man using his daily wage to buy bread. Once he spends his coins and eats his bread, he has *nothing* left to show for his labors."

I wiped my eyes, swallowed hard, and tried to speak in a clear voice. "This is all so difficult to understand."

He smiled at me. "You're using your head to ask the right questions. But *always* trust your heart to give you the right answers." Father stood up. "We should go now. I need to find the man selling ash."

I wiped at the sweat on my forehead, nodded, then followed him down the street.

We walked to an area of the market known to have Greek merchants. The ash Father used could be found only near the fiery mountains in Greece, and it was expensive. This purchase alone was one-fourth the cost of Marcus's project budget, but Father knew from past experience that Marcus would benefit from the investment. To Roman citizens such a costly luxury signaled financial success and divine favor.

At Father's request the trader loaded ten large leather bags onto a cart and followed us to the worksite. When we arrived, Uncle, Jude, and Simeon helped us unload the bags, which weighed more than thirty pounds each. We stacked the bags inside the stable to ensure that the ash remained dry. Tomorrow

Father and Uncle would mix generous portions of the ash with slake and mud to make a brilliant white paste. Covering the bricks with the paste would protect them from the wind and rain, and the white color would offset the light-gray limestone, accenting the home with an opulent magnificence.

After the last bags were loaded into the stable, Marcus toddled out of the house and into the courtyard to pay the trader. Jude, Simeon, and I found a place under the cedar tree and snacked on figs.

When Father and Uncle came out of the stable, Marcus called after Father. "Joseph, may I speak with you?"

Uncle was disgusted with Marcus. He grumbled, "It's getting late, Joseph. We need to leave soon if we are to travel with the others. I'll load the cart and hitch the mule."

Father walked toward the cedar tree. Marcus chased after him.

"James," Father called out to me, "please fetch some water while I speak with Marcus."

I stood and walked across the courtyard, past the two men, to the large stone jars that stored water. There were five of them in the shade of the roofline along the house. Each was approximately four feet tall and two feet wide. I lifted a heavy clay lid off one and dipped a small stone pitcher into the cool, clear water. When I returned I found Father vying for the bag of figs. My brother and cousin had made a game of trying to keep the bag away from him. Marcus laughed as Father raced between each boy, trying to catch the bag. By the time Jude relented and tossed the bag to Father, we were all laughing.

Father took several large gulps from the water pitcher and handed it back to me. He popped a fig into his mouth and handed me the bag. He wiped the sweat off his forehead with his sleeve and, through his chewing, asked, "So what do you want to discuss, Marcus?"

Marcus looked at each of us. His hands trembled. He laced his fingers and rested them against his round belly. As soon as Uncle walked into the courtyard, he motioned for him to join us.

As Uncle approached, he mumbled, "More bad news, Marcus?"

Father glared at Uncle.

There was a curious look to our employer's face, one of unsettling emotion. "I can't begin to tell you how sorry I am for what I have done to you and your family," he said.

"Marcus, we will be fine," Father said abruptly. "You did what you thought was in the best interest of our family. No one would condemn you for such honorable actions."

Uncle placed his fists on his hips and looked at the ground. He didn't share my father's empathy or compassion.

Marcus walked over to Clopas, reached under his own robe, and pulled out the red bag with the gold thread, the one he had received this morning from the Roman prince.

"Do you carry a coin purse, Clopas?"

"Yes, but it is empty most of the time."

Our employer smiled. "Open it and hand it to me."

Uncle looked at Father as if to say, "This man is crazy." But Father gave him a nod of encouragement. Uncle reached into his tunic and untied his coin bag. He pulled the pouch open and handed it to Marcus.

Marcus took the contents of the red bag and dumped them into Uncle's purse. The leather bulged under the weight of the coins. The purse was so full it wouldn't close at the top. Marcus shook the bag to make more room, and when the last of the coins had settled with a clinking sound, the round squatty man handed the leather purse to Uncle.

"There's enough gold and silver here to feed your families for a year. I want you and Joseph to have it." Father stepped toward him to protest, but Marcus lifted his hand to stop him. "I earn a living with my head. You earn your living with your hands. You may not always have your health or a strong back. Your risks do not always reap rewards. But you are a just man, Joseph. Please accept this as a token of my sorrow and concern. I never meant to put your family in harm's way."

Clopas looked at Father. Father looked at us boys. Our eyes bulged at the sight of all that money.

"Joseph!" cried a voice from the road. "Joseph!"

We turned to see Nicodemus, who appeared to be out of breath. Uncle, who still held the bulky purse, plunged it under his tunic.

"Nicodemus!" cried Father. "You are just in time. We're ready to leave for Nazareth."

The scribe, still breathing hard, leaned against the other side of the wall, draping his arms over the top. "The scroll is still on my table," he continued between breaths. "Rabbi Boethus left unexpectedly and has not yet returned. The written agreement is not yet signed, Joseph."

Uncle walked back to the cedar tree. He leaned over and whispered to me, "I told your father not trust him."

Father was still holding the water pitcher. He stared at Nicodemus from the other side of the wall and, in a gesture of kindness, lifted the pitcher to offer him a drink, which the scribe graciously accepted.

"We'll be here, tomorrow, Nicodemus," Father said as the man drank. "I expect you to have something to me by noon.

I want my family's protection assured. If you can't assure their protection, I'll join them in Tiberias so that I might look after their safety."

The scribe nodded, acknowledging Father's plea. He wiped the dripping water from his mouth with the white sleeve of his cloak and handed the pitcher back to Father. "I promise to be here shortly after daybreak."

"Then we'll see you in the morning," Father said.

Nicodemus turned and walked back up the street. When he was more than a block away, Marcus said, "I don't trust him."

Father stroked his beard. "I have to trust him. There is no other way to avoid Tiberias." He turned to face our employer for the final time. "You could have simply employed us for another project or referred us to one of your friends or neighbors. You didn't have to give us your reward from Prince Antipas."

"I realize now that this was never my money," Marcus said quietly. "It was your craftsmanship and your labors that were noticed. I acted the fool." He looked at each of us and smiled. "You still have a job to finish here. Now go, Joseph. Return tomorrow refreshed and ready for a new day!"

Father hugged the sweaty, foul-smelling man and chuckled.

Uncle handed Father the coin-filled bag. Marcus walked over to Clopas and offered him a handshake. When Uncle tried to speak, he found himself struggling for words.

"You're a hard worker and good man, Clopas," said Marcus.

Uncle stared at the ground and kicked at a pebble. All he could manage was a whispered, "Thank you."

CHAPTER NINE

It was dangerous to carry such a large amount of gold and silver. Uncle Clopas gathered all of us together under the cedar tree, lowered his voice, articulated his words, and spoke slowly. "Thieves break into homes. They kill the men. They violate the women. They take away the children as slaves. All in their search for treasures. No one shall be allowed to speak of this fortune."

With the coin purse buried underneath a cart filled with tools, we left the worksite, joined the caravan, and walked solemnly out of Sepphoris. While the other families celebrated the end of the workday with stories, song, and laughter, our clan remained suspiciously silent.

When we arrived at our home in Nazareth, Jude, Simeon, and I unloaded the cart. After we finished, Jude went to milk the goats; Simeon hauled water and gathered firewood; and I took the mule and cart to the fields, where Father and Uncle were gathering fruits and vegetables. Unless a family was overrun by death or debt, land was passed down to the oldest surviving member, usually a son. Father and Uncle had bought our land from a widow who had lost her family to the same type of fever that eventually killed my mother. Father had purchased the land with mother's dowry and some savings, and mother had agreed to care for the widow until she died.

The fields were about a hundred yards away from our home and divided into sections. Divvying up the land made our labors manageable and our yields easier to measure, and helped Father and Uncle prioritize crop irrigation. Each section was small enough for one person to tend but large enough to fill ten bushel baskets full of grain. At that time our family owned five acres of land. We planted grains such as wheat, oats, and barley. Our vegetable plots contained carrots, cucumber, watermelon, chickpeas, onions, and cauliflower. Some of our land holdings were on slopes or hills. We used these parcels for our vineyards, olive groves, fruit orchards, and almond trees.

I arrived in the east fields and began to load bundles of garlic and large watermelons that Father had cut from the vines. I looked to the west and saw him, fifty yards away, standing in the middle of a wheat field. He was spinning in a slow circle under the setting sun, his hands outstretched and palms down, the tips of his fingers barely touching the stalks of wheat. He wore a slight grin, and his eyes, tilted toward the heavens, were closed in prayer. I heard him chanting psalms. He must have sensed my presence, because he stopped, looked in my direction, and walked toward me.

"We will have a good crop this year," he said. He looked to the west. "Is that not the most beautiful sunset you have ever seen, James?"

I smiled at him. "It is."

We stood there watching the sunset for a moment before he said, "Your Uncle and I hid Marcus's gift." He spoke as he kept staring at the sunset. "James, if anything should happen to me, you need to know where we hid the money. It's a big secret to keep from your brother, cousin, aunt, and the rest of our family. Do you think you can do this?"

I did not answer him right away.

Even before Uncle had scared us with stories, I had heard horrible mention of thieves, soldiers, and corrupted men from Israel's own people, torturing men and their wives and children so they would reveal the hiding places of their treasures. The responsibility of knowing our secret hiding place would be one of the first important tasks I would undertake on behalf of our family.

"Father, will you tell Uncle that I know where the money is buried?"

He took in a deep breath, and after he had exhaled, he said, "I don't believe in keeping secrets from my brother. I will tell him at some point. Follow me, and I'll show you where the money is hidden."

I took the mule and cart and followed Father to a red-brick cistern located on the east side our fields, about sixty yards from our house. The cistern, which was hollowed out at the bottom and ten feet deep, stored water for irrigating our fields and gardens. Father picked up a four-gallon wooden bucket and lowered it into the three-foot-wide opening.

"In case anyone is watching, they will think we are getting water," he explained. "Are you listening?"

"I am."

"Do not look down, James, but the treasure is buried in a stone jar wrapped in a leather bag, right under the rock slab on which you are standing. If you are looking west as you face the cistern, the jar will be on your left. Remember, 'The jar points to Jerusalem.' You will need a spade to dig the soil out from around the rock and a masonry bar to lift the slab. Place a stone under the slab so that you can feel around for the jar with your hands. It's not that far under the rock, but give yourself several minutes to dig it out."

Father took the bucket of water out of the cistern, dumped a little back in, and said softly, "Marcus understated the value of his reward. Your uncle and I counted the gold and silver pieces as we put them in the jar. There is enough in that jar to buy several acres of land or feed our family for the next twenty years." He set the bucket on the cistern. "It's going to get dark soon. Please take this bucket of water to the orchards and pour it on the two new almond trees I just planted. Your tired uncle is gathering pomegranates on the north slope. I know you're exhausted, and I don't mean to add to your tasks, but you might take the cart and see if Clopas needs help."

"Yes, Father."

As I led the mule along the walking paths, it occurred to me that Father was most happy when he was in the fields. I was too. There was something about the soft earth stuck between our toes, and the sounds of insects buzzing and birds chirping, that created a sense of being at one with God.

I found Uncle sitting under a pomegranate tree next to a pile of ripe fruit, pushing red seeds into his mouth. He smiled and threw half a piece of fruit at me. "Help yourself, James. You deserve it after all the trouble your father put you through today."

We all had more than enough to eat, and our homes were cozy and comfortable. I was happy for our family's good fortune, but I hoped Uncle wouldn't bring up the subject of money.

"I didn't do much today, Uncle." I pulled some of the red seeds out of the wet pulp and dropped them into my mouth. The tangy sweet taste felt good in my dry throat.

"You did plenty, James. With Jude being married off in a few months, your father is running out of companions. Soon he will only have me to complain to."

I chuckled. It was Uncle Clopas who did most of the complaining in our family.

"We had better pack up this fruit and go home," Uncle said. "Your aunt will give me an earful if we're late to supper."

Uncle and I loaded more than three dozen pomegranates into the cart and headed toward our homes. I expected Clopas to talk about the day's events, but he, like Father always did, kept looking west at the reddish hues of the sunset. With labored breathing and a sweaty brow, we trudged our way back to unload the cart.

Aunt Miriam rushed out of my father's house to meet us. "Clopas, it's time for our meal, and we have a *guest*!"

"What guest?" Uncle replied.

"A scribe from the synagogue of Sepphoris," she announced. "He's in the house talking to Joseph!" My aunt, who always was excited to have company, hardly could contain her joy.

Uncle walked five paces away from her, mumbling, "I don't trust him. I don't trust him. I don't trust him." He threw a pomegranate high into the twilight sky, and I heard it land with a *thud* several yards away.

"What is it, Clopas? Why do you look so strained?"

"It is nothing. Did you offer him some wine, Miriam?" Uncle leaned over and whispered to me, "Maybe the wine will help his disposition."

"Well, of course I did, Clopas!" my aunt shouted. "I also put out a dish of almonds and a bag of raisins. He and Joseph are reclining at the table now."

Aunt Miriam had a bit of a temper, which didn't go well with her loud voice. Father had affectionately nicknamed her "the sieve," because even the best-kept secrets managed to sift through her like wheat from the chaff.

Uncle put his finger to his lips and scowled.

"And James," said my aunt, "the man inquired about you. Wash up, and change your tunic. There are several hanging out to dry behind the house. And put on your light-blue robe."

"Yes, Aunt Miriam."

When I entered our home, Nicodemus got up from his place at the table and greeted me. "You must be surprised to see me, James."

I bowed my head slightly. "It is an honor to have you as our guest."

Father nodded at me and smiled, quietly congratulating me on my hospitality. "Nicodemus will be staying for our meal," he explained. "Please take the place next to him, James."

I walked across the floor to a large table my father had made from an oak tree many years ago. Father had given the table to my mother as a wedding present. The table, now covered with food and candles, hugged the floor and was surrounded by square red cushions with purple thread.

"These are beautiful cushions," said the scribe.

Father smiled and motioned for Aunt Miriam to speak. "Please tell him the story."

Aunt Miriam spoke softly, her eyes focused on the cushions. "Joseph's wife, Salome, was my younger sister. The cushions were one of our first projects together as married women. We dyed the yarn we used for the cushion pieces red, using madder roots we grew in our fields. I wove the yarn into square pieces. Salome sewed up three sides, and together we stuffed the fabric with raw wool then sewed up the last side. The pretty purple thread we used to stitch the cushions together was Joseph's doing. He dyed the thread using mollusk shells he purchased in Sepphoris. It was a gift to Clopas and me on our anniversary."

The cushions still carried the memories and scent of my mother.

"What a beautiful story," the scribe said in a low voice. "I'll bet these cushions remind you of your sister, don't they?"

"Every day," Aunt Miriam said with a smile. "They remind me of all the good times we had together, caring for our homes and children. They were very happy, happy times indeed."

Aunt Miriam's eyes were moist with tears. She bowed her head slightly to indicate the end of the conversation. She went to the hearth, picked up several stone-carved oil lamps, lit them, and placed them near the table. Father invited Nicodemus to say a blessing over the meal. After a long prayer of thanksgiving, he blessed Father, Uncle, Aunt Miriam, Simeon, Jude, and me. When the blessing concluded, Father passed around the food.

The first plate he passed around held flatbreads. I took a piece and ladled some of the vegetable stew Aunt Miriam had made onto the middle of it. I scooped up vegetables with a flat wooden spoon while the broth slowly soaked into the bread. When the vegetables were gone, we ate the broth-soaked bread and mopped up what was left with dry pieces. When the stew was gone, we tore up the leftover pieces of flatbread and used them to scoop up mashed chickpeas mixed with olive oil. Aunt Miriam brought out several bowls of fresh vegetables, fruits, and nuts, all of which we ate with our fingers.

After the meal was over, Father poured each of us a small clay bowl of sweet wine. As I was about to take a sip, Nicodemus asked Father for permission to discuss a business matter. Upon hearing this request, Aunt Miriam fetched a large jug of wine, placed it next to Father, and left us men to discuss our business. Father looked over at me then at Jude, Simeon, and at last my uncle. We each nodded to Father to let him know we were ready to listen.

The scribe placed a five-inch-long scroll on the table. It had a blue piece of ribbon tied around the middle and two wax seals on either side. Next to the scroll the scribe placed a leather pouch that was the size of an apricot.

"Open the bag," Nicodemus ordered.

Father reached for the bag and pulled a clay ring from it. On top of the ring was a carving, a bird, like the one on the clasp worn by Antipas.

"It's a wax seal," Father said quietly.

"Not just any seal," said the scribe. "It is the seal of Prince Antipas. It proves that the proclamation in that scroll is authentic. It also proves that you're on official business."

"I shouldn't own this."

Nicodemus cleared his throat. "You have been called to perform a great service to your people, Joseph."

"But I'm not an agent of Rome. I'm serving the people of Israel by marrying a young girl orphaned by the death of her parents."

"The people of Israel are not the rulers of Palestine, Joseph. For us to afford you the protection you need, you must have possession of this seal at all times."

Father placed the seal on the table. He picked up the scroll and pointed it at the scribe. "What about God's protection? Will he not provide for me through your words alone?"

Nicodemus lifted his head, as if considering Father's point. "You're right, Joseph. God will protect you. But the Roman soldiers don't believe in our God. Consider these worldly things as being God's way of protecting you from *this* world."

Father looked down at the scroll in his hand. "May I break the seals?"

"No," said Nicodemus. "If anyone questions you, the seals must not be broken, lest people suspect the scroll to be a forgery. The scroll says, 'The family of Joseph bar Jacob shall remain undisturbed, so as to complete their duties on behalf of Rabbi Boethus and the prince of Galilee.' "

Uncle stared at the seal for a long time. Father looked at the scroll. Neither seemed sure of what to do.

"It's a Roman idol," Uncle said quietly.

The scribe held up his right hand to display a ring around his finger. It was the seal of Prince Antipas. "Look here! I write, seal, and deliver official correspondence for the rabbi and the prince. The seal is a tool of my trade, just like your hammers and trowels are considered your tools. They are *not* idols!"

"Does anyone else know we have this seal?" Father asked.

"The rabbi knows," said Nicodemus.

Uncle shook his head in disagreement. "It's a symbol of Rome, Joseph, of our oppression and suffering. God will punish us for even having it in our home!"

The scribe let his head fall into his hands and tapped the temples of his head with his fingers. When he spoke again, his voice was tinged with frustration. "Joseph, your condition for accepting this duty was the protection of you and your family from Prince Antipas. Refusing to accept the seal is foolhardy. You need to allow me to protect you in all the ways I know how."

Uncle looked at Father, who was stroking his beard, deep in thought. "Joseph," Uncle began, "I know this decision is yours alone. But our family is woven together by our fields, our faith, and our trade. We should discuss this together."

Nicodemus looked at Father with desperate eyes. He clearly had assumed that Father had made up his mind. While taking on a wife was an ordinary responsibility in the lives of our people, playing a role in Roman politics was an entirely different proposition. To carry the seal of Antipas meant that Father's *duty* was political, and we didn't know why. It was Uncle who realized that my father's marrying this girl could have unforeseen consequences for our family.

Father looked at me. "James, please show Nicodemus to Rabbi Ezra's home. The two of them can talk while our family discusses our situation. Clopas, please call Miriam downstairs. I want to consult with her too."

CHAPTER TEN

It took just minutes to walk Nicodemus to Rabbi Ezra's home. The rabbi welcomed him warmly and invited us both to come inside. I insisted on returning home. When I got there, Aunt Miriam had placed a basket of grapes and six pomegranates on the table. Uncle poured more wine. Father, who had not moved from his place at table, was still staring at the scroll and the seal.

When I took my place, he spoke. "Miriam, Rabbi Boethus sent for me while I was in Sepphoris today. He would like for me to marry a woman from Jerusalem."

Uncle's eyes darted to my aunt then to the rest of us, like those of a scared rabbit who scans the field for signs of a predator. He waited for a reaction from all of us. Jude looked at me, but I just shrugged.

Father stared at my aunt. "My wife was your sister. I want to know what you think of this."

Father didn't have to consult my aunt for an opinion, but he related to women in ways that were different than our custom. He had respected and honored my mother and her opinions, which often had bewildered the men of our synagogue. Father told all of his children, as well as the men who were to marry his daughters, that God created man and woman in his image. Both were equal heirs not only to God's kingdom but also to the blessings and misfortunes on earth.

Aunt Miriam, whose opinions on matters often included a raised voice and a clenched fist, sat quietly. She looked at her bowl of wine, swished it around, and raised it to her lips. She sipped a mouthful, set the bowl down, and folded her hands in her lap. "Your marriage to another woman would hurt me."

Father nodded. "Your sister was my best friend. She will always be my wife."

Aunt Miriam would be expected to help this woman, Mary, learn our family ways. She would have to teach her many things, such as how to grind grain, weave, milk, knead dough, prepare a fire, clean the home, cure our produce and meats, and possibly care for children. Aunt Miriam would be forced to spend many hours with this woman, whose very presence would be a constant reminder of her dead sister.

"The situation would be difficult for me, Joseph," she whispered. She took another sip of wine and spoke louder. "But if this is what the rabbi requests of you, then you must do it—if not for him, then for God. No one has ever suffered under your care, Joseph. And you are so generous with those in the village. If it must be, I will welcome her like an honored guest, and I will teach her everything I know so that she may be a good wife and mother."

Father replied, "I don't have to marry this woman, Miriam. I have a choice in the matter."

My aunt wiped the tears from her eyes with the heel of her hand. She reached for the saucer of wine, but her hand trembled as she raised it to her lips. Father looked down at the table.

After taking a long sip, Aunt Miriam said, "I am not my sister, Joseph. But I'm certain she would tell you that God is calling you to perform this duty. You must do what you are called to do. And I will support you."

Father looked up, then mouthed, "Thank you." He looked over at Clopas. "What do you have to say?"

"Why do you need the seal of Antipas? Since when does betrothal require a Roman seal and scroll?"

"Joazar said that if I marry this woman our family would be protected from having to work in Tiberias."

"And you believe that?" said Uncle.

"I asked for a letter of agreement. What Nicodemus brought us tonight ensures us of much more than that."

"It ensures Joazar's plans." Uncle pointed to the rest of the family. "It does not ensure your safety or ours."

"What else am I to do?" Father protested. "Do you want us to work in Tiberias?"

"Tiberias?" my aunt exclaimed. "Why would you work in Tiberias? It's time for the harvest, Clopas! What would we do about the harvest?"

Father sliced open a pomegranate as Uncle described the events of the day. Aunt Miriam placed her hand over her mouth and began to cry. Uncle reached over to hold her hand. Simeon reached over to hold the other. I sensed he was swallowing his own emotion, as he didn't like to see his mother upset.

When my aunt had calmed herself, Jude spoke up. "Who is the girl, Father?" he asked.

Father took a sip of wine. "Her name is Mary. Both of her parents are deceased."

"Who were her parents?" Miriam asked.

"Rabbi Joachim and his wife, Anna," Father replied.

Uncle's mouth fell open. "Joachim was our father's cousin."

The father to whom Uncle was referring was Heli, his biological father, and my father's stepfather. The legend of Joachim and Anna's pregnancy, and their divine favor with God, was a story that had circulated in the village for many years.

Aunt Miriam gasped and put her hand over her mouth. "The girl's life was dedicated to the glory of God," she exclaimed. "Where is she now, Joseph?"

"I don't know. Joazar wants me to go to Jerusalem, to the Temple, to speak with the priests there. But I don't have to marry her. I'm simply going out of duty and circumstance."

"If she is coming of age, then the priests don't want her to defile their homes," Uncle concluded. "It's one less mouth to feed. They're dumping her on you, Joseph, and if you agree to take her, it will demonstrate that Joazar is willing to compromise with the Pharisees. So what exactly is in this for you?"

"Nothing," said Father. "But we have the means to provide for her and protect her. And if it's true that she is somehow linked to our family, then I have an obligation."

My aunt grinned and nodded at Father. "You could have more children, Joseph."

Father smiled too and reached for a bunch of grapes. "Not with this woman. The Lord already blessed Salome and me with children, and for that I am grateful. But I am willing to provide a home for this girl, on the condition that she keeps to herself. If the legend is true, and she was dedicated to the Lord, then it is my duty is to ensure her safety and purity. With God's help, that is something I can do. Besides, she's James's age. The thought of lying with her does not agree with me."

The entire family sat quietly for several minutes before Father finally spoke again. "I won't proceed without my family's blessing."

Aunt Miriam dabbed at the corners of her eyes with her tunic. Clopas let out a long sigh and gulped down the rest of his wine. I looked at Jude and Simeon. Father's decision was his to make, but we were humbled that he had included us.

Finally Aunt Miriam spoke. "You have my blessing, Joseph. I will do whatever is required to make her a part of this family."

Uncle Clopas nodded in agreement.

Father said, "I haven't heard from the young men in our family."

Jude looked at Simeon. Simeon looked at me. I nodded at them both. Jude turned to Father. "You have our blessing Father," he said. "We are here to help you in any way we can."

As father glanced around the table looking for our approval, a storm of emotions moved within him. In marrying this girl, he would have to let go of my mother. Even though she had been dead for seven years, she was still a part of us. I could tell this would be the hardest part of God's plan for him.

"I am a servant of God," he said softly. "Please pray with me."

It seemed a very long time had passed before Father finished his prayer, but it was the finest prayer I ever had heard. He asked for all the things he would need to make good decisions; he asked God to bless our family, our crops, and our labors; he asked for blessings upon Marcus and his family as well as Nicodemus and Rabbi Boethus; he asked for Mary's heart to be opened to the possibility of a new family. Then he asked God to protect each of us. As he finished he gave glory to God, opened his eyes, and looked over at me.

"I have made my decision. Please summon Nicodemus."

CHAPTER ELEVEN

When I returned from Rabbi Ezra's home with the scribe, my family was gathered at the table. Uncle poured everyone a bowl of wine. Father invited Nicodemus to sit. When Nicodemus noticed Aunt Miriam seated with us, he tilted his head and furrowed his brow. Discussing business around a woman was forbidden, but it was Father's house, and this was how he wanted things.

Once everyone had been served, Father began to speak. "Nicodemus, I apologize for making you wait. We discussed many things, including Rabbi Boethus's proposal."

The room collapsed in silence. Neither Aunt Miriam nor Uncle Clopas would look at the scribe. I kept my eyes focused on Father, who was twirling the seal on the table. He returned the seal to its leather pouch and set the scroll beside it. He looked at Jude, Simeon, and me. "Anything you want to say?" he asked.

No one spoke. Finally I got up the courage to say, "Go on, Father. You may tell him."

The scribe turned to look at him.

"I agree to marry the girl in Jerusalem."

The scribe let out a long breath and smiled. "Very well," he said.

Uncle Clopas looked up to see the expression on his face, but Aunt Miriam did not. "What should I do once I reach Jerusalem?" asked Father.

"Go to the Temple. Seek out the man in charge of the Temple guard. He will direct you to Rabbi Boethus's home. This is the house where Mary is staying."

"Very well," said Father.

"Joseph, you should leave for Jerusalem at first light. The sooner you betroth yourself to this girl, the sooner Joazar can help Antipas forget about you, your family, and your mission in Tiberias."

"I intend to pack first thing in the morning," Father replied.

"Will you be traveling alone?" asked the scribe.

"No. Jude will help Clopas with our building projects and the farm. He is very close to marrying a girl from Nazareth. I suspect he would want to stay behind, if only to spend time with her."

The men chuckled and looked over at my blushing brother. Jude grinned and nodded at them respectfully.

Father looked at me. "James will accompany me."

My insides quaked. Beads of sweat formed on my brow. I could see that Jude was conflicted by Father's decision, but surely he knew Father was right. Jude had the strength and experience to help Uncle with the farm. Plus Leah, the woman to whom he had shown an interest, would be devastated if he went on such a treacherous journey before their betrothal.

Nicodemus smiled in satisfaction. He looked around the table at our faces glowing in the candlelight, glanced to the ceiling, as if to the heavens, and with a low voice, said, "Let us pray."

We bowed our heads.

"Our God," he began, "bless these people, and the instruments of our work, so that we may use these things to do your will. Look favorably upon these your servants so that those they meet may know your glory. Protect Joseph and his family, his lands and crops, and all the work you have given his hands to do, and remain with them all the days of their lives."

When Nicodemus concluded, he reached out, picked up the scroll and the seal from the table, and placed them in my father's hands. Uncle took a deep breath as the seal touched Father's palm, and though it was a warm, humid night, I shivered when my father took hold of the seal of Prince Antipas.

Father poured more wine for everyone. "Nicodemus, I expect you will be staying with us tonight. There are thieves on the roads; the warmer weather allows them to keep to their mischief. I have slept as many as twenty upstairs. There is more than enough room for you."

"Thank you, Joseph. Yes, I will stay."

When we had finished our wine, Father encouraged us to get to bed early. Aunt Miriam, who was preparing sleeping arrangements for everyone, came down from the room upstairs, wished Nicodemus a pleasant evening, and accompanied Uncle Clopas and Simeon to their home next door. Jude went outside to check on the livestock while Father and the scribe made small talk. I collected the remaining bowls and the empty pitcher and placed them by the fireplace for Aunt Miriam to wash in the morning.

When Jude came in, Father was still talking to Nicodemus. Father called him over to the table. "Jude, I assumed that your preference was to stay here so that you could be close to Leah. If you want to go to Jerusalem, you may. You are the older brother."

Jude smiled. "She's not my betrothed yet, Father."

I was stacking wine bowls when Jude looked at me from across the room. I glanced at him but acted as if I were distracted by my work. Jude continued to speak. "I have never been to the Temple. But you're right in asking me to stay. I can take care of the farm by myself and help Uncle finish our work in Sepphoris."

I added, "Your girlfriend will be pleased with your choice." I glanced up to see my brother scowling at me. Both Father and the scribe laughed heartily.

When the laughter subsided, Jude excused himself and went upstairs to bed. I finished stacking the dishes, and Father called me to the table. "My son has a skill for remembering things, Nicodemus. I have taught him, as best I can, to read from the Torah. He also knows how to write a few symbols. He never would say this out loud, out of respect for me, but I know he desires to learn more."

"James," began the scribe, "How would you like to learn from the priests at the Temple one day?"

"I would like that very much," I said.

"Maybe I can help your father find the right person to teach you," the scribe offered. "Would you like that?"

I nodded enthusiastically and smiled.

Father recognized early in my childhood that I had skills for learning. Rabbi Ezra often suggested to him that he send me to tutors in Sepphoris, but Father wanted more for me.

"Well, Joseph, we will have to rise early tomorrow if you're to meet the caravan from Sepphoris. I've arranged for you to meet them outside of Nazareth. You will travel with them through Peraea, along the Jordan and into Jerusalem."

"Will the trip last long?" Father asked. "With a small group of men, I can make it to Jerusalem in four or five days."

"Traveling by caravan is safer, Joseph, but it may take five days, if not seven."

"Then we'll pack enough clothing, food, and drink for ten." Father swallowed the last of his wine and set the bowl on the table. "James, you should go to bed. We'll leave just before daybreak."

I stood, nodded respectfully at the scribe and my father, and climbed the ladder to the second floor to go to sleep. Jude was already asleep and snoring. I kicked at him to get him to roll over, and when he did, the snoring stopped. I found my straw mat in the corner. I lay down to the soft rumblings of the voices of Father and the scribe as they continued their conversation. I barely could make out what they were saying, but as soon as I closed my eyes, my thoughts drifted to the adventure tomorrow morning would bring.

I imagined what the Jordan might look like: the shimmer of its surface, the smell of wild honeysuckle and irises along its fertile banks, the towering poplar trees, the sounds of trickling water. As my imagination wandered between sunlight and darkness, I imagined our camp by the river and the warm fire that would heat my body while I slept. I tried to deepen the colors of my thoughts, and as the sound of rushing water grew louder, my mind drifted off to sleep.

CHAPTER TWELVE

Before we met up with the caravan, Father issued a stern warning. "For our own safety, James, don't discuss the purpose of our business. If anyone asks, tell them we're traveling to Jerusalem to observe the Day of Atonement and celebrate the Feast of the Tabernacles."

It was late August, and the Day of Atonement and the Feast of the Tabernacles were three weeks away. With the harvest approaching, I knew Father had no intention of staying in Jerusalem long enough to observe these feast days. If he was willing to resort to deception to carry out what he believed to be God's will, then I knew our lives were in terrible danger.

The trail we took out of Nazareth intersected with a road that went northwest toward Sepphoris and also southeast to a land known as Decapolis. It was at this crossroad that Father and I joined a caravan of traders. With emotional hugs and handshakes, we parted ways with Uncle Clopas, Simeon, Jude, and Nicodemus.

Our caravan reached the Jordan River at midday the following day. The shoreline faced the city of Bethabara, which means "place of the crossing." We forded the waist-high river with carts, donkeys, mules, and a large group of men numbering about forty, plus women and children. We passed through Bethabara, purchased food and other supplies we would need for the next few days, and continued to the small town of Pella, where rabbis and several villagers welcomed us.

We spent Sabbath eve and day in Pella and left the following morning. Father was friendly and gracious to everyone we met, but we kept to ourselves when we could and spoke few words to our travel companions.

As the trip continued, Father occasionally patted the inner pocket of his tunic to ensure that both the scroll and seal were still there. Each time he did, the pit of my stomach ached with the worry that we might need them in order to stay alive. Without the seal, the high priest's words written on the scroll might mean little to a Pharisee. Without the scroll, the seal would make Father look like a Roman sympathizer, which was the worst possible thing that could happen to someone in a region filled with people who hated Rome.

Our fellow travelers talked incessantly. We learned that most of them were from a large family of salt traders. Their mining operations, which began in the Judean city of near the Dead Sea, ended at the family's vast market in Jerusalem. Their annual Galilean trip occurred in August, just before the harvest, when farmers would need salt as a preservative for meats and vegetables. Once all the salt stores had been traded or sold, the family would hurry back to Jerusalem to prepare for the spike in demand that came from the September feast days.

For three days we walked along commonly known trade routes that crisscrossed the river valley. Every so often Father told me a story about our ancestors and their ties to the river— of Abraham and Lot, Jacob and Joshua, and the many battles our people had fought on both sides of the river.

"The Jordan is more than oasis," Father explained. "The waters, and the plants and animals that surround the river, have been a wellspring of life for many generations. The Jordan is a gift, a beautiful reminder of the one and only God who is our creator."

And beautiful it was.

Mountains surrounded the river's lush green valley. The landscape made me feel confident and secure, as if God were standing right there beside me. When a trail led us close to the river, I heard the sound of rushing waters as whispers from our ancestors. Father walked with a slight grin and a twinkle in his eye, mumbling prayers and repeating verses from the Psalms. Occasionally he identified animals for me, and other times he named the birds, trees, plants, and flowers.

Though Father had been here many times, our journey along the Jordan River was an occasion of personal renewal for him. Throughout our trip he told me stories about our family, recited lessons he had learned in synagogue, and described the things we would see once we arrived in Jerusalem. Anxiety never left us, and the trip was hot and tiring, but I savored every word my father spoke.

On the last night of our trip, we camped south of the village of Adam. After our caravan finished the evening meal, Father and I left for our campsite. We inventoried our supplies, fed and watered our mule, and pounded tent stakes into the rocky soil. When we finished, Father filled our water pouches from a heavy stone jar he used to transport our drinking water. After covering the jar, he secured it in our cart with pieces of twine made from animal hair.

As we worked, he warned me that the most treacherous part of our journey was still ahead. "Jerusalem sits on a hill surrounded by valleys and mountains," he explained. "To reach the city, we will ascend the foothills to the Mount of Olives and then travel beyond the valley, past the eastern entrances. A man could use the eastern gates, but with all the carts and animals, it is better for us to enter the city from the north. The trail we will take from the Jordan River covers a rocky and barren wasteland. If we ford the Jordan successfully and have a safe journey through the valley, we should be in Jerusalem by tomorrow afternoon. You'll need to be mindful of the rocks and be sure of your footing. A man can twist an ankle or fall and break a leg if he is not careful."

When we finished securing our tent and supplies, Father walked ten feet from the tent and cleared a small circle of barren ground. With a small shovel, he dug a shallow trench, six inches wide, around the circle. I gathered sticks and dried shrub brush in my arms and placed them in a pile near the fire ring. In the middle of the circle, Father stacked a small mound of dried grass and placed several sticks over the grass.

He walked across camp to one of the fires used for the evening meal, scooped several hot coals into his shovel, walked carefully to our fire pit, and dumped the coals onto the sticks and grass. The grass smoked as flames began to lap at the sticks. When fire caught the end of a stick, the whole stick became in engulfed in flames, and Father placed larger sticks on top of the smaller ones. Within minutes a fire lit up our campsite.

A breeze swept over the Jordan, cooling the camp. The moon shone brightly, and the sky was full of stars. Without the threat of rain, we could sleep outside the tent and enjoy the cool breeze. We unrolled our sleeping mats on the ground, near the fire, and sat down. Father tossed me a leather pouch of raisins, and I snacked on them as I stared into the crackling flames.

"What beautiful stars," Father said as he looked up at the night sky.

I grunted in acknowledgment and continued to chew a mouthful of raisins. I passed the pouch back to him and swallowed hard. "Father," I said softly, "may I ask you something?"

He nodded.

"I love our home and our farm, but I don't always care for the work we do. Why build things when we can just farm?"

Father emptied the last of the raisins into his hand and popped them into his mouth. He grinned at me with closed lips. "Being a tradesman is hard work," he said after chewing. He tugged at a bug bite on the top of his ear. "Trust me, James. I have often asked myself the same question. For one thing our family would be idle for half the year, with nothing to keep our hands and minds busy."

He stood up to stretch and walked five paces behind us to a small pile of branches and sticks I had gathered earlier. He picked up three limbs as thick as his thumb and broke each one of them over his leg. As he laid the sticks over the fire, he spoke. "The trades we perform allow our family to earn coins, which we can use to pay our tithes and taxes and trade for things we cannot grow or make for ourselves. The coins also pay for tutors, physicians, and other services we need. In the years past, whenever I had leftover coins, I saved them so that I had a dowry for each of your sisters."

Father walked to the cart and came back with a leather pouch of dates. While he snacked on dates, I poked at our fire with a long stick. After a few minutes, I said, "You could trade goods, like these people. Marcus trades goods, and you are definitely smarter than he is."

Father laughed when he heard this. "Well, I am glad you think so, but I am not so sure Marcus would appreciate your assessment of him."

I smiled and lowered my head. I could tell Father was not interested in this idea.

"You're right about one thing, James. You certainly can make more coins as a trader, and you get to journey to many different places. However, most of the traders I know have to live in the city, and they always seem to be traveling away from their families. Marcus complains that his work never stops. He constantly worries about running out of spices to sell or having his home robbed or being cheated by tax collectors."

Father let out a long breath through his nose and took a drink from his water pouch. He swished some around in his mouth to clean the raisins out of his teeth and spat it on the ground. He took another drink that that filled his cheeks. He swallowed the water and continued to speak.

"Rabbi Ezra has often told me that our trade pleases God. He says that many of the prophets and wise men of our ancestors toiled their way through life doing humble jobs. I can't speak for your Uncle Clopas, but I think earning a living as a tradesman *and* as a farmer is a blessing. We have two skills, and both provide us with what we need and plenty of leisure. We are able to leave work at the end of a day and enjoy the things that keep us centered on our family and God. Compared to most men, we have few worries."

Father stopped talking to take another drink then passed the pouch to me.

"A tradesman is not always concerned with schedules, commitments, or money," he continued. "He keeps his own hours, picks his own clients or projects, and most of the time, makes a profit for what he crafts. When I was a young man about Jude's age, my stepfather said, 'If you have enough to eat, enough to wear, and enough to give, then yours is a blessed trade.' I would have to say he was right."

My thoughts drifted to the possibility of studying at the Temple. I wondered if I would forego my chances for learning and, like my father, become a tradesman and farmer. Maybe God would allow me to do all three.

We felt a summer breeze wash over us as we listened to the crickets chirp. Then Father said, "It's still early. Do you have any more questions?"

I wiped a thin layer of sweat from my forehead then backed away from the fire to cool off. I was troubled by my thoughts about the day in the Upper Market. I poked my stick into the dying flames, trying to figure out where to start.

"I have more questions about the man who got his hands cut off."

"Go ahead," Father said, without looking up.

I cleared my throat and spoke softly. "Why did you and the scribe not look at the man? We walked right past him."

Father ran his fingers through his long dark hair twice before he looked at me. "As you get older, James, you will see things that will haunt your memory for years. You will witness violence and suffering, probably more than I. It seems that every time our people protest or revolt, the Romans end up crucifying, spearing, burning, boiling, and ultimately killing anyone in their way, including innocent people."

He looked up at the sky then down at the fire. He took off his brown sandals and leaned back on his hands, his legs outstretched and his dirty brown toes inches away from the fire.

"You may have to watch the people you love suffer or be put to death at the hands of the Romans. I have seen more than my share of brutality, and so has Nicodemus. This may come as a surprise to you, but we choose to ignore violence that does not concern us."

I shook my head in despair. "I don't understand this."

Father swallowed hard. The sparkle in his eyes was gone, replaced by the reflection of the flames. "A man's eyes can see only so much injustice or violence. It's like when we are gathering grain from the threshing floor. What is it that I tell you?"

"Don't overfill the baskets, or we will lose part of the harvest."

Father nodded. "And when you see grain that you worked so hard to cut and gather spilled onto the ground, how do you feel?"

"Very sad, as if I have wasted something precious God has given us."

"James, when your eyes have seen as much violence as I have, your soul feels like an overfilled basket. You cannot see it, and you cannot touch it, but the pain you feel is real. When I don't have to see violence, it is as if I have kept the basket from overturning."

Father let those words sit with me, like fresh egg yolks dumped into a pot of boiling water. His next words were said so quietly that I almost missed them. "Sometimes you become numb to watching horrible things. You know what you are seeing is terribly wrong, but on the other hand, you are so grateful that the situation is not affecting you or your family."

Father's statements were very difficult for me to hear. Twice in the last week, nightmares had overtaken my sleep. I couldn't get the images of the woman being stoned to death out of my head, and now Father was telling me my eyes would be windows to a cruel and violent world. I now understood why Uncle Clopas didn't want to witness the stoning. I also wondered whether my father's heart had hardened too much over the years.

I took several swallows of what was left in Father's water pouch and handed it back to him. I said no more about the man who had lost his hands. As the fire collapsed into coals and smoke, one last question burned in my mind.

"Father, I overheard some people in the caravan arguing about Samaria. Some say we should have avoided crossing the river. Others say we'll need to cross it again when we reach the city of Jericho. Why did we cross the river in the first place?" Father motioned for my poking stick, and I handed it to him. He used the stick to collect the hot coals together. The summer breeze had turned cooler, and there was a slight chill in the air. We heard the sounds of people laughing, talking, and telling stories, and from a distance, we saw the dark outlines of women herding children into tents. Father stared into the fire. He broke the poking stick in half and threw it onto the coals to give us some light. As soon as the sticks touched the coals, they popped and crackled.

"You have heard of Samaria before, James?"

"I have heard people in our village talk about it. They say that it's close to Galilee and that evil people live there."

Father nodded. "The first part is true. It *is* close to Galilee. The second part troubles me. I'm not so sure that the people there are evil. But don't share my views with your uncle or Rabbi Ezra."

"Why did we have to cross the river?"

"Some believe the Samaritans don't hold fast to the laws of Moses. Others feel they have shaped the teachings of the

Torah to fit their way of life, rather than bending their lives around its teachings. By crossing the river, we avoided traveling through Samaria to keep us clean and pure so that we can enter the Temple."

I picked a couple of lice out of my hair and scratched my head. "Why not simply ignore them while traveling through Samaria?"

Father let out a long yawn. "We are taught, as they are, to avoid each other at all costs, even if it means avoiding each other's lands." He straightened his sleeping mat. "One day I would like to visit Jacob's Well, but it is in the heart of Samaria. I fear I may never see it in my lifetime."

Father stood and walked to our cart and tent. He placed the water pouch in the cart, inspected our supplies, and checked on our mule. When he was satisfied that everything was ready for our journey tomorrow, he joined me near the waning fire.

"Are some problems too big for God to fix?" I asked him.

Father began to babble quietly to himself. "I never understood why we couldn't find ways to heal our differences. It seems as though we've never really tried. David managed to unite all of us. It was only after Solomon that the tribes split up again. Maybe there will come a day when another leader will rise up and join the tribes of Israel once more." He looked over at me. "I didn't mean to ignore your question, James." He looked up at the yellow moon as he spoke. "God created the heavens, the seas, the sun, the moon, the mountains, the rains, the animals, and man. Whatever problems man designs, simple or complex, God already knows how to solve them."

Father said no more.

We sat in silence for several minutes. Finally he let out another long yawn. "We should sleep. We're close to Jericho, and the caravan is hoping to get an early start tomorrow morning."

The fire, now reduced to a mound of ash, smoked out. Father and I lay down on our mats, covered ourselves with wool blankets to keep off the chill, and stared at the heavens above us. The night sky was clear, and the stars shone brightly. From the northeast to the southwest, I saw what looked like wisps of white clouds, like long strands of cotton, weaved throughout the stars.

I closed my eyes for only a second before falling into a peaceful sleep.

CHAPTER THIRTEEN

We forded the Jordan River at a shallow crossing just north of Jericho. I was disappointed to learn that we wouldn't be going into the city. The Jordan became wider and deeper as it flowed south, and our caravan leader didn't want to risk losing any possessions, people, or time.

From a distance I made out buildings and the city walls, and while I stood in awe at the sight of Jericho, I imagined Joshua's warriors storming the city. Until Jerusalem it would be the largest city I ever had seen.

I stared across the river, which was much wider now, and wondered if it would be shallow enough to cross, or if it would swallow me up like an Egyptian trying to cross the Red Sea. Father must have sensed my fear. As we took our first steps into the water, he struck up a conversation.

"James, what do you remember about the story of Joshua's battle at Jericho?"

"The priests traveling with Joshua carried the Ark of Covenant around the city once a day for six days. On the seventh day, Joshua's army marched around the city seven times. When Joshua commanded them to yell, God used their battle cries to break down the city's walls. Joshua's army stormed the city, destroyed everything and everyone, and defeated the Canaanites."

"Very good," Father said, smiling. "Have I ever told you the story of Achan, one of Joshua's soldiers at Jericho?"

I shook my head, keeping my mouth shut to avoid swallowing a gulp of muddy river water. The water was up to my chest, and I was holding a leather satchel over my head to keep our midafternoon meal from getting soggy. I loved the stories about warriors, and despite these distractions, I listened intently.

Father cleared his throat and projected his voice over the sounds of the rushing river. "Achan was a soldier, a handsome man with a large family, much land, many possessions, and the most gifted warrior in Joshua's army. But before Joshua stormed Jericho, God told him no one was to take any spoils of war. Joshua gave his army the order, but his command angered Achan, for it was the spoils of war that had helped him build up his land and possessions."

Father paused. With one hand on the bit of our mule, and an eye on our cart, he looked over our own possessions to ensure they were secure. At first I didn't notice that we were approaching the middle of the river. Once I realized the middle didn't get any deeper, nor would it swallow me up, I relaxed some. I kept my ear tilted in Father's direction.

"What happened next, Father?" I asked impatiently.

"Oh, you want me to continue?"

"Father, please!"

He laughed and said, "Well as you know, the trumpets sounded, the people cried out, and the walls of Jericho fell. Joshua took half the army and went one way into the city, while Achan took the other half and led them in the other direction. They killed all the Canaanite families but one."

"Rahab's family," I interjected.

Father nodded. "But there was also an Israelite family killed that day."

"Whose?" I shouted over the Jordan's waters.

"There used to be a small town near Jericho called Ai. Joshua sent three thousand men to take over a city of three hundred, but they were defeated. When Joshua asked God about his defeat in Ai, God said that it was his punishment for taking spoils from Jericho. "

"But Joshua ordered his men to avoid taking anything from the city," I protested.

"Eventually he learned that Achan took treasures out of Jericho."

The roar of the river diminished with each step. The waters became shallower, and walking became easier.

"What happened next?"

He looked at me with a stern face. "Joshua had Achan and his entire family executed for taking the spoils of war, even the women and the children."

I looked away, stunned beyond belief.

A moment later we were climbing the other side of the bank. I helped Father with the mule and cart, and we joined the others on the road that would lead us to Jerusalem. My whole body shivered, and I didn't know if it was because of my wet clothes or hearing of Joshua's cruelty. I felt dizzy at the thought of my family being killed for something I had done.

By the time the caravan reached the shoreline, we already had started up the trail to Jerusalem. I took a drink from my water pouch and tried to focus on the steep hills ahead. A mile into our journey, I said to Father, "That wasn't the ending I expected."

Father was tired from crossing the river. He labored under his breath as he spoke. "What surprises me is that Achan was the only soldier who disobeyed God. Personally I'm grateful that the whole of Joshua's army followed his command."

"I see things differently," I pleaded. Emotion raided my words. "God protected Achan and his family and gifted him with a sound mind and a warrior's spirit. I don't understand why Joshua would kill him after one mistake."

Father waited for a moment, allowing me to regain my composure. "You're always willing to show mercy, James. I'm grateful that God has gifted you with a sense of compassion. I can tell you wish to side with both the leader in Joshua and the warrior in Achan. Both men had desirable qualities. However, if God's commands can go unheard like whispers in the wind, it means even good men can succumb to desires of the world. God's way is always good, and I hope you never have a heart that stops listening to him."

"Then how does anyone know when to listen?"

"Hopefully we're listening all the time, James."

Was I always listening to God? Sometimes I barely could keep focus enough to listen to Father or Uncle, let alone God.

Father sensed that I was confused. "This story ties into the discussion we had last night." He wiped the sweat from his forehead. "Our days are not consumed by our livelihood or a quest for money or things. We make time for one another and for our friends and neighbors. We rejoice in the home we have, the community in which we live, and the synagogue where we worship. And not only do we have time to listen to God, but we also *make time* to listen to God."

I nodded slowly and took time to think about Father's point. After a few minutes, I said, "Your words are beginning to make sense to me."

He winked at me and smiled.

The trail to Mount Olivet steepened. As our caravan continued its ascent, Father and I stopped talking. I felt a dull ache grow along the lower part of my ribcage as I struggled to catch my breath. I was hot, sweaty, and thirsty, and the dust from the desert caked the inside of my mouth. I spat on the ground in disgust.

If I had been alone, I would have been lost by now. When we were children, Father had taught us how to keep our sense of direction by locating the sun in its course or the stars in the sky. But these twisting paths were disorienting. I listened to the rocky ground crunch under my sandals, and with each step, I grew tired and weary. Thirst grabbed hold of my body like a screaming child to a mother's skirt. There was a gnawing inside my heart and a sloshing in my stomach. At one point I wanted to cry. There was nothing beautiful about this place. The hills and mountains were everywhere and threatened to devour us. The sun baked me like bread in a stone oven, and I felt empty and alone.

The children cried, and the older ones complained. The mothers tried to shush them with sweet dates and water, but they grumbled that the water was warm and had an unpleasant taste.

"The waters of the Jordan have quenched the thirsts of many," said Father. "But in these times, many people and animals cross the shallow parts of the river, making the water there unclean. This is why I filled our jug from the well in Adam. You are to drink only from that water. Don't drink water from the shallows of the river."

There was a strange smell to the river, and the water had swirled to a deep, bark-like brown from all the people and animals crossing it. Around midday many of the people who had drunk the river water were overcome with stomach pain. Some vomited; others soiled their tunics and skirts. I watched as people all around me become sick. I heard their retching and flatulence for hours.

The sounds made me sick to my stomach. I felt as if my breakfast of nuts, dates, and dried bread could bubble up at any moment. I stayed focused on the trail; sipped cool, clean water from my pouch; and kept my feet moving in rhythm with my breathing. The trail ascended until we reached a plateau, and just when I thought I would have to sit down to rest, our caravan stopped.

Father pointed west, and I saw, in the distance, for the first time, Jerusalem, the holy city of David.

"You are on Mount Olivet, James. This is the mountain on which our ancestors are buried."

I heard Father, but I was too caught up by the magnificence of Jerusalem. The white limestone walls that surrounded the city glistened in the sunlight. Sepphoris was a speck on a hillside compared to Jerusalem. I saw trees and lush green spaces at the foot of the mountain, but most impressive of all was the sun in a westerly course, sitting like an orange ball over the city.

"The Abode of Peace," Father said quietly.

Everyone in our caravan paused to look at the city. Many of the women whispered prayers. Some of the men prayed too. The older boys simply stared. While I stood there, peace washed over me. My aches and pains disappeared; my stomach relaxed; and my spirits lifted. Then I noticed a thin trail of smoke rising up from the city toward the sky.

"Why is there smoke coming from the city, Father?"

"The smoke is coming from the Temple." He pointed at a large structure. "The smoke comes from the incense and sacrifices offered there. That's where we'll be in a couple of hours."

The trail into Jerusalem provided a view of the city for the rest of our walk. I wished Jude were here to share the experience, and for a brief moment, my heart filled with sadness as I thought about my family. Right now they would be finishing their work at our master's house.

I realized that Father and I would be sleeping in a strange city, under a blanket of fear, without the comfort and security of our family. Camping along the Jordan was an adventure, but now that we were here, I remembered the reason for our journey. We were no longer in the safe, fertile valley of Galilee. We were in Judea, where both Herod and Rome were not only feared but also despised, and Zealots terrorized the Jews by killing sympathizers.

Father heard my sniffles. "What's troubling you?"

"We've traveled such a long way, and to see Jerusalem is amazing."

I kept my response short and curt, trying to hide my emotion. I didn't want Father to think I might become a burden this far from home.

He grinned and spoke with reassurance. "Whenever I travel I always miss home at moment when I want to share something with my family. The journey along the Jordan is amazing, but to enter Jerusalem for the first time is an experience you wish you could share with everyone. It's especially moving for me, because our ancestry is tied to David."

I nodded but didn't look up.

"James, look at me." I swallowed hard and looked up at Father. "I'm pleased to have shared this experience with you. You are a fine son." He smiled then laughed loudly. It was as if he could sense my realization. "God has blessed us in many ways!" he announced.

A murmur of agreement erupted from the caravan. I shucked the sadness from my heart like husks from an ear of corn. My spirits lifted; my heart rejoiced; and I listened with both ears as Father talked with excitement about what we would see at the Temple.

CHAPTER FOURTEEN

*G*od's power went ahead of his people, and they claimed victory on *Mount Moriah, and Solomon became king. At God's command, Solomon built the Temple, and inside the Holy of Holies, they placed the Ark of the Covenant, which held the Ten Commandments. And only Solomon could enter there, for it was the holy place where God dwelled on the earth.*

Rabbi Ezra's teachings filled my thoughts like a bucket of cool water drawn from a well. As the caravan marched toward Jerusalem, the walls of the city loomed before us, and grown men were made tiny as they stood next to these walls. The people within them created sounds that bounced back and forth, the noise climbing the rocks and stone as if on ladders. Once the noise reached the top of the walls, it filled the air with a buzz, like bees, and became louder and more distinct as the caravan reached the city.

That's when I realized the men I'd seen walking outside of the walls were Roman soldiers. My heart began to pound.

"Remember, because of the all the carts, wagons, and live-stock in our caravan, we'll have to bypass the eastern entrances and come into the city from the north," said Father.

He pointed out several pools on the outskirts of the city that were used for ritual cleansing and healing illnesses. He also pointed to a rocky, hill-like outcropping dotted with overhangs and crevices. The crevices along the rock looked like hollow faces without eyes or teeth.

"Your late grandfather called those caves, the faces of fear. He believed God carved those niches out of the rock to scare away opposing armies and evil intruders."

I didn't care for that hillside, and I grew happier when I could no longer see it from the trail.

Before we entered an enormous gate on the north side of the city, Father invited me to gaze at the stonework. Each square stone had been cut by hand by slaves and made to fit without any gaps. I rubbed my hand along the wall and wondered how many men it took to build it.

"James," said Father, "we could be standing where Solomon stood while inspecting the masonry."

My eyes went wide as I turned around to look at him. "Is it possible?"

He nodded. "Yes."

I ran my hands along the stone, the soft, smooth texture tickling my dusty fingertips.

Hundreds of people passed us, too busy to notice or care. I couldn't help linger near the wall and arch. If I could have reached them, I would have touched every square stone.

"Do you know what masons in this area call this type of stone, James?"

I shook my head.

"It's called the royal stone. It has been used in palaces, walls, and buildings as far back as our ancestor David."

"Where do they find it?"

"In the hills and nearby mountains. It's a very soft stone, so soft you could carve it with a mason's knife. But once the sun's rays strike it, the stone begins to cure and harden, and as it does, it becomes almost a pure white."

Those around me couldn't have cared less about the gate. I stood still, staring straight up into the crux of the archway.

"The arch is as tall as ten men," I said to Father.

He lifted his head to look at the arch. "It would take more than ten men to reach the top. They would have used a system of ropes, pulleys, and ramps to set the upper stones." He smiled at me. "It's an incredible thing to see, isn't it?" I nodded. "Come, James. We must continue."

I followed Father through the gate and into Jerusalem. A small bridge made of rock and stone covered an aqueduct. Father pointed to a pool that served as a collection point for water. "That's Hezekiah's Pool. I've heard this is one of the places where Isaiah delivered his prophecies to the king."

Father knew Isaiah was my favorite prophet, and I looked upon the pool with wonder and reverence. Though I didn't know what they looked like, I imagined a skinny, dark-bearded man in a thin brown tunic, speaking to a king, resplendent in royal red.

"How did King Hezekiah know he should listen to Isaiah?" I asked in a whisper.

"God must have revealed himself to Hezekiah in some way. But even then, the king could have done whatever he wished. He didn't have to listen to Isaiah, and he didn't have to be a good king. Nor did Hezekiah have to command our people to return to the ways of Moses. I find the stories of Hezekiah remarkable."

I stared at the pool. "Father?"

"Yes, James?"

I looked up at the crowds of people walking past us. "How do you know if a man is really speaking on behalf of God?"

Father chuckled and shook his head. "I have no idea, but if you ever meet a prophet, would you introduce me?" He put his hand on my shoulder, his mouth drawn up in a grin, his eyes shining like stars. "If God sent a man on this earth to speak to me, I trust that God would open my heart as well as my ears."

I liked Father's answer and nodded approvingly.

"Come, James. We should make our inquiries at the Temple. Nightfall is coming, and the Sabbath will be upon us in a matter of hours."

We walked farther along, and the travelers around us became instantly quiet.

"What has happened?" I asked Father.

He nodded to the right at an enormous white marble structure, with rooftops full of Roman guards armed with bows and spears. "King Herod's palace," he whispered. "No one will speak, pray, or rejoice while near his house."

My head spun toward Father, and I watched him pat the seal and the scroll hidden in his tunic. He pulled me close then leaned down to whisper. "It didn't occur to me that carrying the seal of Prince Antipas might be treason. I don't know if he and his father are getting along. If they're not, then having this in our possession may do us more harm than good. I'll be happy when we are rid of these things."

Once the caravan passed Herod's palace, it disbanded. Father expressed his appreciation to their leader, and we continued our journey on our own. We snaked our way around the city, avoiding the merchants and beggars, walking as fast as we could with a mule and a cart in a sea of people. The air was filled with the sound of people bartering, animals baying, metal clanging, and beggars begging. The streets smelled of dung, spices, food, and incense, and were overcrowded with traders, merchants, and Roman soldiers. My mind was overwhelmed at the sight of it all, but we walked by so quickly that I had no chance to process everything I saw.

"First we'll pass from the Upper City to the Lower City, James. Then we'll need to cross a bridge over an aqueduct. When we do, you'll see the front of the Temple and the stairs that lead to the Court of Gentiles." Father looked down at me. "Son, do you remember where the Temple is built?"

"Mount Moriah, where Abraham planned to offer up Isaac for sacrifice."

"Very good," said Father. "And it's directly over the site on which Solomon built the first Temple."

We rounded the corner of a busy street, and Father stopped the mule and cart. There was a pleasant demeanor about his face. He pointed to a building lined with white granite columns. When I looked up, I was overcome with both wonder and fear.

There the Temple stood in all its majesty. Dozens of people from faraway places congregated around the entrances. The streets were jammed with animals and carts. My feet were frozen. Father waited patiently while I stared. Then he knelt on one knee and leaned in close so I could hear him over the roar of the crowds. "The Temple is a sacred place, a holy place, where God can be on earth. Kings, prophets, and other wise men have walked these streets. Not only did we purify ourselves in the Jordan River, as they once did, but we also entered the gates of Jerusalem in the same manner. And now you will walk in the footsteps of our ancestors."

I knew why we were here. I also knew why my father had answered what he believed was God's call to him. Those first steps inside the Temple would be our way of showing God that we were listening to him.

"There is one more thing I want to say," said Father. "Great deeds have been performed on this mountain, but evil lurks in shadows of our people's past. Much blood has been spilled here, in both sacrifice and hatred. I want your heart to rejoice, James, but I also want you to be mindful of both the living and the dead. Evil continues to assault not only the Temple but also the whole of Jerusalem. You must pray with intention."

"Yes, Father," I said softly.

There were many walls within Jerusalem, and most served to guard the Temple. I touched many of the smooth, white stones as we walked past.

"The Temple Mount covers forty acres, which is larger than all of our village in Nazareth," said Father.

As we came closer to the entrance of the Temple, I heard the cooing of doves and the bawling of sheep, goats, and cattle. The smoke from the Temple incense stung my eyes and burned my throat, and the smells of dung and smoked animal flesh cloaked the air like heavy wool. We turned the corner and walked down a street that put us directly in front of the steps that led to the Court of Gentiles.

"We must go inside and find the high priest," said Father.

With tired legs and sore backs, we climbed dozens of stairs to the Court of Gentiles. There I saw the men who changed Roman money for Temple money, along with hordes of booths and merchants selling everything from turtledoves, to livestock, to wooden trinkets, and food. The columns inside the Temple were made of solid marble and were so big that it would take eight men, their hands joined, to encircle just one. Father stood beside me, but he often looked down to see the expression of wonder on my face. Finally he put his hand on the middle of my back to push me along.

"How did they manage to cut and move these columns?" I asked.

"The walls of the Temple Mount were built by outcasts who were worked to their deaths. Jewish tradesmen like us built the inner courts, such as the Court of Women. Priests who were schooled specifically in the arts of masonry built the sanctuary and the Holy of Holies. Only they were allowed to build those parts of the Temple."

I shuddered. "Could we be worked to death in Tiberias?"

Father shrugged. "It's unlikely but possible. That is why we're here, to protect ourselves and our family, and to provide a refuge for a young woman with no home."

From where we stood, we saw the high wall that made up the Temple's south side. The left side of the building housed the Holy of Holies, while the right side was filled with priests performing sacrifices. Father's eyes roamed all over the building, and he rambled as he spoke.

"It's obvious that the priests no longer want to support her. If her life was dedicated to God, our people shouldn't discard her calling or throw her out on the street like an animal carcass. She is to be cared for, nurtured, and loved, and she will find all of this and more by being a part of our family."

It seemed unbelievable that after this journey I would have a new mother.

Father walked to the back of the Court of Gentiles and found a Temple guard. An older man of fifty dressed in a blue tunic, he met Father's request with suspicion. "Why do you wish to see the captain?"

"I am Joseph bar Jacob of Bethlehem, now living in Nazareth. I am here at the request of Rabbi Boethus," Father replied with a shaky voice.

The guard gave my father a curious look. "Why should I trust you? What proof do you have that I might believe you, Joseph bar Jacob?"

With an ache in my stomach, I glanced up at Father. I wondered if he would pull the seal of Antipas from his tunic pocket, but he didn't.

"Please tell the captain that Rabbi Boethus's scribe, Nicodemus, sends his gratitude."

The officer's face softened at the mention of the scribe's name. "Is he doing well?"

"Rabbi Boethus is very busy, and—"

"I meant the scribe," the guard interrupted.

"Why, yes. He stayed in my home the night before we left Nazareth. He discharges his duties with dignity and reverence and is most certainly a son of Abraham. Do you know him?"

The officer grinned then looked at the ground and back up at my father. "Nicodemus is my son," he said softly. "I haven't seen him since his move to Sepphoris three years ago."

Father returned the grin. His twinkling eyes appeared. The conversation was no longer between a pilgrim Jew and Temple guard. It was one father talking to another.

"Then take heart, and know that your son is doing well," said Father. He offered the guard an outstretched hand.

"Thank you for showing hospitality to my son. It means much to me," said the guard. He shook Father's hand. "Please wait here while I summon the captain."

While we waited, Father led me to Solomon's Porch, which overlooked the Cedron Valley and Mount Olivet. "There's the mountain we crossed," he said, pointing. "And those are the gardens below."

The setting sun cast a deep red glow over the valley.

"Father, is this really where God will stand when he comes to judge us?"

He shrugged. "I don't know, but I can't think of a more beautiful place for God to be."

We turned around in time to see the high priest, Rabbi Boethus, accompanied by the Temple captain, a scribe, a servant, and the Temple guard Father had just met. We were surprised to see Rabbi Boethus. He frightened me even more in his ceremonial dress. He wore a white undergarment with a royal-blue tunic and a tall white hat with a gold headband. Draped across his chest was an apron of many colors, and a plate of jewels covered his chest. A row of small bells sewn into the hem of his tunic jingled as he walked.

After Father's confrontation with the rabbi at the synagogue, my heart and mind were mixed up. Rabbi Ezra always taught us that the high priest was the holiest of all holy men, but I felt conflicted about this after he had belittled Father. Today, however, I realized that despite my feelings about what Rabbi Boethus had said to my father, he was still the high priest. He was indeed powerful, if not the holiest of men, and I was grateful that Father was here.

Father closed his eyes and bowed slightly in the high priest's direction.

"Joseph bar Jacob," Rabbi Boethus said in a firm voice, "I was told by Nicodemus to expect you."

"Yes, Rabbi," Father said in a low voice.

"Your journey went well?"

"Very well. Thank you."

The high priest stared in my direction. "I see you brought along your son, James."

"This is his first visit to Jerusalem."

"I see," said the high priest. He looked me over with a watchful eye then turned his attention to Father. "You both must be tired and hungry."

"We are," said Father.

"You will be staying at my home in the Upper City."

"Thank you, Rabbi," Father said softly.

"Come. We must fix you and your son something to eat before the sun sets. I will have my servant take you to my home. Where have you hitched your mule and cart?"

"They are at a stable not far from here," said Father.

"My servant will help you fetch your belongings."

"When may I take my son on a tour of the Temple?"

Rabbi Boethus folded his arms and frowned. "I can't allow you or your son to enter the Temple."

I was devastated. To come all this way from Nazareth and not be able to enter the Temple hurt worse than any pain I had known. I felt sick to my stomach, but I didn't dare move in front of the high priest.

Father bowed in respect. "Thank you for your hospitality, Rabbi."

"One more thing, Joseph," said Rabbi Boethus. "Nicodemus insists that your family is from the line of David."

"It is," Father replied confidently.

The high priest stared at Father for several seconds. "I suppose that is good."

I wasn't sure how to interpret Rabbi Boethus's stare, but I could tell Father was anxious.

"You and your son should get some rest," said the rabbi. "We'll have much to discuss tomorrow night. Ethan, my servant, will show you the way to my house. Once you arrive, prepare yourselves for the Sabbath. We'll conduct our affairs at sundown tomorrow."

The high priest turned and walked away. Father looked at the guard, who had greeted us so warmly just minutes ago, with a look of confusion. The man offered no words. He turned and followed Rabbi Boethus, the scribe, and the Temple captain.

The servant, a short, wiry man who was younger than Father, motioned for us to follow. Father allowed him to get ahead of us and leaned down to whisper. "I'm sorry about the Temple, James."

I wiped at my eyes. "Perhaps I will see it another day."

"I hope to be with you when that day comes," said Father.

The servant gave Father a disapproving glance.

"Why were my son and I denied access to the Temple?" Father asked.

The servant stopped, turned around, and walked up to my father. He patted my father's chest, and when he found the lumpy mass that contained the seal and the scroll, Father instinctively backed away.

"The things you carry are not holy," the servant whispered to Father. "You won't be allowed to enter the Temple as long as you carry these things. Once you are rid of them, you must purify yourself."

I stared up at Father, whose eyes were filled with rage at the judgment passed onto him by the servant. "I never wished to carry these things," Father said firmly.

"But carry them you must, if you wish to survive," said the servant. Then he pointed to the setting sun. "We must hurry. The Sabbath is coming."

We quickly collected our mule and cart and followed the servant through the city to the Upper Side.

I could tell by the way Father's lips were pressed together that he was bitterly angry. Maybe Uncle was right. Maybe God had cursed us for carrying the seal and the scroll.

CHAPTER FIFTEEN

When we arrived at the high priest's home, we were escorted to a large room where several servants were dining. They seemed irritated that we had interrupted their meal but found places for us at a table in a small room just off the main entrance. In silence we ate a meal of lamb stew and fresh fruit. Another servant, a tall lean man, then led us to a room upstairs that contained padded mats as thick as my leg, covered in blue silk.

"What about my mule and cart?" Father asked.

"They're safe," huffed the servant. He slammed the door behind him, leaving Father and me confused and concerned.

"This isn't the kind of hospitality I would expect from the leader of our people," Father remarked. "I expected, at the very least, to meet Joazar's wife. It would have been a typical and honorable thing to do."

"I don't know what to think," I mumbled.

Father came over and put a hand on my shoulder. "I'm sorry about the Temple. We should get our rest. We have a busy day tomorrow."

Our change of clothes was with the rest of our belongings in the cart. Father stepped outside and called for a servant, but no one answered. He came back to our room, shut the door, and prepared his mat. I sighed out loud for both of us to hear.

"What is it, James?"

"Nothing feels right to me. It's as if we're not wanted here."

"I agree with you, but we're together, and that's what is important."

The next morning, we awoke to a knock. Another servant, different from the others we had met, stood at our door with a basket that contained two pieces of dried fish, two pears, two apples, and almonds.

"If you must relieve yourselves, there is a place at the end of the hall," said the servant. He shut the door before Father and I had time to rub the sleep from our eyes.

When we finished our breakfast, we gathered the courage to venture from our room. We climbed down the ladder from the second floor to the first and wandered around eight large rooms, including the kitchen, dining, and living areas.

But there was no one in the house to greet us.

"Come on, James," Father said sternly. "We must make our way to a synagogue."

We found the front door, and Father opened it. Standing there were a Temple guard and Ethan, the servant who had helped us with our mule and cart the day before.

"Where are you going?" Ethan asked.

"It is the Sabbath, young man, and we are going to find a synagogue to praise God and celebrate our safe trip to Jerusalem."

"I can't let you do that," he replied.

"And why not?" asked Father. His anger turned to defiance, and with each word, he raised his voice. "I am a man of God! I have a duty and an obligation!"

"Joseph bar Jacob!" shouted a voice from behind us. It was a man in priestly robes, but it was not the high priest.

Father took a moment to study the man. "How does this matter concern you?" Father asked in a commanding voice. "My son and I will not be indolent concerning our obligations to God!"

The priest closed his eyes and bowed his head slightly. He spoke softly and respectfully to Father. "Come, Joseph. You and your son will observe the Sabbath with the members of this priestly household. We are honored to have a descendant of David among us."

Father, put off by the gentleness in the priest's voice, took a deep breath and nodded. We followed him through the house, along several stone corridors, to a room with no windows and only candles for light. The room smelled of incense and sweat. Inside were more than fifty men, most of whom appeared to be priests. In the front of the room stood the largest altar I had ever seen, carved from rare, black rock that came from the fiery mountains. Its opulence was reserved for only the rich and powerful.

The walls were adorned with intricate tapestries and the altar with gold candleholders. Father and I stared in shock at the assembly, which included Temple guardsmen, the Temple captain we had met yesterday, scribes, and priests of various ranks, including Pharisees, Levites, and Sadducees.

"Joseph, you and James may take your place in the front," said the priest.

Father and I walked across the room, trying to avoid the stares and painful silence that followed. I wanted to ask him how this man knew my name, but I was too frightened to move, much less speak.

"You will worship with us today, as our honored guests," said another priest from behind the altar. With those final words, the chanting began, followed by prayers, lessons, and discussions.

Because there weren't any windows in this room, we couldn't know what hour it was. With each passing prayer, I grew hungrier and hungrier, and at one point, I felt as though I might pass out. Father listened to the rabbis and elders and early on kept his comments to himself. Even though the words and language used by these men was unlike anything I had ever heard, Father seemed to grasp every word.

At one point the men began to question Father. There were questions about Daniel and Esther, David and Goliath, Solomon, and the fall of our people. Some men chose to question him regarding his positions on various laws, and one priest asked him about his views concerning Rome and the Samaritans. These latter questions were meant to trick Father, but he answered with words and phrases beyond my learning and understanding. He was experienced with the ways of men, and this became apparent to everyone in the room. More discussion ensued, and by the end of our worship, Father had earned the respect of every rabbi present.

It was three hours past midday when the services finally ended. We were given a snack of dried fruits and nuts, with the promise of a feast following the end of the Sabbath. We were welcome to wander the house, the grounds, and the many splendid gardens, but we weren't allowed to leave the premises.

Father and I walked through the gardens and talked of the lessons and discussions, strolling through the grounds as prisoners of our own people. It wasn't an unpleasant experience by any means, though, for during those hours, I learned much from him. We could tell by the shadows that the sun was going down, and in some ways, I wished that the day would never end. The conversations Father and I shared that day not only gave me new ways of thinking but also offered me a new appreciation for my father and our family.

"Father, I was very proud of you at synagogue," I said. "I'm always proud of course, but today I saw you in ways I never had seen before. You never speak that much in our own synagogue or with such words."

Father gave me a hug. "It's a wonderful thing to hear, James. When I was your age, growing up in Bethlehem, your grandfather made sure I had some Temple schooling. I was fortunate enough to spend many Sabbath days in Jerusalem at the Temple and surrounding synagogues. It was in those days that I met one of my best friends."

"Rabbi Ezra?"

Father laughed. "Yes."

"But you never shared any of these stories with Jude or me, or any of my other brothers or sisters."

Father picked up a sliced pomegranate from a nearby basket of fruit. He took two halves and handed one to me. "Eat before you dry up and blow away," he said. "This will hold us over until the feast tonight."

I took four seeds out of the fruit and placed them in my mouth. I ate while Father spoke. Between bites he explained why he and my uncle chose not to discuss their experiences in Judea. "When we made the decision to move to Nazareth, I did so with the intention of raising my family in peace and safety. Bethlehem and Jerusalem had become dangerous places under Roman rule. Descendants of David and Solomon were tracked down and killed, just so Herod could avoid the threat of a Jewish king. Anyone who even mentioned the word *messiah* was suspect, and many were brought up on false charges of treason and crucified." Father finished eating his pomegranate seeds and tossed the rind into the garden. "By the time my stepfather had passed, my mother had been dead for years. It was some time after his burial before your uncle and I decided to move to Galilee. We knew we could live, farm, and pray in Nazareth and, as we were able, work as masons and carpenters in Sepphoris. We left our schooling, our big words, and our fancy arguments back in Bethlehem, in favor of a simple, quiet life. Rabbi Ezra is the only one in Galilee who previously knew your Uncle and me, because of our childhood days in Bethlehem."

Even though there was still light outside, it was officially sundown. A thin, boyish-looking servant interrupted us. "Your presence is requested at the table of the high priest. Follow me."

CHAPTER SIXTEEN

The servant led us into the great dining room. Five dining rooms could have fit inside this space. Large heavy tapestries of Jewish symbols, woven in a multitude of colors, hung from the white stone walls. The table, made of sandstone, seated up to twenty people. Thick cushions covered in deep green and purple silk encircled it.

At the end of the table sat a girl in a beautiful white dress. Her eyes were cast down, and a thin white veil covered her head and face.

"Is that Mary?" I said in a low voice.

Father didn't answer.

The high priest and his wife greeted us, then seated Father at the end of the table opposite the girl. Rabbi Boethus motioned for his servants to serve the food and drink. Fourteen servants— seven boys and seven girls about my age—moved about the room. The servants scurried about the dining room like mice, filling the table with bowls and platters of meats, vegetables, flatbreads, and fruit.

The high priest pointed at the girl, as if pointing out a prized sheep in the middle of a flock. With a gruff voice, he said, "This is Mary, daughter of Joachim. Her family is of the line of Aaron."

Father nodded to the point of bowing and smiled, but the girl looked away. Many of the rabbis who had celebrated the Sabbath with us were in the room. A servant called for everyone to sit at the table, and when everyone was seated, the high priest commanded Mary to remove her veil. He offered a prayer of thanksgiving over the meal, which consisted of lamb, beef, spiced sauces, and thick vegetable stews. The servants offered us a tart wine, and at the end of the meal, a sweet wine. When everyone finished eating, the high priest motioned for his wife and Mary to stand up and then dismissed them.

Other than pleasantries used for passing food, everyone at the table had remained silent throughout the meal. I had tried to sneak a glance of my new mother, but Father always interrupted me by passing a plate of food. We were sitting at the most coveted banquet table in all of Palestine, but the experiences that had led up to this point were riddled with contradictions. We didn't feel welcome, and the most respected person in our tradition had embarrassed Father. Confining us to the house and gardens did little to warm our hearts or lift our spirits. Even the servants seemed to dislike us.

The business of our journey—its mission and purpose—was now the focus of our discussion. Rabbi Boethus began the conversation immediately. "Joseph, you need to understand why I couldn't let you into the Temple yesterday."

"You don't have to explain your reasons."

I could tell by the high priest's facial expressions that Father's graciousness and humility impressed him.

"Now that you are under the safety of my house and destined to complete your betrothal to Mary, you may hand over the seal of Prince Antipas." The high priest stretched out his hand and pointed at the table. "Place the seal here."

Father took in a deep breath and reached into the inner pocket of his tunic. He laid both the seal and the scroll on the table then eyed the high priest.

"What is this?" Rabbi Boethus asked.

"It is a scroll from Nicodemus, stating my purpose and who I am serving."

The high priest peeled the dry parchment from the wax, breaking the seals. He opened the scroll and read its contents aloud. The words in the scroll matched those we had heard from Nicodemus many nights ago.

Nicodemus was a Pharisee. Pharisees believed in an afterlife. Rabbi Boethus was a Sadducee. Sadducees didn't believe an afterlife existed. A rivalry between the Sadducees and Pharisees had raged for hundreds of years and at times was just as dangerous as the politics played out by the Jews and the Romans. Father was a Pharisee, as were our ancestors, which put us at odds with the high priest. He would have to choose his words carefully. If he said the wrong thing, our family could be banished from the synagogue or accused of blasphemy and executed.

"So it wasn't just the seal of Antipas that Nicodemus sent forth with you. He also sent my personal regards."

"I am only here to do the will of my people," Father said quietly.

"Then whom do you serve?" hissed the high priest.

"I serve God," said Father. "And I know the Sadducees and the Pharisees seek a husband for Mary, who was orphaned by her parents many years ago."

"Anna was too old to bear children," huffed the high priest, "but God blessed her. There is no question that God made Joachim and Anna righteous in the sight of Israel."

Father nodded. The high priest took in a deep breath and let it out slowly, as if making a final judgment. "Very well, Joseph. I will hand Mary over to you. Consider her your betrothed."

"Thank you, Rabbi," said Father.

"Is that is all you wish to say? Do you not wish to know more about her?"

"There were rumors about Mary's miraculous birth many years ago," Father replied. "I know her life has been dedicated to God. I also know we are distantly related, and—"

With a fist, the high priest pounded the table. "But there is one thing, Joseph, that you don't know," interrupted the priest. "Because of Mary's descent from the line of Aaron, and her miraculous birth, we believe God's divine favor rests with her. She *must* marry a descendant of David."

The sparkle left Father's eyes. His mouth dropped slightly, and his breathing quickened as he opened and closed his hands.

It took me a moment to grasp the full meaning of our journey and our trip to Jerusalem. For hundreds of years, our people have waited for a messiah, the one foretold by the prophet Isaiah. By arranging someone from the line of David with a virgin from the line of Aaron, the Pharisees hoped to hasten the messiah's arrival. The Sadducees, especially Rabbi Boethus, had political aspirations. Prince Antipas already knew that Father was from the line of David. If Father and Mary ever produced a son, the prince would have our entire family executed to keep Isaiah's prophecies from being fulfilled.

As I began to realize the danger this union meant for our family, fear took hold of my heart and mind. Father cleared his throat, looked at me, then shook his head, as if to say, "Do not say a word."

Then he turned to face the high priest and spoke. "When will I have chance to speak with Mary?"

"You may speak with her tomorrow morning." The high priest motioned for a servant who stood at far end of the room. "Bring the gift, Ethan."

The servant, who had helped us yesterday, appeared from the back of the room carrying a large leather bag. The bag clinked when he set it on the table in front of the high priest. The high priest opened the bag and pushed it to the middle of the table.

"Joachim entrusted the Temple with the dowry for his daughter. This silver represents two years of his wages. This is his gift to the one who would marry his daughter. It is now yours, Joseph."

Father neglected to share his intentions to remain chaste. Not once during our visit to Jerusalem did he mention this to the high priest or any of his servants or officials. The high priest was about to pay a dowry on a marriage that never would produce children.

Father looked at the bag but didn't reach for it. He knew that refusing the gift would insult the high priest. He also knew that if he took the money to our sleeping quarters, we were sure to be robbed. Father took a moment to think about his reply before addressing the high priest. "Thank you, Rabbi," he finally said. "This is a generous gift, and it will be used to care for Mary. Perhaps it would be better if your treasurers guarded the silver until we left for Galilee."

The high priest nodded. "That is probably wise, Joseph."

A servant removed the bag from the table and disappeared from the dining room.

"Tomorrow morning, after breakfast," Rabbi Boethus said, "I will arrange a meeting between you and Mary in the privacy of the gardens." Then he stared directly at me. "While your father is visiting with your new mother, I will arrange a tour of the Temple for you. There is a purification bath on the lower level of my house. You will go there after breakfast. After you prepare your heart, mind, and body for Temple worship, I will send one of my personal scribes to accompany you."

My heart soared, and I choked out a soft, "Thank you, Rabbi," and gave him a respectful nod.

"Then we are set for tomorrow," announced the high priest. Ethan suddenly appeared in the room. The high priest motioned for him to come to the table. "Please show them to their beds."

Father and I rose to our feet. I followed his lead, bowing slightly in the direction of the high priest, who nodded in our direction, then abruptly left the room.

We followed the servant upstairs. Inside our sleeping room was a stone basin full of water. We washed our hands and faces and dried them with white-linen towels. As we were finishing, Ethan returned with a stone pitcher of water and two silver goblets. "I will wake you in the morning," he said, and closed the door behind him.

Father and I prepared for bed in silence. When we both had reclined on our mats, he spoke to me in a quiet voice. "Your Temple tour should be exciting, James, but don't linger too long. I want to leave Jerusalem as soon as possible, maybe after our midday meal."

"I sense that Rabbi Boethus's servant does not like us."

Father shifted on his mat. "You have good instincts. I sense that there are a lot of people here who don't like us."

The shutters were open in order to let in the cool summer breezes. Our windows faced the garden, and through these windows, we heard voices. Father rose halfway on his mat.

Moonlight lit up our room, and I saw the whites of Father's eyes looking at the open window then at me. Neither of us dared to get up to see who was below. I lay on my mat, staring at the stone ceiling above me and listening to the rumblings of angry voices coming from the darkness.

It was several minutes before the voices were gone.

Father crawled over to the table that held the washbasin, careful not to make any noise. He picked it up and placed it in front of our door. "To alert us of intruders," he said in a whisper, then went back to his mat.

I wonder whether Father lay awake for as long as I did, for it was twilight before I felt safe enough to close my eyes.

CHAPTER SEVENTEEN

We awoke at daybreak to the sound of footsteps in the hall. Father rushed to the door to collect the stone basin filled with water. As the door flew open, he stumbled backward, spilling some of the water on the floor.

Ethan paused to stare at him with a curious look then said, "Rabbi Boethus asked me to summon you. He says you have an urgent matter to tend to in Galilee."

I sprung from my sleeping mat and put on my sandals while Father spoke to the servant. "What kind of matter?" he asked.

"I don't know, but there is a courier who appears to have traveled throughout the night to get here. He collapsed when he entered our door. He carries a scroll."

When I finished fastening my sandal straps, we followed Ethan down the ladder to the main room. In a wooden chair sat a young man, two or three years older than me; his legs, arms, and hair were grayed by dirt and dust. The white tunic was colored brown by the filth of the desert and his body looked frail and weak from lack of food and water.

From across the room, we saw him shovel cold stew from a clay bowl into his mouth. The young man's eyes appeared wild with fear; his dirty fingers pushed through the gravy to gobble up chunks of meat and vegetables. When the boy saw Father, he rushed from the table and collapsed in his arms. When the tearstained face parted from Father's chest, he looked up.

My eyes grew wide, and my jaw dropped.

"Jude!" Father cried. "What has happened? Where is Clopas?"

Father walked my brother over to the chair and sat him down to rest. He knelt in front of Jude, who was still trembling.

"I left with a group of herdsman from Judea, Father, but they weren't moving fast enough. I didn't think I would get lost, but the desert is so big..."

His voice trailed off, and Father held him to his chest. Father turned to me and spoke. "James, have Ethan help you get the mule and cart ready. Gather our things and enough supplies to last seven days."

I did as Father asked. When I returned an hour later, Jude was holding a bowl of stew, his third, and drinking water from a large silver cup that Father held. Ethan arrived with Mary and the high priest. Ethan stood on her right, holding her by the upper arm. Rabbi Boethus held the leather bag of coins.

Father looked at my cousin then at the high priest and servant. "Unhand that woman," Father said sternly.

Ethan released his grip from Mary.

Rabbi Boethus walked over to Father. "Is your son all right, Joseph?"

"I think so," said Father.

"Shall I send for my physician?" the rabbi asked.

Jude handed the empty bowl to Father and cleared his throat. The high priest motioned to another servant, who then left the room, presumably to seek out the physician. Father looked at me with a mixture of worry and despair. He handed the bowl and cup to Ethan and knelt in front of Jude, who was still sitting in the chair. "Can you speak, son?"

"Yes, Father." Jude nodded, and everyone in the room stood where they were, in silence, ready to listen. As Jude spoke, I noticed that Mary had knelt, her head still bowed in respect. The servants and the high priest showed little interest in her piety, but this small gesture captivated me. I wondered what her life must have been like all these years. The way Ethan had handled her—like an unruly mule—troubled me.

Jude spoke in a raspy voice through a dust-caked throat. "It was the last day of Marcus's project. Uncle Clopas asked me to stay behind and sharpen the tools for the harvest. Around lunchtime Marcus arrived in Nazareth, out of breath, yelling for help. He ran the entire way." Jude looked at the high priest and Ethan and began to shake. "Wh-wh-who is that?" Jude asked Father.

"That is the high priest, Rabbi Boethus, and his servant, Ethan. Ethan is the one who prepared this food for you," said Father. He smiled at Jude as if he were a young child learning to play. "Can you talk, son?"

Jude leaned back in the chair, his eyes wide with fear. The temples on the sides of his head flared, and he blinked rapidly. He wrapped his arms around his stomach and leaned over, as if to vomit.

Father knelt in front of him. "Do you feel sick?"

Jude shook his head quickly. He leaned over to speak to Father. "I've seen him before," he whispered through clenched teeth.

"Who have you seen before?"

Jude pointed at Ethan. Father turned around to look at the servant and the high priest. "He is delirious," Father said quickly.

"My physician will be here soon," the high priest announced.

Father looked at Jude again. "Son, what else do you remember?"

With a quavering voice, my brother said, "Soldiers came and took Uncle Clopas and Simeon."

"Where did they take them?" Father asked slowly.

"Tiberias."

The high priest bristled at the mention of the city. He stroked his long white beard rapidly, leaned over, and whispered something to Ethan, then motioned for him to leave. Father turned around when he heard the door close then looked at the high priest.

"I sent Ethan to hurry my physician along," Rabbi Boethus said gruffly.

Father stared at the rabbi for a few extra seconds before he turned back to face Jude. "Did you see Clopas or Simeon before you left?"

Jude shook his head. He swallowed hard. "Marcus told me to leave as soon as possible. He said not to return to Sepphoris. He said he would—"

Jude erupted into a fit of coughing. Father patted him on the back and shouted, "Would someone please get us more water?"

A servant filled the silver cup that sat on the floor next to Father. He lifted it to Jude's lips and waited for him to catch his breath.

"You don't have to talk," Father said as he stroked Jude's hair.

Jude shook his head. "Marcus followed the Romans to Tiberias to look after Uncle and Simeon. He told me to find you in Jerusalem."

The look Father gave Rabbi Boethus was enough to jolt me out of my despair. There was no question that Father held the high priest responsible.

"How did you find me, son?"

"He collapsed on the road, in front of Herod's palace," said Ethan. He was standing in the doorway next to a short elderly man with wild white hair who was dressed in a light-brown tunic and purple robe.

"Soldiers were about to stab the boy when I heard him cry out that he was Judas bar Joseph, son of Joseph bar Jacob. I asked the soldiers to relent, in the name of Joseph bar Jacob, the honored guest of the high priest. They threw the boy at my feet, and I brought him here."

"You didn't tell me this when you woke us," Father said sternly.

"I didn't know if the boy was lying," said Ethan. "There are many people who want to assassinate the high priest."

Father's hands went up to his face. He rubbed his forehead with his fingertips. "James," he said loudly, "Are we ready to travel?"

I walked over to him. "We are, Father. The mule and cart are ready; the provisions are loaded; and there is water in our jar. I found a milking stool for Mary so that she may sit in the cart without getting dirty."

At the sound of her name, Mary looked up from her prayers. Her eyes found me. She stood and let her hands fall to her side. In a room of men, Mary needed permission to speak. Father nodded at her immediately.

"Thank you, James," she said, bowing slightly.

Her voice was like the songs of birds in the morning, her words like cool winds on a sunny harvest day. Even Jude, whose face had been intently focused on Father, looked up to see the face of the woman who spoke those words. Father cocked his head to one side, confused, but only initially, by the authority in her voice. He smiled at her approvingly.

"My physician is ready to examine your son," announced the high priest.

Father nodded. "I will check on our things. James, stay with Mary until I return."

There were nine of us in the room, including my brother, the physician, the high priests, the servants, and me. Of all the Jewish men standing in that room, Father trusted only me to watch over Mary. I sidled up next to her while the physician examined my brother. We stood in silence while the physician asked Jude a series of questions. He examined his body, inquired about his hunger and thirst, and gave him a bitter brown liquid to drink. Jude coughed after he drank it.

As he was coughing, Father entered the room. "How is he?" he inquired.

"He is dehydrated," replied the physician. "I have given him some salt water mixed with herbs to help his body recover. But it is my opinion that he shouldn't travel. He needs to rest."

Father shook his head. "That is impossible. I must return home."

The high priest stepped forward. In one hand he held a scroll, in the other the leather bag that contained the dowry of silver coins. With a disapproving look, he handed both to Father. "The scroll says your brother and nephew are laboring on the royal palace of Prince Antipas. The scroll contains directions to the worksite. It is signed, 'Marcus.' "

"Thank you, Rabbi," Father said quietly.

"Marcus is an educated man," said the high priest. "He is too educated to be a Galilean."

All eyes were on Father. He glanced around the room, expecting a fierce reprimand for having labored for a Roman. There were so many more important things worrying Father, and this detail was nothing more than a pebble on the side of a mountain.

"Marcus can't decide if he is a Jew or a Roman," Father said to the high priest. "It is not for me to make up his mind, particularly when he pays for his services in advance."

The servants snickered. Even the high priest's face softened. Without warning Father walked past the high priest to confront Ethan, who stood by himself along the far wall of the Great Room. Father reached into the bag of silver, which contained more than forty coins, and pulled out five.

"To give all this money away would show disrespect for Joachim. To give too little would show disrespect for you. My hope is that this is enough to show you respect. I will be forever indebted to you for saving my son's life."

The servant closed his eyes and held up a hand. A moment later he opened his eyes, took Father's hand—the one containing the five silver coins—and closed it over the coins. Then he shook his head.

"The scribe in Sepphoris, the one you favor, is my brother." He looked at me then back at Father. "Please look after him."

Generations upon generations of families served the Temple. My father had explained this to me, but I didn't realize these families were all tied together. Now I understood why the guard didn't offer Father any words when we were turned away from the Temple the day we arrived. He knew his own son would be looking after us in the high priest's house. It wasn't our custom to refuse a gift, but in some sense, the debt Father looked to repay already had been paid by his own hospitality and goodwill. With his hand still clenched in a fist, he offered a nod and smile to Ethan.

Father turned to the physician and handed him the coins. "For your services," he said. Then he turned to me. "Help your brother and Mary into the cart. We must cross the Jordan before nightfall."

I went to my brother and helped him to his feet. I motioned for Mary to join us. With one of his arms draped across my shoulders, and the other across Mary's, we helped Jude walk out of the high priest's house to our cart, which was waiting outside the door.

I stacked our provisions toward the front of the cart and placed the tent and bedrolls toward the back. We placed Jude on these. Mary found the stool that I had placed on the other side and sat there, but only after drawing a pouch of water from the jar. She handed it to Jude, who drank furiously. Father came out with the bag of silver. He offered his gratitude once more to the high priest and Ethan, and walked to the mule. He grabbed the mule by its harness and called out to me. "James, press on," he said loudly.

Father signaled for the mule to move forward, and I pushed the cart from behind. As the cart pulled away, I turned to see the faces of the high priest, the physician, and Ethan. They watched curiously as we disappeared into the crowd. After several minutes I turned around again, but I couldn't see them, for the streets of Jerusalem were filled with people.

Father called out to me once more, and I ran up to meet him. "We must hurry," he said frantically. "We will leave Jerusalem by the north gate, but I don't want the soldiers to recognize Jude."

I repeated what Father had said to Mary. She moved quickly, helping Jude lie down in the cart. She partially unfolded the tent and used it to cover my brother.

I walked on the opposite side of Father, next to the cart. At first we traveled along the street unnoticed, just another pilgrim family among many. But when Father pulled the mule past Herod's palace, we encountered a small crowd of soldiers shouting insults at Jews. One of them ran up to Father and walked alongside him, taunting him.

"Your mule won't make it through the desert. It will die, and you will have to eat it to survive. You and your Jew children will die of thirst, and the meat from your bones will be ripped off by wolves."

The soldiers laughed, but Father kept walking as if he heard nothing. When we had made it out of the gate safely, he picked up the pace. "James," he yelled to me, "get your brother up."

Mary pulled the tent off Jude. He sat up on the bedrolls and drank from the leather pouch. I walked around the cart and ran to catch up with Father.

He turned to me and spoke in a low voice that Jude and Mary could not hear. "We are not going to cross the Jordan, James. We can be home in three or four days if we take the trail through Samaria."

I nodded.

"The sun is already hot, and the desert winds are sure to start blowing later in the afternoon. If Jude gets overheated, he could get sick again, and it could kill him. He must keep drinking water. Promise me you will keep him drinking."

"I will. It is already midday. Should we stop to eat?"

He shook his head. "Pull some dried fish from our supplies. We can eat while we walk. We need to hurry if we're to make it to the river before nightfall."

I sensed panic in his voice. If I could have kept from the sun from setting to soon, I would have. "Is there anything else I can do, Father?"

I watched a tear roll down his cheek and disappear into his beard. "You can pray. I'll keep us moving across the desert. You just keep your brother alive."

The trek seemed to last longer than the one Father and I had made three days earlier. Mary and I kept forcing water on Jude, and after ten pouches, he finally refused to drink any more.

We reached the outskirts of Qumran safely, and Father found a small group of Roman traders numbering six men who were on their way to Sepphoris. At the mention of Marcus's name, four of the men laughed and spewed insults at our master's expense. Still they invited us to travel with them, and Father accepted. I prayed their good humor made them trustworthy, but we really had no choice. We needed to travel in numbers for safety, and these men were the only group heading to Galilee by way of Samaria.

While Father worked out the travel schedule, Mary approached me. "Why is a son of David traveling through Samaria?" she asked. "And why travel with Romans?"

"It is the fastest way to Nazareth," I replied. "We will shorten our trip by several days."

"Your father would make himself impure?"

Mary had no right to question me, but I looked so young that she may have mistaken me for a boy. If she had known my age, she would have chosen different words. Even so, I didn't want to offend her out of respect for Father.

"These men are following the roads along the Jordan, Mary. I'm sure we'll try to avoid the Samaritans, just as they try to avoid us."

"Why does your father consort with Romans?" Mary asked sharply. "Has he no fear of God?"

Jude, who had been lying in the back of the cart, overheard her comment. Mary and I heard the cart creak as he stood up and climbed out. He walked over to where we were standing.

"Father fears God," Judas said smugly. "And you have no right to question him, or James, about this matter."

Mary turned to me, and I shrugged. "We are a close family," I explained. "If you were in trouble, Father would do whatever he could to protect you."

Mary took a step back and looked me up and down. Her judgment of not only me but also Father concerned me.

"No man has ever showed me kindness. What makes you think your Father is any different?"

Jude was furious. He opened and closed his dirty hands in anger and walked back to the cart. It would have been perfectly acceptable for him to strike Mary for her disrespect. But Father never struck a woman, nor did he respect men who did.

Mary continued to press me. "Do you not have an opinion of your father?"

My new mother was proving to be more like Aunt Miriam than a woman dedicated to God.

I shook my head and gritted my teeth. "Father is a good man," I said sternly. "You can trust him. But I would suggest that from now on you don't speak another word to Jude or criticize Father. If you want to question someone, question me."

"How old are you?" Mary blurted out.

I smiled at her. "Fifteen."

Mary bowed her head. "I am sorry for my disrespect." She walked back to the cart, sulking.

Father appeared with a handful of small bags. He handed them to Mary and Jude. "Dried fruits and nuts," he said.

We left Qumran with the Roman traders. I led the mule while Father ate his snack. At one point he turned to me and asked, "What were you three discussing back there?"

The noise of the mules, carts, and footsteps were enough to shield my voice from Mary and Jude. "Nothing important," I said.

Father nodded and kept watching the trail. "What did Mary have to say?" "Not much," I replied.

I looked at Father and saw him grinning. "She questioned you about the Romans and Samarian trail?"

"She did," I said.

"Sounds like something your mother would have done," Father said with a twinkle in his eye. "What did you tell her?"

"I told her that Jude doesn't travel well and that she would be wise not to aggravate him."

Father and I glanced back at the cart. All we could see were the backs of Mary and Jude's heads. They sat apart from each other, staring in opposite directions.

Father looked back at me, raised his eyebrows, and chuckled.

CHAPTER EIGHTEEN

We nibbled on cakes made of dried dates and flatbread. In the stillness of the evening, we heard our Roman counterparts laughing and yelling from their campsite, a hundred yards away. Father suspected they had been drinking. Jude shook from the cold. Father had given him two servings of food and an extra pouch of water. I ate slowly, my mind and body exhausted by the events in Jerusalem. Mary sat quietly between Jude and me, eating her bread.

Father invited her to speak. "Mary, is there anything you want to talk about?"

She kept her eyes focused on her bread and continued to take small bites.

Jude cleared his throat. "You can talk, you know. Father welcomes the conversation of women."

Mary tore the rest of her flatbread in half and handed a piece to Jude. Then she looked up at him. "What should I say?"

Jude grinned and looked at Father. "What should she say?"

In the firelight I saw Father wearing a pleasant smile. He closed his eyes and shook his head.

Jude's joking shamed Mary, and she dropped her head to avoid looking at us. An untouched cake sat on top of her water pouch. I reached over, picked it up, and handed it to her.

"Father believes a woman should have a voice in her husband's home," I said over the sounds of the crackling fire.

The reflections of the orange flames were much brighter against the pale skin of Mary's face. Her dark hair flowed down to the middle of her back, and her eyes were a soft brown, like those of lambs. Her hands were much smaller than mine, and her fingers were thin, short, and feminine. Without question she would be the prettiest girl in all of Nazareth. She took the cake in the palm of her hand and lifted it to her lips. She stared at me while taking a bite then rested the cake on her right leg, which was covered by a cream-colored tunic.

When Mary looked up, she saw all of us staring at her. "What?" she said.

Her movements were slow and elegant, but her actions were purposeful. I really wanted to get to know her, to understand what her life was like and what she did to fill her days. Like a determined fisherman, Jude cast his net one more time. "We were kind of hoping you would talk to us," he said politely.

Mary took another nibble from her cake. "I want to know why we're in Samaria and why we're traveling with Romans."

Jude and I looked down at the fire.

"You can bathe in the Jordan," I said.

"There are ritual purification baths in both Nazareth and Sepphoris," Jude remarked.

"And I'll be happy to take you to either," Father replied.

Mary finished chewing and took a sip from her water pouch. "A man of God wouldn't travel with a young woman through a defiled nation or make her share a camp with gentiles."

I never had spoken to Father in this way. I was surprised to hear these words coming from Mary's mouth. At the same time, I wondered how a Temple girl would fit into the lives of tradesmen and farmers. Would she get along with Aunt Miriam?

"I share your concerns, Mary," Father began. "But my brother and his son are in trouble. Your *family* is in trouble. I would take the same risks for you as I would anyone else."

"You are breaking the laws of Moses," Mary retorted.

"I may be breaking commandments set forth by our ancestors, but I'm not breaking any of the Ten Commandments set forth by God."

"Who are you to decide which commandments shall be kept and which shall be broken? You *must* be from the line of David if you think yourself so wise!"

Father would have punished us for this kind of talk.

"Unlike David I'm not sending another man to war just so I can marry his widow," Father said softly. "I only wish to save a young woman dedicated to God from a lifetime of despair and loneliness and, at the same time, save the lives of my brother and his son."

Father's voice was calm but stern, and his eyes were fixed to Mary's. He conducted the conversation as if he were walking a narrow trail lined with scorpions. If she were to be his wife, he needed her trust.

After several minutes Father let out a sigh and grinned. "I can't imagine how difficult this must be for you, Mary. I assure you, in our family, you will find joy, laughter, meaning, and purpose. You will be free to move about as you wish and make your own decisions. Your opinion will be counted among those most important to me when our family faces difficult times."

"Why do you treat me this way, Joseph bar Jacob?" asked Mary.

"You are a part of our family," said Father.

"But how will I know what to do?" Mary pleaded. "I know nothing of commanding a household or its tasks."

"My sister-in-law Miriam will teach you these things."

Mary sat quietly. Her hands didn't move from her lap, nor did her legs or feet twitch. She stared into the fire for several minutes before she spoke. "Who is this woman?" she asked. "Tell me more about your family."

Father looked away from Mary and into the fire. "Our houses are next to each other. Our families, at times, almost seem like one. Miriam lost her sister, Salome, to fever." Father abruptly stopped talking.

The days leading up to Mother's death were filled with horrible pain for me, Jude, and especially Father. As she lay dying on her bed, she cried out in suffering and confusion from the fever. Father and Aunt Miriam tended to her the best they could. Rabbi Ezra called in a physician from Sepphoris and paid him with coins from the synagogue. No amount of money or medicine could have saved my mother, and Father's worst fear was realized. Toward the end of her life, she no longer recognized him, nor did she ever hear him say good-bye.

Mary looked up to see him staring into the dancing flames. He waited a moment before he spoke again. His eyes remained fixed on our campfire. He cleared his throat to speak. "Salome was my wife," he choked out. "When she passed away, three of our children already were married with families of their own. But I still had two young boys at home. Miriam helped me raise and care for them."

Father looked up; the flickering flames reflected the tiredness in his eyes. The hairline along his aged cheeks, where his dark beard began, was matted from tears. He took a deep breath and let it out. "Those two boys are the young men seated on your right and left." Father's eyes were lost in the embers of our past; his ears were clogged like the streets of Jerusalem with memories of my mother talking and laughing.

We sat silently while the night breezes and crackling fire filled the void.

"I'm sorry about your wife," Mary finally said.

Father's voice continued in a steady rhythm, perhaps to reassure Mary, but his eyes never left our fire. "I traveled with gentiles because they were willing to leave Qumran immediately. Otherwise we would have had to wait another eight days for the next caravan. I didn't feel we could wait that long, and I don't want to arrive to a dead brother and nephew. These gentiles were kind enough to offer to travel the east shore of the Jordan. I was the one who suggested that we travel through Samaria to cut our trip short. Not only will we return home faster, but we also will return home before the Sabbath."

Mary remained silent.

"Where are you from?" Jude asked her.

She looked over at him and shook her head, as if to say, "I'm not speaking."

"Mary," I said, "you could start by telling us what you know of your family. We only know what we've heard in stories."

Mary opened her mouth then closed it.

"It's appropriate for you to speak among us and with us," said Father. "And yes, we will have our disagreements, but we will resolve them together."

Mary looked at Father.

"Joachim was my second cousin," said Father. "We are, in essence, your family."

Mary took a big bite of the leftover cake and handed the rest to Jude. Then she took several swallows from the water pouch. When she finally spoke, I was stunned by the confident tone in her voice.

"My father was a priest at the Temple. My mother, whom I have heard was a beautiful woman, struggled throughout her life to have children. One year my father was chosen to light the incense for the Feast of the Tabernacles. It is a great honor, one that most priests only get to do once in a lifetime. When Father went to perform his duty, an angel of God spoke to him. The angel said that his prayers had been heard and that my mother, Anna, would bear a child."

Mary fidgeted to get comfortable on the hard ground.

Jude stood up and fetched our bedrolls. When he finished passing them out, I asked Mary a question. "What did your father tell your mother about this angel?"

"An angel also had visited my mother. By the time my father returned home, she already knew. At least that's what I was told."

Jude and I looked at each other and then at Father. None of us was quite sure how to respond.

"Mary," Father said in a deep voice, "do you know how old your parents were when you were born?"

"They were near the end of their lives."

The moon was set like a large, orange-yellow ball in the sky, which signified the coming harvest. Father pointed and remarked on its enormous shape and size. While everyone was looking at the moon, Jude continued to question Mary. "Why did your parents leave you in the Temple? Why not leave you with family?"

"I have one living cousin, Elizabeth, and her husband, Zachariah," said Mary. "But Father and Mother dedicated my life to God. I would have had to live with the Temple community anyway."

"What does that mean?" pressed Jude.

"It means my life was boring," Mary said sternly. "I wove ceremonial clothes, baked ceremonial bread and candles, and grinded resins into little incense pebbles. I had no friends and very little interaction with the wives or the other women, and the rabbis would hit me if I tried to protest. When I wasn't working, I was confined to my room or the gardens."

"Were you lonely?" Jude asked.

"Yes." Mary bowed her head. "I was miserable—dedicated to God, yes, but miserable." She looked over at Jude. When she did this, I saw the trail of a single tear in the light of the moon.

"You did a great job of taking care of me today," said Jude. "Thank you for helping me drink and eat."

"You are better?" Mary asked.

Jude nodded and smiled.

"I promise you, Mary," said Father, "that you will never be alone again."

Mary smiled at him. "Thank you," she said softly.

"We should sleep," Father announced. "We have at least two days left on our trip."

The last two days of our trip back to Nazareth were pleasant. Mary spoke often, and when she did, it was usually with Jude or me. Father said that was because we were closer to her in age. As our little group snaked around the trails of Samaria, Father walked in step with the mule and kept the cart on an even path. By the middle of the second day, Jude was strong enough to walk on his own. By midday on the third day, we reached the tip of Galilee.

Father insisted that we stop to bathe in the Jordan.

When we finished bathing, he took Mary on a long walk near the river. When they returned, Mary walked with her arms crossed. She looked as if she had been crying. Then Father said something to her that neither Jude nor I could hear. She broke away in a slow run toward the river, stumbled down its banks, and flung herself into the water.

Father walked up to Jude and me. "I told her."

"Told her what?" asked Jude.

"That they wouldn't be having children," I interjected.

Father let out a long sigh. "She said that I was a monster, that I had tricked the high priest into giving me money in exchange for the marriage. She accused me of being a Canaanite."

We watched as Mary covered herself in the waters of the Jordan, her thin girlish figure bobbing up and down in the water, her white tunic sticking to the outlines of her form, and her wet hair clinging to her neck and back.

"She is a beautiful woman, Father," Jude remarked.

"That she is. She is also a Temple virgin, born and raised in the city of Jerusalem, with little life experience. She was meant to spend the rest of her life weaving clothes for the high priest. She is beautiful, intelligent, and as it has become apparent, quite a powerful force."

Father smiled. We watched as Mary continued to immerse herself in the Jordan. The day was sunny, and a soft breeze brushed the valley with wisps of cool air.

"Will everything be all right, Father?" Jude asked.

"With God's help it will. I have prayed that she and your Aunt Miriam can find ways to get along. Without her help Mary might feel like she went from one prison to another."

We left the Jordan River to begin our descent northwest to a valley in Galilee. The branches of the poplar trees hung heavy with leaves; the air smelled honeysuckle fresh; and the brown fields announced the coming harvest. I would have savored every single moment had I known they were about to dry up.

CHAPTER NINETEEN

We began the final leg of our journey early in the morning so that we might make it to Nazareth before the Sabbath began at sundown. When we were a few miles from home, Father called out for me. "James, run ahead and scout the village for soldiers or anything that might look suspicious. We'll wait a mile outside the village. If you don't return, I'll take Mary and Jude and head back toward the Jordan."

I nodded and ran as fast as I could.

When I could see our village, I decided to enter from the fields. I couldn't hear any voices, which was unusual. I crawled along in the tall grasses to keep from knocking down the wheat. It was hot, and the grass was hard and crunchy. My stomach ached with worry as I neared one of the cisterns that we used for irrigating the crops. I heard a voice coming from the village and flung myself into the wheat.

I was itchy and breathing hard. I got on my knees and slowly peeked over the wheat stalks toward the village. I saw a man in a dirty tunic looking to the sky and pacing. I stood and walked toward him. As I got closer, I recognized Rabbi Ezra. I smiled and began to run.

"James!" Rabbi shouted. He caught me in his arms and gave me a long hug. "Where is your father?"

"He's waiting for me a mile out of town. I was supposed to make sure it was safe."

"Your father is wise," Rabbi said. He put a hand on my shoulder. "Is Jude with you?"

I nodded. "He's all right now. He found us in Jerusalem."

Rabbi Ezra dropped his head. "Thanks be to God."

"Mary is with us too. Come. You should go with me to meet them."

As we walked along the road, I said, "There is no one tending the fields. Where is everyone?"

"All the able-bodied men are in Tiberias, which is where your Uncle Clopas and Cousin Simeon are today."

"And the women?"

"The Romans raided the village twice this past week. I have ordered the women and children to stay inside, at least during the day. It isn't safe."

I saw Father leading the mule and pointed ahead of us. "There he is, Rabbi," I said.

We waved and Father waved back. When we reached them, Father gave Rabbi Ezra a long hug. "It is good to be home," said Father.

"We're glad you're back," said the rabbi. He walked past the mule to the cart, where Jude and Mary sat.

"Hello, Jude," Rabbi Ezra said, smiling. "I see you found your father and brother."

Jude nodded. "Yes, Rabbi, I did."

"And you must be Mary," the rabbi said. Mary lifted her face, which had been shielded by her head cover. She nodded politely but didn't speak.

"She is very beautiful, Joseph," Rabbi Ezra concluded, "and soft-spoken."

Jude looked at me and chuckled. I dropped my head to smile. Mary turned away from Rabbi Ezra and pulled the head cover past her cheeks to shield her face.

Father looked at Rabbi, smiled, and shrugged. "Is it safe for us to enter Nazareth?"

"Yes," said Rabbi Ezra. "Clopas and Simeon have not yet returned from Tiberias. They should be here in a few hours."

As we walked toward home, Rabbi Ezra talked to Father about the Roman raids on Nazareth. When we arrived, Father handed me the reins and went to the cart to help Mary. Rabbi Ezra knocked on Uncle Clopas's door.

"Miriam, it's Ezra. Open the door."

My aunt cracked the door open and peeked out. The door flung open, and there stood my aunt, her hands covering her mouth.

"Oh, Joseph!" she cried. She ran into my father's arms and sobbed. "Oh, Joseph, it was so terrifying. They took them all!"

Father held her in silence while she grieved. When she looked up from his chest, she noticed Mary. She wiped the tears from her cheeks.

"You must be Mary," she said with shaky voice. "We're honored that you're here."

Aunt Miriam walked over to Mary, gave her a welcoming hug, and held her hands as she stared at her. "She is so young and beautiful, Joseph."

Father nodded.

"We must get you into some fresh clothes, dear," she told Mary. "I'll get you some water to wash up and something cool to drink. Are you hungry? Would you like some fresh fruit?"

The hardened look on Mary's face softened, and she nodded.

Aunt Miriam hugged her once more. "Come. We must get you fed and refreshed!"

Jude and I looked at Father. Father raised his eyebrows and chuckled. Rabbi Ezra patted Father's shoulder. "Your dear sister-in-law has been bored these last few days. Mary will give her a much-needed distraction."

Rabbi Ezra helped us unload and unhitch the cart. Just as I was returning from the stable, I heard Jude shout, "Simeon! Simeon!" I appeared from the stables and ran out to the road. Simeon and Jude hugged, and then Jude hugged Uncle Clopas. When they turned to face me, I saw that their cheeks and foreheads were badly burned by the sun. Their work tunics were soiled in dried mortar, and cuts and bruises marked their feet. Uncle's beard was gray from dust, the lines around his eyes filled with sand.

Father and Uncle exchanged an emotional greeting that lasted several moments. Uncle began to weep, and Father held him until he finished.

"Let's wash up and go inside, dear brother," said Father.

When the men had finished washing, we went inside Uncle Clopas's home. The interior was similar to ours, except that Aunt Miriam insisted on lighting more candles. As each of us reclined at the table, Aunt Miriam and Mary came to us from the cooking area.

"Clopas," said my aunt, "this is Mary."

Mary respectfully bowed her head.

Uncle looked at Father in disbelief. "She is like the first warm morning of spring, Joseph. Or a soft rain right after planting the fields. Where on earth did you find her?"

"Jerusalem," Father said with a laugh.

Uncle walked over to Father and gave him another hug. "I can't believe our family is both alive and together."

Aunt Miriam gave Mary instructions, gently, on where to find the wine goblets and pitcher. As my aunt poured the water, Mary began to the pour the wine.

"We have about an hour before sundown," Rabbi Ezra said to Father.

Father turned to Aunt Miriam, but she already knew what was on his mind.

"She's doing very well," she said, smiling. Mary set down the pitcher of wine and stood next to Aunt Miriam. "She knows much about hospitality, Joseph." Her eyes swelled with emotion. "It is *so good* to have you as a part of our family, Mary. Thank you for helping me this evening."

Mary hadn't spoken since we had arrived in Nazareth. Her first words were solely for my aunt. She said softly, "It is an honor to serve *you*."

Aunt Miriam set down the water pitcher and hugged her. Uncle Clopas and Rabbi Ezra nodded their approval.

Aunt Miriam and Mary began to arrange candles throughout the room and prepare place settings for the Sabbath meal.

"Tell me what happened, Clopas," said Father.

As Uncle began to tell of the terror that befell Nazareth, I was secretly thankful we had been away. Three days after our departure, Roman soldiers came to Nazareth looking for able men to work in Tiberias. There was no warning or recourse. An older man, John, who had stopped working a year ago on account of the shakes in his hands, refused to go, and the Romans ran a spear through him.

"John's wife collapsed on top of him and sobbed," Uncle said quietly. He paused for a moment to wipe his eyes then continued. "They lined us up in rows, counted us, then marched us to Tiberias. We were forced to work on the synagogue. An hour before sunset, they rounded us up from the worksite and told us to go to our homes and return the next day. They said that if we didn't return they would burn our homes and kill our women and children."

Father turned to Jude. "Where were you?"

"He was the lucky one," Uncle said with a chuckle.

"I was in the fields," said Jude. "I saw the horses and just lay flat in the fields all afternoon. When I thought they were gone, I went back to the house."

"Since they hadn't counted Jude, I thought he would be safe. He could manage the farm and fields. But the Romans started raiding nearby towns, which was why I sent him to Jerusalem."

"Where is Nicodemus?" Father asked. "We were supposed to be protected."

"I don't know, Joseph." Uncle wagged his head. "I didn't want to send Jude to Sepphoris to look for him with Romans on the roads. Jude volunteered to go to Jerusalem, and at the time, it seemed like the only good idea."

"He almost died looking for us," said Father.

"I got lost in the desert," Jude interjected.

"Who found you?" Rabbi Ezra asked.

"A servant from Rabbi Boethus's home," Jude replied.

Father ran a hand over his face. "Do you report back tomorrow?"

"No," said Uncle. "Jews are allowed a day off for the Sabbath."

"And the Romans don't have me, James, or Jude factored into their count?"

"No," said Uncle.

"Where is Nicodemus?" Father asked again through gritted teeth.

"I told you he and Joazar weren't to be trusted," Uncle replied.

Father sat quietly, allowing the words to settle. "We will observe the Sabbath and then accompany you to Tiberias. Reporting for duty is better than risking the lives of our families."

"I think that's wise, Joseph," said Rabbi Ezra.

With a puzzled look, Father stared at the table.

"What is it?" Uncle asked.

"In a sense, I'm grateful that James and I weren't here when the raid took place. I can't explain how it came to be that we're all sitting here, tonight, as a family."

Rabbi Ezra nodded. "It is good, isn't it?" All of us nodded. "Then let us pray."

The pleasant scent of Sabbath bread baking in the oven filled the room as Rabbi Ezra gave thanks for the many blessings bestowed on our village and family, and for our safe journey from Jerusalem. I looked up to see Mary and Miriam's eyes closed also in prayer. Mary must have felt my gaze and opened her eyes. She looked at me for only a second before bowing her head. I closed my eyes again and thought about this past week. Mary's presence filled a painful void that had lingered since my mother's death, and her care and concern for Jude had helped him survive.

If God was watching over her, then he was certainly watching over us.

CHAPTER TWENTY

The day following the Sabbath, we set out for Tiberias. To reach the city, travelers must climb a small hill covered with green grasses and an ancient olive grove. The trees number in the hundreds, and one in particular is the largest in Galilee. Many have claimed that a descendant of Noah planted it.

This morning a young man about my age was hanging on that tree.

Just before we arrived in Tiberias, I witnessed the desecration of that beautiful hill and those ancient groves. I also saw, for the first time, the awesome power of the Roman army. As we approached the hill, I heard people screaming and shouting over the sounds of clanging metal. Father ran ahead to see if we were in danger. He reached the top of the hill and abruptly turned back.

"They're crucifying Zealots!" he said as he gasped for air.

Jude began to walk up the road, but Father reached out and grabbed him.

"You are the perfect age for a Zealot recruit! Do *not* go any farther or they may seize you by mistake!"

Uncle Clopas stepped toward Father. "Let him go, Joseph. He doesn't understand."

"He will soon enough. Walk with me. Stay together."

At the top of the hill, a hundred yards away, was the most disgusting sight I had ever seen. More than a thousand Roman legionnaires were nailing young Jewish men to the olive trees on the backside of the hill, near the road that led into Tiberias. At the clump of trees nearest to us, Roman soldiers were beating three young men with clubs.

"Do you see what they're doing, Jude? The soldiers aim for the ribs and upper legs so that they weaken them but don't injure them," Uncle Clopas explained.

The soldiers stopped beating the men and dragged them by their wrists to the olive grove.

"Why have the soldiers stopped beating them?" I asked.

"You will soon see," said Uncle Clopas, his voice seeped in sadness.

Father motioned for all of us to sit down on the road. "If we remain standing, we may be perceived as a threat."

We watched as the soldiers tied the bodies of the boys to the olive trees, extending their arms and legs to the nearest branches. Using sharp iron stakes the width of a man's thumb, the Romans nailed their wrists and ankles into the wood.

Each hammer blow brought forth a shrieking cry of agony. I pulled my legs to my chest and buried my head against my knees. I raised my head again just as the Romans poured on more pain and suffering. One of the soldiers arrived on horseback, carrying a clay pot with a stirring stick. When Father saw this, he bowed his head, shut his eyes, and placed a hand over his mouth.

Uncle Clopas spoke quietly. "When you are crucified on a cross beam, like the ones you have seen in Sepphoris, your body cannot let out air properly with your arms outstretched, and you suffocate to death. It is different for these men; it could be days before they die, especially if their loved ones bring them food and water and chase away the wild dogs."

As Uncle spoke, the soldiers smeared a tarlike substance on the faces, beards, and chests of the victims. Before I could process the horror in front of me, Jude asked, "What are they doing?"

With his head still bowed and his eyes shut, Father said, "They are coating them in honey."

The three boys looked at one another. We were horrified.

"The bees and hornets will deter loved ones from trying to feed, water, or rescue the boys," said Clopas softly. "The stings either will poison their bodies to the point of death or make them so weak that they can't breathe."

Screams and groans flew like arrows up the hillside. As the condemned suffered, Father had to speak louder to be heard over their cries. "Clopas, you and Simeon must report to work. I don't want either of you suffering the same fate. James and I will go with you. The bag of silver I received for Mary's dowry is in the cart under our tools. We can use this money to bribe the overseers."

Father motioned for us to walk down the hill, away from the city, but I couldn't get my feet to move, for they were frozen by fear. As Father walked past me, he grabbed me by the arm and kept talking to Uncle Clopas. "If we can bribe the officials into suspending your work detail, we might have enough time to bring in the harvest."

Uncle Clopas scowled at Father. "I don't like this plan. What if they press us all into service? What if they decide to raid Nazareth again? If we are all here, we'll have no way of protecting the women."

Father stood for moment, pondering what to do. Then he looked at Jude. "Do you think you can take care of the farm and the women?"

"Yes, Father," said Jude.

Father pointed down the road. "There's an old shepherd's trail off the main road that leads back to Nazareth. The soldiers generally avoid it. Use that trail to get back home. Tell Aunt Miriam and Mary our plan, and then go to Sepphoris. Find Marcus. Tell him what's happened. He will help you find Nicodemus. Don't leave Sepphoris until you've spoken to Nicodemus. Only he can help us."

"Can you handle all of this, Jude?" asked Uncle Clopas. "It's a lot of responsibility."

Jude nodded. "Yes."

"Then go," said Father.

We watched as he ran down the road. When we could no longer see him, Father, Uncle, and I headed toward Tiberias.

I dreaded having to walk past all those crucified men.

Some of the men's faces were covered in bees. Many twitched in pain. The cries were fewer, as dozens began to lose consciousness. An older man had been crucified on one of the olive trees close to the road. His eyes were open, and his head swayed back and forth. Tiny drops of the man's blood had streaked across the leaves, turning them from green to red.

I stared at the tree for what seemed like an eternity. It was a younger tree with many branches, surely enough to fill thirty or forty large baskets with olives. But the olives lay in piles all around the tree.

"Our family could be fed for weeks," I mumbled. "We could press enough oil to sell at market."

Father looked at me with raised eyebrows. "Is that all you see, son?"

I swallowed hard. "It was once a tree of life. Now it's a tree of death. I would never want to eat from this tree." I turned to Father in desperation. "I want these men to die quickly."

Father put a hand on my shoulder. "I also want their suffering to end, James." He knelt next to me. "Many will lose consciousness soon. Some will lose their will to live and simply die from despair. Until the time when they will pass, God will find a way to ease their suffering."

"These men were someone's sons and grandsons," I protested.

"Or fathers, grandfathers, uncles, or brothers," added Father.

"I feel so scared."

"That is exactly how the Romans want you to feel, James. Do remember that day in the Upper Market when we talked about violence?"

I nodded and wiped my eye with the heel of my hand.

"Remember this day too."

Uncle Clopas was several yards away; I assumed he was having a similar talk with Simeon. Father motioned for him to join us.

As we walked farther, I saw a young man about Jude's age writhing in pain and moaning. I studied the nails in his wrists and ankles and heard the buzzing of hornets. The boy howled and cried for his mother, who stood nearby. She screamed at us to help her then flung herself onto Father.

He held her as she grieved.

"You must let her go, Joseph," said Uncle.

Father placed two silver coins in her hand. As he let go, she fell to the ground and wailed.

"God be with her," prayed Father.

When we finally reached the gates of Tiberias, a tall Roman soldier stopped us.

"Where are you going?" the soldier shouted.

"We are masons. We're here to work on the synagogue," Uncle answered. "We work on behalf of the high priest, Rabbi Joazar ben Boethus of Sepphoris."

The soldier laughed. "Your work is at the prince's palace, not the synagogue." "But sir, I worked on the synagogue just last week," pleaded Uncle.

"Move!" the man shouted, and three other soldiers joined him.

Father gave Uncle a worried look. As the soldiers grumbled about their pay and duties, Uncle spoke in a low voice to Father. "We are slaves now, Joseph. We are here for good."

We were taken to a chaotic worksite filled with yelling and screaming and cries of pain. We stood in a long line of men waiting for their assignments. From our position, we saw the Romans whipping and beating slaves who either refused to work or were too tired to perform their duties. When a worker collapsed from exhaustion, injury, or death, the Romans tossed the body into a deep pit where dirt had been dug out to level off the worksite. Bodies were piled upon bodies; some were still moving.

Father turned his head away. "I pray for them," he said quietly.

With no clean water or latrines, the worksite stunk of spoiled vegetables, animal dung, and human waste. The putrid air was filled with the sounds of trowels scraping against stone, paddles churning in pots filled with mortar, and pained groans from the workers. Father noticed a small group of young men carrying water. Each carried a wooden pole across his back. Two large buckets hung from opposite ends of the pole.

"Who are those people?" Simeon asked in a soft voice.

"They are water slaves," said Father. "You need a lot of water to make mortar. These men haul it from Lake Tiberias."

"Why not haul water from the wells or the cisterns?" I asked.

"If a bucket, or one of these men, fell into the well, the whole town might be poisoned," Uncle explained.

One of the water slaves fell to the ground near us. Three Roman soldiers rushed over to the man and whipped his shoulders where the pole had rested moments before.

When we reached the front of the line, I saw a Roman official seated at a small table. He asked Father and Uncle to announce their names, place of residence, and the nature of their work.

"We're undertaking a task for a prominent Roman in Sepphoris," explained Father. "We're also performing a service for the high priest. Is it possible that we might pay some sort of restitution that would exempt us from working in Tiberias?"

The Roman roared back in laughter. "The Romans don't need money, you fool. They need men!"

Uncle Clopas cast a worried look in Father's direction.

"Where are we to report?" Father asked quietly.

"Are you Jews?" the Roman asked.

Father and Uncle nodded.

"You will be allowed to leave the worksite each day. At the end of each week, you will be allowed to leave early to prepare for the Sabbath. Do not be late for work, or you will haul water as your punishment for that day. For each month of work, you will be paid a silver coin. Do you understand?"

Father and Uncle nodded again.

"Show them to the site," grumbled the official.

Two soldiers led us to the far corner of the new palace. As we walked I saw large square limestone blocks being hoisted in the air by a system of ropes then lowered onto other blocks that made up the wall.

"If one of those blocks were to come loose," said Father, "it would crush the man underneath it."

"It happens more often than you would think," added Uncle.

Simeon and I looked at the limestone blocks and shuddered.

When we arrived at the worksite, we discovered our job was to help build the palace foundation and retaining walls. The blocks were tightly joined next to one another—so tightly that a leaf couldn't pass through the cracks. If there were spaces, masons filled the cracks with mortar so the entire foundation was made to look as if it were one huge piece of limestone.

The soldiers left us at the corner of the foundation and walked away.

A man about the same age as my father walked over to us. His beard was full of dirt and grit, his lips chapped and gray, and his brown tunic covered in dried mortar clumps.

"My name is Aaron. What is your skill?"

Father introduced our family and the skills we had to offer.

The man looked at Simeon and me and frowned. "Keep those boys close. You don't want the Romans to mistake them for water slaves. The Romans usually leave us Jews alone, but look for what needs to be done and stay busy. If you need direction, ask me. Don't ask a soldier. They'll whip you and beat you just for speaking to them."

"How long will we have to work here?" Uncle asked.

"Until the palace is built," Aaron replied, "or until we are dead."

"What if we choose to desert Tiberias?" Father asked.

"Where do you live?" Aaron asked.

"Nazareth," Uncle replied.

"That's too close. They will come after you, and if they find you, the soldiers will kill the women and children, burn your homes, and take you as slaves. It has happened to many men. I have seen it with my own eyes."

Father ran his hand over his face. "We should head to the cart and collect our tools."

Aaron grabbed Father by the sleeve. "If you wish to keep your mule and cart, don't bring them tomorrow. The Romans will confiscate your property. Carry what you need."

"We will do as you suggest," said Father.

"Then it is time," Aaron replied. "If you want to live, work hard."

CHAPTER TWENTY-ONE

The trip to Tiberias took about two hours each way. At the end of the shift, we were all so exhausted we barely could walk. Our water pouches were dry; we had no food; and the summer sun blasted down on us.

"It will be autumn soon," said Father as we trudged our way home. "The cooler weather will lift our spirits."

Aunt Miriam and Mary rushed out to meet us. I saw Jude coming in from the fields. He ran to greet us. Simeon gave his mother a kiss and went inside the house. He was the weakest of us, and his wiry frame and little fingers worked twice as hard to keep up with the adults.

"Will he be all right?" Aunt Miriam asked Clopas.

"He will manage, just like the rest of us," Uncle replied.

Mary gave Father a hug. "I was worried about you and James," she said quietly.

"We're in good physical condition. We know how to do this work. If Jude can help us pull through the harvest season, we should be all right. How was your day with Miriam?"

Mary looked at my aunt, who was still holding on to Uncle Clopas. She stared at Mary, waiting for her response.

Aunt Miriam answered for her. "She's homesick."

After supper, with the family gathered around the table, Father spoke of the changes that would come to our daily life. With the help of Rabbi Ezra and the elders in the village, Jude would run the farm. Mary and Miriam would have to work the fields in addition to their regular housework. Father warned Simeon and me that we would have to work in the fields too. Simeon groaned.

"We're falling on harder times," my uncle said sternly. "You will become stronger for it, and we will survive this. We only have a month or two to complete the harvest. Then we'll have only four more months to complete the work in Tiberias, well before planting time."

I wish I could say that Uncle was right. In the weeks and months that followed, our family worked harder than any of us had in our lives. September brought forth a bountiful harvest, more than Father could ever remember. But the added labors made all of us weary. It was the end of October before all the produce had been gathered and the grain stored away for the winter. Over time Mary learned the things she needed to know to be a good wife. Aunt Miriam remarked that she was a fast learner but too quiet. Father guessed that Aunt Miriam probably talked enough for the both of them.

One cold morning, early in December, we were awakened by a knock on our door. Jude and I were upstairs sleeping when I heard the banging. We scampered from our bedrolls and shimmied down the ladder. When Father opened the door, I couldn't believe my eyes. It was my oldest brother, who lived in Bethlehem.

"Simon!" Father exclaimed. He wrapped his arms around my brother. The cold air snuck inside our home, and I begged Father to shut the door. The commotion caused Uncle Clopas and his family to stir. Within minutes our entire family was assembled in the front room, welcoming Simon home.

Aunt Miriam started the oven fire, while Mary served Simon a cup of water and a piece of flatbread left over from the night before. He sat on a cushion, reclined in his usual way, his legs crossed with his arms resting on the table. His hair was much longer than I remembered, but his dark eyes had the same sparkle as Father's. The whole family fidgeted in silence while Simon ate and drank. When he had finished the bread, he said, "It is good to be home."

"Why are you here, Simon, and where is your family? Is everything fine?" inquired Father.

"Everyone is fine, Father," said Simon. "My wife, my children, my trade—everything is good. I understand that you were in Jerusalem."

"James and I were there. I am now betrothed to Mary, the daughter of the late Rabbi Joachim."

"And you couldn't make the extra few miles to Bethlehem?" hinted Simon.

"Your father returned home when he heard about our situation," Uncle explained. "We were pressed into service by the Romans."

"I heard this from some Temple priests who serve at my synagogue," said Simon. "Are you well?"

"Better than most," said Father. "God is watching over us."

Simon nodded and took another drink from his cup.

"If you traveled through the night, there must be something urgent you have yet to tell us," Uncle asserted.

"Mary's cousin, Elizabeth, the one in Juttah, is due to have a child soon. She wants Mary to come to her home and help her."

Mary walked over to my brother. "Is Elizabeth all right?" she asked quietly.

"She's fine," Simon said with a smile.

"What about her husband, Zachariah?" Mary asked.

Simon shook his head. "He is having some trouble, I'm afraid." He looked around at the rest of us. "Like Mary's mother, Elizabeth is too old to have children. But God blessed Zachariah and Elizabeth, and she became pregnant. She's due in March, about three months from now."

"What's wrong with Zachariah?" Father asked.

Simon shrugged. "Right after Elizabeth became pregnant, he came down with a fever that left him unable to speak. He mumbles and stutters as if his tongue is swollen. Though he would like to proclaim the greatness of God from Mount Olivet, he can't. If you bring up the subject of the baby, he tears up. The physicians and other Temple priests are hoping the swelling of his tongue goes away on its own."

Mary cleared her throat.

"Speak whenever you wish, Mary. Simon allows the women in his home to do the same," Father said.

Mary swallowed hard. Her pleasant voice fell on my ears like soft rain. "Elizabeth must feel both joy and sorrow," she said softly.

"She's doing remarkably well," Simon assured her. "But she really wants you there with her. Many of the other Temple priests' wives have offered to help her. She only wants you."

Mary looked at the floor. "Joseph is working very hard right now. With all my duties, I'm not sure I can make the trip to Juttah. I want to, but I am betrothed to Joseph and am an important part of this family."

After struggling through her first few weeks, Mary had become enchanted by the rhythm of life on our farm in Nazareth. She enjoyed going to the well and taking short walks.

The women of the village were captivated by her personal life, particularly her Temple schooling and teachings. And Mary was astounded by all the things they knew how to do, such as weave, dye, milk, farm, and raise children. With humility, she embraced their instruction and learned much. By the end of October, Mary was recognized as being one of the most productive workers in our village and known for her strength and wisdom.

Father tugged at his beard. "She can't go alone. Who would go with her to Juttah, Simon?"

"She would be fine traveling with me. I can get her to Zachariah's home. Assuming that she would want to stay to help take care of Elizabeth after the birth, the return trip in the spring would concern me. With less food and work available then, the roads will be teeming with thieves, and I can't escort her back to Nazareth—"

"Because it's planting time," Father said with a smile.

Simon grinned and nodded. "Forgive me, Father, but I also have a family to watch over."

"The Romans are snatching up every able body they can find to finish the work in Tiberias," said Father. "They have stormed two more villages near us already. It's not safe for you to be here, Simon. If they press you into service, you can't go back to Bethlehem." Father looked over at Mary. "Do you want to help your cousin?"

Mary nodded. "I do. But this is our home. I am needed here first."

"Someone from this house could go with you," suggested Father.

Mary looked over at Jude. From the day Mary had nursed him back to health, to their labors in the fields, the experiences had helped them form a special bond. Father was grateful that Mary had someone her own age for company. Aunt Miriam was thankful that Jude was there to help teach Mary in the ways of farming.

Father looked around the table at our family. "The harvest is over, and our work in Tiberias will be completed before the planting season begins. If Mary is to visit Elizabeth, I want someone from my family to watch over her. Jude, would you be willing to accompany her?"

Jude looked at Mary then back at Father. "Would I get to go to Jerusalem?" he asked. "And actually spend time there?"

"Yes," Father said with a laugh. "I'm sure Zachariah could use some help at his home. He also would make sure to show you the holy places and the Temple."

My face became hot, and I was flushed with envy. But Father knew, as I did, that the Romans would kill my family and come looking for me if I didn't show up to work the next day.

Father turned to Simon. "It is settled. Jude will accompany Mary to Juttah. Tell Zachariah that they both have my permission to stay through the spring and into the summer. Antipas will have returned; the work in Tiberias will be complete; and there will be no more danger to our village or our lives. Until that time, Juttah will be the safest place for Mary."

"I have an extra mule they can use, Father," said Simon.

Father stood and hugged my brother.

Mary and Aunt Miriam scurried around the house, trying to seat everyone for breakfast. I smelled vegetables cooking in the pans and the scent of honey from small pitchers on the table.

Simon turned to Jude. "If we leave today, we should arrive in time to observe the Festival of Lights."

Before saying the blessing, Father patted Simon on the back. "It is good to have you home, son."

"It is good to be home, Father."

When Father finished the blessing, the table buzzed with chatter about Elizabeth's miraculous pregnancy and Zachariah's speech impediment.

"The poor man can't even celebrate his family's good fortune," Aunt Miriam lamented. "Do they know what happened?"

"Apparently it came on suddenly," Simon explained. "He gestures with his hands and writes things down."

"Can he eat or drink?" Mary asked.

Simon nodded. "He can eat, drink, and breathe, just like he always did. It's his speech that has everyone concerned."

"He could be going mad," suggested Uncle Clopas.

Mary cringed when she heard this and looked at Aunt Miriam for answers.

"Clopas!" my aunt said in a loud voice. "The man and his wife found favor with God! He is not going mad! He may be scared or nervous, or he may simply be overwhelmed from the thought of having a child at such an old age. Many men have their tongues tied when their wife is pregnant."

"Usually by force," Clopas said in a low voice.

The table roared with laughter.

Father looked at Jude. "When you return from Juttah, use the main roads near Jerusalem. Make sure you travel in a group, preferably with Jewish traders or pilgrims, but use your own judgment." He glanced at Mary. "She has been dedicated to God. I am entrusting you with her care."

Jude nodded and looked at Mary. She smiled at him.

"Good," Father said with a grin. "We need to get ready for our workday. Simon, you need to collect supplies for your journey."

I felt as if our lives were finally returning to the normal we once knew many months ago. I thought about my last day at the Jordan, in the company of my brother, Father, and my new mother. It was a moment I had returned to many times during those long walks to Tiberias.

As I watched my family move about our home, I felt at peace, as if God had firmly planted his presence in our home. I hadn't felt so at ease since that day by the Jordan. I mumbled a prayer of gratitude and rushed outside to help Simon and Jude prepare for their long journey.

Chapter Twenty-Two

In the months that passed, we focused on our work in Tiberias. It was one of the cooler winters Father could remember, with more rainy days than sunny ones, and with all the rain, progress on Prince Antipas's royal palace slowed. When the Romans heard that their duties would be extended into June, they became violent toward the slaves and barely tolerant of the Jews. Prince Antipas delayed his return from Rome. Both Rabbi Boethus and Nicodemus were called upon to travel with him as his advisors, which meant we couldn't expect relief from our harsh work conditions until the end of the summer, when Jude and Mary would return home.

Father tried desperately to keep up with our farm, often working late into the night. He battled against time, heat, and a field thick with weeds. Through August and into September, the Romans kept us laboring into the evenings. After returning from our worksite, we had about thirty minutes of daylight, and we used every minute with great efficiency.

"James, go out to the stable and count the number of containers we have for gathering grain. Simeon, check on the orchards and nut groves. Note any of the trees that need to be cut back. Clopas, please clean our tools so that all we'll have to do in the morning is pack them. I'll go down to the fields and see if the crops are ready. We may have to start harvesting a little each day."

I walked to the stable, which was the halfway point to our well. As I passed the well, I noticed that the dirt around the rock ledge had been pounded flat by the winter rains, and I hoped no one had discovered the gold and silver coins. The sunset cast a beautiful red glow over the valley, and as I faced west to watch for a moment, I saw the shadow of a mule and rider. A young man walked ahead of the mule, leading it along.

"Jude!" I shouted with all my lungs. "Jude!" I ran as fast as I could along a trail that led through our fields. When I reached my brother, I noticed he had a scornful look. He halted the mule and pointed back at Mary. Thinking she might speak first, I looked up at her, but she stared at me in silence. I looked back at Jude and lifted my hands.

"Mary is pregnant," Jude said smugly.

Mary pulled away a thin wool blanket to reveal a large bump where her tiny waist and flat belly used to be.

There were no joyful greetings, no tears of joy, no laughter. There was just a weight that came pressing down upon my mind and heart and stomach. My eyes bulged; my stomach felt sick. I placed my hands on my hips and looked up at Jude, whose mouth was crinkled in a frown so pathetic it looked like he had eaten a handful of sour grapes.

"What happened?" I asked.

"If I knew what happened, James, I would tell you."

I looked up at her, then over at Jude. "What are you going to tell Father?"

Jude dropped the leader. "I don't know."

I searched my thoughts for the right questions to ask, but all I could think to do was skip to the one question that was in my heart. The setting sun was pointing right at the trail. I closed one eye and squinted with the other.

I cocked my head toward Jude. "Did you lie with her?" I asked him.

Mary sniffled and buried her face in the blanket.

Jude stomped over to me. "She is Father's wife!" he said through gritted teeth. He grabbed me by my tunic. "How can you ask me such a thing?"

"You two have spent almost a year together, Jude!" I protested.

Before I could finish, he threw the weight of his body into me, knocking me to the ground. He knelt on my chest and pounded my face with his fists. "I did nothing! I did nothing!" he screamed.

One of my eyes began to swell. A warm liquid dripped down my upper lip and oozed its way into the crack of my mouth, and I recognized the salty bitterness as the taste of my own blood.

I heard Mary yell, "Jude! Please stop! Jude! You're hurting him!"

The sound of leather sandals thumped against the dirt-packed ground. As my older brother threw punch after punch, the shadow of a figure covered my face. When the shadow moved, I felt the sun warming my face, and I heard the sound of a body hitting the ground.

I looked up to see who was there, but I couldn't. Both of my eyes were swollen shut.

"What is the meaning of this?" I heard Father shout.

After a few seconds, I heard Uncle's voice. "Joseph, you'd better take a look at Mary."

I felt a piece of soft cloth fall against my toes. Mary dropped the blanket she was holding onto my sandals. She had been the one who had pulled Jude away.

I desperately wanted to see the reactions of my family. I tried to speak, but as soon as I moved my mouth and jaw, I was overcome with pain. I grunted. Two large hands grabbed my shoulders and helped me stand. I could tell by the smell of the wine on his breath that it was Uncle Clopas.

"Who did this?" I heard him ask.

I shook my head. I would not betray my brother. The few times we ever disagreed, we always had kept it between us. There are some secrets that only brothers share.

"Who did this?" Uncle Clopas asked again.

"I did," said Jude.

"But he didn't mean it," Mary protested.

"Silence!" screamed Uncle.

One voice I didn't hear was Father's. When the talking ceased, I heard the sound of wheezing, the kind that comes from deep within a man's chest. It was the exact same sound I'd heard in Tiberias, near the crucifixions, and on my mother's deathbed just before she died.

"Joseph," I heard Uncle say in a gentle tone. "Joseph."

There was no answer.

I saw three dark shapes move toward the mule. As I stepped closer, I saw a fourth figure draped across the back of the mule, as if leaning against it. The figure slumped to the ground near the mule. I heard him take a deep breath and cry out loud. It was the same dreadful sound Father had made shortly after my mother's passing, as if God's hand had come out of the sky and torn his heart from his chest.

Pain shot through my head and face. Every time I tried to blink a salty tear away, my eyes stung horribly. But the tears cleared away some of the cloudiness, and I saw Uncle kneel next to Father.

"What am I to do, brother?" Father pleaded. "We are slaves to the Romans, the harvest is small, my wife…this child…"

I looked to the west. As my vision continued to clear, I saw the evening sun setting like a red-hot coal of a dying fire. I heard footsteps coming up the trail and turned to see a small figure walking briskly toward us.

"Oh, my," I heard Aunt Miriam say. "Oh, Joseph! Oh, poor Joseph!"

Father sat with his legs crossed in the middle of the trail, his head bobbing in despair.

"Do you want me to get the rabbi?" Uncle asked.

If Father called upon Rabbi Ezra, then the matter would be settled. A courier would be sent to Sepphoris to fetch someone of power, someone in the Sanhedrin. Mary would be charged with adultery and stoned to death. And since Jude was the only man traveling with her, his guilt already was assumed.

Uncle tried to break through to my father once more. "They could hold court as early as tomorrow, Joseph." Father sniffled and stared at him. "Let me help you put this behind you. We have enough coins to buy food through the winter and into next spring. We can start planting again and resume our work in Sepphoris. Please, let me help you."

"What about Jude?" Father asked slowly. Uncle backed away from Father. "I won't do this, Clopas. I won't kill my own family."

"You aren't thinking clearly, Joseph. Something needs to be done and soon. The whole village will know in a matter of minutes."

Father shook his head. "No, Clopas," he said sternly. "We can't allow our people to kill Mary."

"A village mob may want to kill them both," Clopas said softly.

A stained family could be banished from the village. A stained family would be banished from the synagogue. While Uncle sought to preserve our family's good name, Father faced yet another loss to add to an otherwise long list. His own father had passed away when he was young. He had lost my mother eight years ago. But Father fought back his own grief, spending each and every day of his life trying to hold his family together.

Uncle looked at Aunt Miriam, who had knelt beside the two men. Then I saw Father look at me. There was very little left of the man I knew him to be. His passion for living was all but gone.

Jude had yet to speak. He had the right to state his case, but he was so angry that he refused. Mary peeled herself off the mule, since the rest of us had assumed she was unclean. Now both of them walked slowly away from our family, down the trail toward Nazareth, with Mary's round belly exposed for everyone to see.

"The village has heard us," I heard Uncle say. "Joseph, give me permission to call on the rabbi."

Father turned to me. "James." He took a deep breath to collect himself. "James, I'm sorry." I walked over and sat next to him. "Did you speak to Jude?"

I nodded. Everything on my face was swollen. Dried blood had crusted on my lips; my eyes had swollen shut; and my jaw was bruised so badly that I wondered how I ever would be able to open my mouth to eat or drink.

"Can you speak to me, son?"

I nodded again. Emotion coursed through my veins like the Roman horses that galloped in and out of Tiberias. My face pounded in pain with every beat of my heart.

"What is it?" Clopas said, hurrying me along.

I looked at Father. My words were garbled, as if I were chewing and speaking at the same time. "*Rachamim*," I said, grunting. "*Rachamim!*"

Father pulled me close to him. The pain in my face increased from the pressure of being pulled so close to Father, but nothing would have made me let go.

"Joseph," said Clopas, "you know what you must do fulfill the law."

Father shook his head. "I will speak to Rabbi Ezra tomorrow but not about this. Take Jude and Mary home and feed them. Give them the sweet wine we were saving for their return. We'll discuss this tomorrow."

"You could be banned from the synagogue," said Uncle.

"This is my decision. I give, I sacrifice, and I love with all my heart, brother. If all this is wrong, let the Lord punish me according to his will."

"I can't let you do this," Uncle pleaded.

"The sun has set. The village is dark. Walk Mary and Jude to the house. If anyone asks, tell them the cart ran over my foot, and I cried out in pain. I need to take care of James."

Uncle looked at me in despair. "Say something to him, James," he insisted. "Wake your Father up from his despair so that he may do the right thing."

I shook my head. Uncle stared at me in anger then looked at Father. "How long will you be?" Uncle asked.

"I'll take James down to the well and clean him up. We'll have a drink of water and talk."

"If Jude and Mary want to see you, what should I tell them?"

By now Father had collected himself. His grief had waned, and his voice was clear. "Tell them I will always love them and to get some rest."

Uncle lifted his head, as if questioning Father's answer.

"Go, brother."

Uncle nodded and, like a reluctant servant, walked away in quiet disgust.

I followed Father to the stable, where he unhitched the mule and cart. He lit an oil lamp, handed it to me, and gathered Jude and Mary's belongings. As he unloaded the cart, he talked to himself. "Zachariah ensured that they were prepared for the trip. There are several blankets in here, probably to keep Mary's belly covered or to provide her padding for the trip. There is a jar of water and several paper packages containing dried fish, fruit, bread, and nuts."

I heard a clink as Father picked up a coin purse the size of a fist. "There's enough silver in here to a keep a traveler comfortable for months," he mumbled. "Zachariah intended to take great care of Jude and Mary." Father took the lamp from me and looked into the leather pouch. "What is this?" He handed the lamp back to me. He reached into the pouch and pulled out a scroll. "It must be from Zachariah."

Father picked up an empty bucket. He placed some of the cloth scraps we used for polishing tools inside it then threw in several handfuls of salt from a wool bag. This wasn't the salt we used on our food but the salt we used to fertilize our fields. It came from the Dead Sea and had special minerals that kept the weeds down and ensured healthy crops.

"You carry the bucket, and I'll take the lamp," said Father.

I held onto his arm as we walked slowly toward the well. When we reached it, Father dunked the old rags into the cool water and used them to wash my face. After several minutes he caked the special salts onto the rags and told me to hold them against my swollen eyes and bruised cheeks.

"The salt will ease the swelling in your face and take away some of the pain. Keep your eyes shut, James, or the salt will hurt worse than the bruises."

I sat on the stone ledge of the well, pressing the salts to my eyes and face. Father set the lamp down next to me. "I'm going to read this scroll while we are here," he said. "It's the only place I feel safe, and I may need it to save your brother."

"He hit me." My words were muffled through swollen lips and the bundle of cold salted cloths.

"I know he did, James," Father said.

"Listen," I said. Though my words sounded like those of child just learning to speak, I needed Father to hear what I had to say.

Father looked at up at me. "You don't have to explain anything right now. Just sit there with the salts, and let me read this scroll."

I shook my head vigorously, feeling every shake as a sharp pain. "No, no," I said.

Father sighed. "What is it?"

"He didn't lie with her," I struggled to say.

He looked confused, and his hands began to tremble. "How do you know?"

"When I asked him, he hit me," I said again. Heavy emotion bubbled up behind my eyes, and I couldn't say another word.

Father turned around, leaned against the well, and peeled the two wax seals from the scroll. He read to himself for several minutes.

"You want to know what it says?" he asked.

I nodded.

He cleared his throat and read the letter out loud.

Dear Joseph,

I can't explain the wondrous events that have transpired over these past months. Elizabeth gave birth to a healthy boy, and I regained my speech several days later. Given our old age, this is nothing short of a miracle. Elizabeth and I are not sure when or how she became pregnant. As I have learned, it is not for me, or Elizabeth, to question.

I want to express my concern for you and for Mary. How this happened is a story only she can tell. Believe what she tells you.

I am confident that Jude is a dutiful son. He is, in many ways, much like his father. He spent the past several months shielding Mary, like an older brother guarding his sister's honor. This will seem like a difficult time, Joseph, but I know you will do what is right for your family.

- Zachariah

I looked at Father and shrugged. He was rinsing bandages in the bucket of water. "This will have to wait until morning."

He helped me off the ledge and handed me the lamp. He dumped out the bloody salt water, wrung out the rags, and placed them in the empty bucket. When this was finished, he traded me the bucket for the lamp.

"Follow me," I heard him say.

Together we walked, guided by a single flame in the middle of a cool, dark September night, along a rocky path that led to our home.

For the next two days, I rarely left my mat. The pain in my face was so horribly intense that all I wanted to do was sleep. Aunt Miriam visited on the morning of the first day to remove the salted wrappings and apply new ones. She offered me a cup of water and several spoonfuls of mashed chickpeas. I barely could open my mouth, and it hurt to swallow. Rabbi Ezra visited me shortly after, prayed over my face and body, then forced me to drink a bitter-tasting liquid that made me very sleepy.

On the morning of the second day, I awoke to footsteps near my sleeping mat. I rolled over and saw the figure of man's tunic but couldn't make out the face. The figure reached down to hold my hand, and I closed my sleepy eyes to drift off to sleep. The hand felt warm but rough. It was a laborer's hand, with cuts on the fingers and palms. The thought of the fields comforted me. I slowly rolled my head from side to side, trying to open my eyes, but couldn't.

I thought I heard the sound of sniffling and cocked my head to one side. Then I heard the figure speak. "Go back to sleep, James," he whispered. "I will watch over you."

I wanted to smile, to rejoice in all the mercy that was shown him. For if my father had shown mercy toward Jude, he must have shown mercy toward Mary. With thin rough hands gently squeezing mine, I fell back asleep, resting peacefully in the house of my father and in the company of my brother.

CHAPTER TWENTY-THREE

When I woke up on the third day, much of the swelling in my face had receded. I heard Uncle Clopas yelling downstairs and my father screaming for him to get out of his house. I slowly rose from my mat and hobbled down the ladder. To my left, Jude and Mary, along with Aunt Miriam, sat at our family's gathering table. Straight ahead I heard Father greet Rabbi Ezra, who stood just inside the doorway.

Rabbi Ezra looked behind Father and saw me standing at the foot of the ladder. "Good morning, James." The rabbi smiled. "Did you fall off the side of a mountain?"

"Good morning," I mumbled back. "No, Rabbi. The side of the mountain fell on me."

Rabbi Ezra chuckled. "I see."

Father walked over to see me. "Are you feeling better?"

I nodded.

"Neither of the boys will say anything, but I think James was merely the convenient target of all the anger and frustration that had been building in Jude," said Father.

"I understand," the rabbi said.

His blue sash helped all to recognize him as a rabbi, but his homespun tunics were as modest as ours. He didn't dress like the priests in Sepphoris or Jerusalem, nor did he wear his sash when he was working in the fields. And though he was more educated than anyone in our village, including Father and Uncle, he never spoke of it, nor did he ever shun hard work.

"I don't suppose that you've eaten, James?" Rabbi Ezra asked.

"No, Rabbi," I said. I tried to squeeze the crusted ooze from my eyes by shutting my eyelids tightly and rubbing my finger over my eyelashes.

"Has anyone eaten yet?" he asked.

To my surprise, no one in the room had broken the fast.

"If it's all right, Joseph, we could have the women prepare a meal while we talk," the rabbi suggested, "unless you want this conversation just between us."

Father shook his head. "I think everyone should be here for the discussion, Ezra."

"And your brother?" asked the rabbi.

I was surprised when Aunt Miriam said nothing.

Father looked at her when he spoke. "Clopas and I disagree about how to handle the situation with Mary."

"Only Clopas?" the rabbi asked.

Father nodded.

"Then Clopas needs to be here," said the rabbi, "and Simeon for that matter. He is of age, just like James."

"I'll get them," said Aunt Miriam.

A moment later she returned with Uncle Clopas and Simeon. Both were red with anger, Uncle so much that he stomped like a child to the table. He took the cushion next to Father.

Rabbi Ezra said a long prayer. He asked God to bless our home and our conversation. After the prayer Father handed Rabbi the scroll from Zachariah. He read it aloud then passed it to Clopas, who in turn reread the scroll.

"Did you know that Zachariah wrote this for you?" the rabbi asked Jude.

"No," said Jude.

"Did you know he buried a bag of silver in the back of your cart?" Father asked.

"No." Jude looked over at Mary. "Did you know of this?"

Mary shook her head. "No."

"Did Rabbi Zachariah ever question you about what happened to Mary?" Rabbi asked.

"He didn't," Jude answered.

Clopas glared at Jude but held his tongue.

"Why?" asked the rabbi.

Jude said nothing.

"Please answer the rabbi, son," Father said softly.

"Shortly after we arrived in Juttah, Mary told me she had been visited by a messenger from God. I took Mary's story to Rabbi Zachariah immediately," said Jude.

"What did you tell Rabbi Zachariah?" the rabbi asked.

"I told him a messenger had spoken to Mary. The messenger said that a life was stirring inside her womb but that she shouldn't be afraid. The messenger said this life was a gift from God, just like the life stirring inside Elizabeth. The messenger said Father would help her protect the child."

"Did Rabbi Zachariah believe this *story*?" asked the rabbi.

"He believed it immediately," said Jude. "Rabbi said that God helped Elizabeth to become pregnant. He said we shouldn't doubt his power to do all things. If the messenger told Mary that the power of God would come upon her to make this life possible, that is what she should believe."

Jude paused for a moment. Father rubbed his forehead and wouldn't look up at Jude.

Uncle Clopas was far more resolute. "Why should we believe this story?" he yelled. "Who would believe such as story? Do you take your father for a fool?"

Simeon's eyebrows were furrowed like Uncle's. If Simeon had a beard, he would have looked just like his father. The moment would have been an occasion for laughter, if not for the seriousness of the situation.

Jude looked across the table at Uncle. He answered him in a soft voice. "I never once worried what others might think until we started preparing for the trip back to Nazareth. Rabbi Zachariah didn't question me, nor did he accuse me."

"Why is that?" Rabbi Ezra asked.

"When his wife, Elizabeth, became pregnant, Rabbi Zachariah said a messenger spoke to him also. Initially he dismissed the messenger as nothing more than voices in his head, so the messenger cursed him for not listening, and he was struck dumb. Everyone in Juttah and Jerusalem knows this. Mary and I saw his infirmity with our own eyes. Three days after Elizabeth gave birth, the rabbi came down with a nasty cough. After spitting out what he had brought up from his lungs, he finally was able to speak."

"So it is true!" exclaimed Aunt Miriam. "He lost his speech for the whole of Elizabeth's pregnancy!"

Knowing that this piece of juicy gossip bore some truth was cause for celebration as far as Aunt Miriam was concerned. She alone would have the honor of telling all the other women in the village about it.

Jude nodded and said, "It's true. Zachariah couldn't say a word. He motioned with his hands and wrote things in the sand. It was his only form of communication."

Father looked at Rabbi Ezra. The rabbi looked at Clopas. The three men glanced at one another for several minutes before Rabbi Ezra broke the silence. "I heard Mary's testimony yesterday. This messenger you describe...do you think it was an angel, Jude?"

Father looked over at Jude. It was the first time since Jude's arrival that I saw him stare into my older brother's eyes. Father cast an approving glance of compassion, but the skin around his eyes and cheeks looked as if they had been stretched across his face. The difficult times we endured this past year had aged him. His eyes had lost their shine and his graying beard seemed to swallow the rest of his face. He was desperate, and ready to accept any answer that would help him save his son.

"Rabbi, I didn't see the things that Mary saw," Jude said. "On our journey home, I thought maybe God would send me an angel so that I could defend her, but he didn't."

"But do you believe her story?" Father asked.

Jude sat in thought for a minute, searching for words. He looked at Mary. He looked at Father. Then he looked at me.

During the two days I had spent in bed, wild rumors spread throughout the village. Because our family's reputation was in question, Jude's upcoming betrothal to Leah was postponed. Leah's father wouldn't speak to Father or Uncle, nor would her mother speak to Aunt Miriam. On top of the shame Jude felt, Rabbi Ezra had yet to decide whether to ban him from the synagogue, and as such, Jude's every word was measured.

Jude loved Mary, and the two of them had shared much in the way of work, loneliness, and personal suffering in the months that had led up to their departure. Yet I knew he never thought any more of her than a brother would a sister. In some ways she had become a curse to him. He only spoke of it to me once, but he resented Father for leaving him alone to look after her and our farm while we worked in Tiberias. Still he did what Father asked of him, as any dutiful son would.

Jude cleared his throat. "When Mary told me of her visit with the angel, I almost left Juttah."

"Go on," said the rabbi.

"But she begged me to stay with her so that I might help her tell her story. Rabbi Zachariah urged me to do the same. He convinced me it was possible for an angel to speak to Mary in the same way the angel was trying to speak to him."

Rabbi Ezra took a drink of water and slowly set the goblet on the table. "I could believe the story about the angel, but the story concerning her pregnancy seems contrived. Was she ever alone? Is it possible she could have been violated and simply doesn't want to reveal the man's name?"

"No. That's not Mary's nature," Jude said firmly. "She has been watched and cared for since her arrival in Nazareth."

Rabbi continued, "Do you think Zachariah readily accepted Mary's story because of what happened to Elizabeth?"

Jude nodded. "When Rabbi Zachariah regained his speech, he told me Elizabeth became pregnant because of God's favor. He believed the same could happen to Mary, especially since her life had been dedicated to God."

Uncle Clopas shook his fists above his head and slammed them on the table, knocking over several cups of wine. "You fool! How can you believe these lies! You made that child with her! Admit it!"

Jude stood up, his hands opening and closing into fists. Father made a move to stand, but Rabbi Ezra pushed him back down.

"How dare you call me a fool, Uncle? When I saw with my own eyes our cousin struck dumb by the hand of God! And here I stand, giving true testimony to the things I have witnessed, and yet you still don't believe!"

"What do you believe, Jude?" Rabbi interrupted.

The weight of the question hung in the air like smoke from a clogged chimney. In the space of this silence, Rabbi Ezra managed to get Uncle Clopas to sit down at the table, while Aunt Miriam and Mary scurried about, wiping up the spills from the stone floors.

Jude looked at Father. "You made us leave Nazareth in December. Elizabeth's son was born in March. During that time I watched Zachariah endure taunting, whispers, and gossip. Our cousin suffered greatly, while his wife, Elizabeth, rejoiced. When his mouth and tongue finally worked, he praised God the entire day, singing, yelling, joking, and crying." Jude sat down and looked at Uncle. "To deny God the power to have created this life is to deny that God's hand moved over the waters of creation, to deny that he alone created day and night and the animals and the beasts and the heavens and the earth."

Jude pointed at Mary. "To deny that God could create a life inside this woman is to deny him the very power he used to create Adam! If he wills the existence of this child, who am I to question him? I am nothing more than a servant to her and to God and my father." His eyes moved from Uncle's to Father's. "For the past nine months, I have been her servant, not by my own choice but yours. This woman—this woman whose very life was presented in the Temple and dedicated to God—is your betrothed, Father. You asked me to watch over her. This I have done. And I have not failed her...or you...or God!"

As Jude choked back his emotion, Father got up from the table and walked to him. They embraced for what seemed an eternity. Both of them wept. Rabbi Ezra lowered his head in prayer.

Uncle Clopas finally knew Jude had spoken the truth. He lowered his head in shame.

After several moments had passed, it was Mary who broke the silence. Her gentle voice seemed to float like clouds on a warm summer day. "May we serve breakfast?"

Rabbi Ezra opened his eyes and looked at her. "Yes, please," he said, smiling.

Aunt Miriam and Mary served us cakes made of wheat flour then brought out small stone pitchers of honey. While Mary poured warm honey over our cakes, Aunt Miriam placed a bowl of dried dates in front of each person. The rhythm of these menial tasks comforted me, and I felt a sense of peace descend on our home. It squeezed between the cracks in our walls, forcing its way in until every empty crevice of our home had been touched.

Once Aunt Miriam and Mary had placed pitchers of sweet wine on the table, they joined us. Rabbi Ezra blessed the meal, and we ate in silence. When we were near the end of the meal, he asked Mary to pour us all more wine. When she had finished, he asked her to sit down near him.

"When you knew you were pregnant, who did you tell first?" he asked her.

Mary cleared her throat. "I told Jude then Elizabeth."

"What did you tell her?" the rabbi asked.

"She didn't say anything-" Jude interrupted. "Elizabeth knew Mary was pregnant before she opened her mouth."

"What do you mean, son?" Father asked.

Rabbi Ezra looked over at Jude.

"Elizabeth said that God had revealed Mary's mystery to her."

"What exactly did Elizabeth say?" Father asked.

Mary stared at Father. "I don't know if I am worthy enough to repeat it."

Rabbi Ezra stood. "Mary, this is a serious matter. I must know what the angel said to you and to Elizabeth."

Mary looked away like a little girl who had been reprimanded. "I don't know if I can say," she said then looked at us as if we were all strangers.

"You have to say something, Mary," grumbled Miriam. "If nothing else, preserve Jude's honor and the honor of this family."

I saw the emotion in Mary's face, and I wanted to rescue her. From what I didn't know, but Jude seemed to run out of words.

"Mary," I said softly, "is it because you are afraid or because the angel told you not to reveal what was said?"

"I don't know. I can't remember," Mary said. She stuttered much as she spoke, and she began to shake and cry.

I stood up from the table and walked over to her. "You could whisper it to the rabbi," I suggested. "He's a man of God. He's fit to hear God's word and the words of his angels. None of us would have to hear what you share."

It would have been improper for the men in the room to leave Mary in private with another man. Women's affairs were the responsibility of the husband, father, or oldest brother. Women had no authority over their own matters. Whatever Mary revealed, she needed to do so in the company of the men in our family.

I wasn't surprised when Mary walked over to Rabbi Ezra, who stood in the middle of the room. She leaned into his ear and whispered the holy words she had heard from the lips of the angel. It took her less than a minute, and when she had finished, the rabbi stood motionless, his eyes darting from person to person, before settling in on my father.

He cleared his throat. "Joseph, I am convinced of your son's innocence in the matter at hand. It is evident that Zachariah found no fault with the boy. The way that Jude has looked after and cared for your betrothed is not only remarkable but also commendable, especially under the circumstances."

The rabbi looked at Jude. "Suspicions and accusations are like smoke, my son. They rise up and spread quickly, and when the fire is put out, the scent of the smoke still lingers. I'm afraid your clothes will smell like smoke for quite some time, and for this I am sorry."

He then looked at Uncle, who sat at the table with his head still bowed in shame. "Clopas, I want you to ask for forgiveness from your nephew, in the presence of all in this room. And when you are finished here, I want you to go to everyone in this village with whom you planted the seeds of doubt and restore your nephew's honor with your apologies. When you have finished speaking to every household in our village, seek out every weed that has grown in your field, along with a hearty measure of grain, and burn them as a sacrifice for your sin. Now I would like for everyone in the room to leave," Rabbi announced, "except Mary and Jude. I want to bestow upon them a blessing."

CHAPTER TWENTY-FOUR

Father and I walked slowly to the well, the loose pebbles crunching under our feet. "It's unusually warm today," he said, as he looked to the sky.

I expected him to look back to see if I was behind him, but he didn't. The clouds gathered around the sun like shrubs, but the rays shone through like yellow staircases to the heavens.

He stopped when he reached the well, turned around, and leaned against it, his arms crossed and face pointed at the ground. His beard, matted in places on his face, made him look much older than his years. His eyes sagged, and the unkempt hair about his shoulders blew in clumps with the breeze. He smelled of sweat. His cream-colored tunic was almost gray with dust. I stared at him, wondering what I would do if something ever happened to him. When I reached the well, I stood next to him and looked out over our fields.

"The crops look thin, don't they, James?"

"They do." I glanced at him. "We did the best we could. Please don't shame yourself over this."

He wiped a sniffle with his sleeve. "Thank you, but it still bothers a man when he thinks his fields are only partially tended."

"Father?"

"Yes, James?"

"What are you going to do? We are *we* going to do?"

"I don't want to see your brother killed for a crime he didn't commit. I also don't want Mary to die."

"Do you think she's innocent?"

Father looked at me, and for the first time that day, he smiled. "I think they're both innocent. The problem is your dear uncle already opened his big mouth, and because of these rumors, I may have to divorce Mary."

"Why?"

Father cleared his throat. "If there is anyone who can right this wrong, it is Ezra. But until that time has passed, we may not be able to practice in Nazareth's synagogue. I can't bear the thought of that." He inhaled a deep breath and exhaled a sigh. His eyes became wet, and he turned away from me to face the sun. We were startled out of our despair by the cheerful voice of Rabbi Ezra.

"Joseph! James!" he called out. "We need to talk!"

Father turned around and leaned against the well. Rabbi Ezra walked right up to him and put his arms around him, and Father began to weep. Rabbi Ezra held him for several moments, much in the same way he held him after the death of my mother. Theirs was a childhood bond, a friendship that had once been broken apart by time then put back together when Mother and Father moved from Bethlehem to Nazareth. Rabbi Ezra often remarked how honored he was to be a part of our family.

"Joseph, it will be all right."

"I know," Father mumbled. He wiped the tears from his eyes. "Maybe I should just divorce her. Zachariah will take her in and care for her. I still have her father's dowry and Zachariah's silver."

Rabbi Ezra smiled. "Joseph, you never have abandoned anything in your life, be it a failed building project or a poor crop or problems with your family. This girl needs your family more than ever right now. She especially needs you."

"What about the child?" Father asked. "This child isn't mine."

Rabbi Ezra spoke in a fierce whisper. "Then make it *yours*, Joseph. Register Mary and the child in Bethlehem."

"Do you think she was unfaithful, Ezra?"

Rabbi Ezra took a step back and spoke sternly. "Did you not read Zachariah's letter? Did you not hear your own son bear powerful witness to God and to all of us?"

Father bowed his head in despair. "If I take Mary as my wife, and I legitimize this child, then what? I can't live *here*. The whole village will think me accursed! I am a leader in the synagogue. I have a business and fertile lands. What will people say to their leader? What about Leah and her family? Poor Jude is heartbroken. He wanted to marry her next spring."

Rabbi Ezra motioned for me to come over to him. He spoke to me in a quiet voice. "Maybe he'll listen to you. Is there anything you can say, James, to help your father?"

I walked over to Father and leaned against the well. I crossed my arms and looked up to the sun. It was a glorious day, despite our dire situation. We had rejoiced, and yet suffered, so much this past year.

"Do you remember the stoning of the woman last year, Father?" He nodded. "We were walking to the execution site outside of Sepphoris, and you prayed for the *mamzers* begging in the streets. You were praying for them, remember?" He nodded again. "Father, I never asked you about your prayer, and Uncle Clopas wouldn't let me disturb you. I couldn't think of what to pray then, so I prayed to God that he would hear yours." Father cracked a smile and looked at me. "What did you ask God to do, Father?"

He kicked at the dusty ground and sent a pebble flying. Then he uncrossed his arms and moved closer to where I stood. "I asked God to forgive me my sins so that I might come to him with a pure heart. Then I asked him to have mercy on the children and the families that had abandoned them. I asked him to watch over those children, like a shepherd watching over a flock, and to find some way to remind all of us that these children were still children of Israel, deserving of shelter, food, drink, and a place in the synagogue, and—"

"And then you threw one of the boys a denarius," I interjected.

"Yes, I gave him some money to buy food."

"Mary's child will need shelter and food and drink. So will Mary. Maybe God answered your prayer by delivering Mary and this child to you."

Father swallowed hard and put his hand on my shoulder. "I cannot pretend to know the mind of God," he said, "but maybe Mary and this child *are* part of God's plan for us. We are sons of David, are we not? Did God not expect David to lead the Israelites in ways that were different than the ones before?"

I looked over at Rabbi Ezra, hoping I hadn't offended him. He made one of his hands into a fist and held it up to his mouth, as if it to prevent himself from speaking.

"Father, we can't stay in Nazareth. There are too many rumors, too many superstitions. If we stayed, a mob could come in the middle of the night to take matters into their own hands. We couldn't protect Jude or Mary from such a tragedy. We have the money from Marcus as well as Mary's dowry. You said it yourself. We have resources to last us five years, if not longer."

"Ezra, what do you think?" Father asked.

Rabbi Ezra dropped his fist and exclaimed, "Listen to the boy, Joseph. His words are blessed with wisdom."

"Mary's almost to term. Do you think she would be up to traveling?" Father asked me.

I nodded. "She's strong, Father. If we took the cart and the mule through Samaria, we would make it in four or five days."

"Mary couldn't travel for long periods without resting. It might take longer."

"And Jude…he must come with us," I said.

Father nodded then looked over at Ezra. "What do I do about Clopas? The farm? My business? We are due back to Tiberias tomorrow."

Ezra stepped toward Father. "Send for Clopas once you get to Bethlehem, or whenever you are ready to accept him back into your graces. He, Miriam, and Simeon can tend the farm, with the help of others in the community. I will summon Nicodemus to help negate your assignment in Tiberias. He'll know how to convince Joazar to commute the work order."

Rabbi Ezra cast Father a worried look. "This money you speak of, where is it?"

Father laughed. "You're standing on it."

Rabbi Ezra looked at the ground. "There is no money here. Have you gone mad, Joseph?"

I couldn't help laugh out loud. "It's buried underneath you, Rabbi."

The laughter soothed our souls like a cool wet cloth on sunburned skin.

Father gave me a big hug. "Thank you, James, for your words."

"He is quite a rare young man," Rabbi Ezra added. "He would make a fine rabbi one day."

"If we decide to stay in Bethlehem, James, you could study at the Temple," said Father.

"That is true," said Rabbi Ezra. "And I have no doubt that Mary's father would be happy to know his dowry would be put to such use."

Father gave his friend a long hug. "I am grateful to you, old friend."

"You would do the same for me, Joseph."

Rabbi Ezra signaled to both Father and me. "Now come, both of you. There is much to do and very little time. If a mob is to form, they will do so tonight, after the workday has ended. You should leave as soon as possible."

CHAPTER TWENTY-FIVE

Jude and I packed the work cart with food, water, blankets, clothes, and carpentry tools. There were enough provisions to last two weeks, more than enough for the five-day journey Father anticipated.

"God willing," said Father, "we may make it in time for the Day of the Atonement."

"Why the tools, Father?" Jude asked.

"We may have to stay with Simon for some time. We should do our part to help their family. Competition for building projects is high, but we can make goods and sell them in Jerusalem. He'll also have three more men to help in the fields."

Father hitched the mule to the cart and handed me the leader. "Did you two prepare a place for Mary to sit?"

Jude pointed to two pillows and a stack of blankets. "She can lie on the blankets and lean against the pillows, Father."

"Did you check the axle on the cart, James?"

"I examined it carefully, Father. It's in good shape."

"Is the mule fitted for travel, Jude?"

"She is."

Father grabbed a single blanket from a stack in the cart. "Come with me."

Jude and I followed him to the well, where he looked out at the fields. "Do you think Uncle Clopas can handle the fields with the village's help?" he asked us.

"Of course he can," I said.

Father smiled. "I'll miss the harvest this year. We've worked so hard for so little, but it would still be fun."

"There will be four less mouths to feed, though," said Jude.

Father nodded. "This is true." He motioned to the ground next to the well. "James, show your brother where we hid the money we received from Marcus. Hide it under this blanket until you can get it onto the cart. Make sure to hide it well."

"Where are you going, Father?" I asked.

"To make peace with my brother and his family."

Father turned to walk up the hill, leaving Jude and me to pull up the rock and dig out the bag of coins.

"How much of Marcus's money is buried here?" Jude asked.

I pulled away the big flat rock with a loud grunt. "All of it."

Using our hands, Jude and I dug up a small mound of earth before finding the bag of coins. The soft leather was mushy from being exposed to damp soil and was beginning to rot through. I sifted the dirt with my fingers to make sure we didn't leave any coins behind. Jude pulled the bag from the dirt and examined it.

"The bag is rotting, James."

I stood up and rubbed the soil from my hands. "Once we get to the house, we can put it in a different bag."

I wrapped the bag in the blanket and trudged up the hill to the cart. Then I moved our possessions around in search of a suitable hiding place.

"You know what we should do," Jude said softly. "We should split the coins into two pouches. We can put one in the cart, and I can carry the other."

"Why would we do that?"

"If something were to happen to the cart, or if Father were robbed, then only some of the coins would be lost."

The idea seemed reasonable enough, so I agreed. "I'll go into the house to see if I can find two food pouches. Divide the coins equally, between silver and gold."

Jude spilled the coins into the middle of the cart and began to sort them.

I went to the house. As I walked inside, I saw Father and Uncle Clopas hugging each other. Aunt Miriam sat at our table, her hand covering her mouth as she cried. Rabbi Ezra sat next to her, holding her other hand.

"Where is Mary?" I whispered to Rabbi Ezra.

"She is at your uncle's, collecting her things. Do you need something?"

"Two small food pouches," I whispered.

Aunt Miriam wiped the tears from her cheeks. "I keep several pouches in a storage box upstairs. Take as many as you need, James."

I crept up the ladder to our sleeping room, found the box, and took out two small pouches. As I climbed down the ladder, I heard Father and Rabbi Ezra talking. Uncle Clopas and Aunt Miriam were gone, and Mary was reclining at our table.

"Did you find what you were looking for, James?" Father asked.

"Yes," I said.

I scratched my head and looked around. "Where did Uncle Clopas and Aunt Miriam go?"

"Home," said Rabbi Ezra.

I looked at Mary. "Are you doing all right?" Mary's eyes looked tired, almost sleepy, but her voice carried the sharpness of an ax. "I'm not all right, James. I've just returned from a long, hard journey, and now I'm leaving on another one. I'm hungry, uncomfortable, and very close to having this baby."

Her voice became softer with each word, her eyes filled with tears. "I'm scared."

Father looked at me and nodded. I went over to Mary and knelt beside her. "Why are you scared?" I asked softly.

Mary crossed her arms and rocked back and forth. "I wanted a baby, James, but not this baby." Her blue eyes became like polished marble. "I don't know if I want this child."

I looked at Father and Rabbi Ezra, searching for help. Rabbi Ezra nodded, as if to say, "Go on."

When I turned back to Mary, I noticed her face looked sunken, her cheeks appeared hollow, and her skin was pasty white. She reached for my hand. "You have to help me, James," she begged. "I don't know if I will live to bear this child."

Jude burst through the door. "Where is James?" he said with a tone of impatience.

Father held a finger to his lips and pointed to the two of us sitting on the floor. Jude stood with Father and Rabbi Ezra.

"How can I help you, Mary?" I asked. She appeared close to fainting. I turned to Jude. "Fetch her some water."

Mary started rocking back and forth again, her motions so quick it made me sick to my stomach just to watch her. She cried out and lay down on the floor, curled up on her side. Jude returned with a jar of fresh water. Father retrieved a cup from the shelf, filled it half full of water, and handed the cup to me.

"Mary," I said in a raised voice. "Mary."

She closed her eyes. At that moment, her legs started to kick, and her whole body shivered. She lifted her head slightly to speak. "I am not fit to carry this child."

"Why do you say this?" I asked her.

"The child isn't mine."

I looked up at Father, Jude, and Rabbi Ezra. "Whose child is it, Mary?" I asked.

She didn't answer. She lay on the floor with her eyes closed. "Mary, please drink," I begged.

Rabbi Ezra rushed over, placed his hand on Mary's forehead, and began to pray. Father and Jude stood behind him and watched as Mary began to stir.

Jude began to weep. "Mary, please wake up," he said over Rabbi Ezra's prayers.

Mary still didn't stir. Her breathing slowed from its rapid pace, and her chest continued to lift and fall, showing us signs that she was still alive.

Father prayed out loud. He prayed for Mary's soul, for her protection, and for the baby in her womb. He prayed for our family, for Jude and Uncle Clopas, and for forgiveness for all the wrong he ever had done in his life. He prayed for me, that I might live to use the good wisdom that God had bestowed on me to help men from all the places of the earth. He prayed for Miriam and her deceased sister, Salome, his beloved wife and mother to his holy family. He prayed that God might spare them the loss of two lives, a tragedy he claimed he couldn't live through again. Then Father asked God to leave Mary in his care, to grant them protection according to his will. When he finished, he took the cup of water and drank it. Then he set the cup on the table and knelt by Mary's side.

"Mary, please wake up," he pleaded.

As his first tears began to fall, Mary's foot twitched, then both her feet, and then her legs. She rolled over on her back and opened her eyes. She looked at Father, then at Jude and me, then Rabbi Ezra. She sat up. Her white tunic fell across her girlish figure, and her hair spilled over her shoulders. Father supported her with his arm around her back.

"I'm thirsty," she said softly.

Father looked at Jude, who was already moving toward the table. He took the cup from the table, dipped it into the water jar, and handed it to Father, who passed it to Mary.

Rabbi Ezra knelt at Mary's feet. "What happened?" he asked.

Mary took several gulps of water and handed the cup to Father. "I don't know, Rabbi. But if we are to go, then let's go. We can't wait any longer."

Father looked at Jude and me. "Get the mule. Finish loading the provisions."

I rushed out to the cart to find the coins scattered between two piles. I ran back into the house, collected the leather pouches, and ran outside. When I had finished, I concealed one bag in the cart, under the blankets where Mary would sit. The other I gave to Jude.

Father appeared from Uncle Clopas's home, along with Aunt Miriam, Simeon, and Rabbi Ezra. We exchanged few words, but words weren't needed when Uncle Clopas hugged my brother. Father helped Mary into the cart. After she had made herself comfortable on the blankets, he took the leader from Jude and nudged the mule forward.

The old wooden cart creaked at the axle, but Father never looked back.

CHAPTER TWENTY-SIX

For a small group of traders, the trip to Bethlehem would take three to five days, but our two-wheeled cart was no match for the stony trails that curved around the Jordan River. Father led our mule slowly to avoid large stones, and the ruts and holes left by washouts. Despite every possible care Father took, Mary felt every bump and rock. Jude walked on one side of the cart and I on the other. We did our best to keep her comfortable with pillows and blankets, but it was useless.

"Is it possible that I may walk?" Mary called from the cart.

Father kept his hand on the mule as he turned around. "I fear we don't have the extra time to spare."

"Where will we spend the night?" Mary asked.

"We'll camp near Scythopolis and resupply in the morning."

"Do we have stop to there?" Mary begged. "It's an unholy place filled with mercenaries and idol worshipers."

Father called Jude up to hold the lead rope then walked back to the cart to talk to Mary. "I know this is hard for you. It's hard for all of us. But the sooner we arrive in Bethlehem, the safer we will be, and the safer this child will be. I don't want any of us to be defiled by the land or its people, nor do I wish to put us in the way of robbers or bandits. I know these trails, Mary. I have traveled them for work and for trade and used them extensively in my younger years." Father sighed. "I need you to trust me. If not out of duty as a wife, then out of love for this child you carry."

Normally Mary would look to Jude or me for a sign of what to do. Instead she looked up at Father and dropped her shoulders in acceptance. The early-evening sun shone on her face as her soft lips spoke not with resignation but certainty.

"I trust you, Joseph."

Father lingered for a moment. Mary always looked beautiful, but with the sunlight shining down upon her, she appeared radiant. He smiled, nodded in respect, and walked back to Jude to retrieve the lead. Father commanded the mule to move, and the cart began to creak once more.

We spent the night camped outside the city of Scythopolis. As we sat by the fire, we saw that the city was lit up by torches and heard the shouting and laughter of hundreds of people.

"Some of the finest artisans in all the land live there," said Father. "It is there where I learned about building materials, carving, and iron shaping."

"It's a modern-day Sodom," mumbled Mary. "Not a city fit for a son of David."

Jude and I looked to Father, who was smiling. "Not everyone who taught or advised David was of the tribe of Israel. We could learn much from these people."

"What do you mean?" Mary asked. "All they would do is pollute our minds and ruin the very nation we struggle to rebuild."

"I have set many cornerstones during this rebuilding effort," said Father. "But we don't own our nation. The Romans own it. We are merely allowed to exist through God's divine intervention and his manipulation of the systems and governments of our day."

"Since when do you know the mind of God, Joseph?" Mary asked.

Father looked as if he were a child with his hand caught in a jar of honey.

Jude and I tried not to laugh. "I'm not saying I know the mind of God," Father said, smiling. "I'm simply sharing my opinion."

Jude and I chuckled.

"Well, then what would your opinion be of my unborn child?" Mary asked.

Father stopped smiling. Jude and I put away our laughter and looked at her. "You have yet to ask me about this child," she said. "Will you not acknowledge that I am pregnant with a child that is not yours? If you want my trust, Joseph, then I want your thoughts."

In the firelight I saw Father take a drink of water. The light-hearted mood he had tried to create was now overcast like the dark clouds of an approaching storm.

"I will acknowledge that the child is mine," Father said sternly. "Why else would I risk our lives for such a journey?"

"Do you still distrust my testimony?" Mary asked.

It occurred to me that now that we were out of Nazareth, Mary might be willing to expose her suitor. I wanted to look over at Jude but thought better of turning my head in his direction.

Father shook his head. "I don't need to know whose child this is, nor do I want to know. My duty is to you and this child."

Mary began to weep. "But you must know, Joseph!"

"I don't want to know!" yelled Father.

Jude stood up and looked at him. "She needs to tell you, Father. It's a story that I'm not worthy to share. You *must* listen to her," he begged.

My ears weren't meant to hear the words that befell her lips, yet I found them difficult to believe. Mary spoke of conversations with heavenly beings dressed in dazzling white. They told her she was to have a boy named Jesus and that his name would be known above all others, both in this life and the next.

"When the angels left me, I went to Zachariah for comfort," she said quietly. "And as he held his infant, John, he told me that my child was a fulfillment of Isaiah's prophecy. He said I was to accept the favor showered upon me by God and to welcome this child as if welcoming God himself."

Father looked at her. He closed his eyes for a moment then opened them again. "Is this the secret you told Ezra?" Mary nodded. "I don't know what to make of all this. My mind is tired, my feet hurt, and all that concerns me is keeping you and this baby safe."

I watched as Mary replaced her anger with worry. "I'm a child of the Temple, Joseph. I know no sin, nor have I ever lain with a man, yet I carry a life inside me—a life that stirs at every mention of the name of God." She placed a hand on her belly. "While on earth, this boy will be our son, and he will be called a son of David, just as you are called a son of David. If I complain it's because I do not want anything dreadful to happen to you or me that could cause me to lose this child, or for any of us to lose favor with God." Mary shook with weeping. "I couldn't live with myself if something happened to this baby."

Father leapt from his place at the fire and sat next to her. He cradled her in his arms, rocking her gently. "What must I do to keep you from worrying?" he asked.

"Believe what I say, Joseph, and get us to Bethlehem safely," she replied.

We traveled three more days, spending our nights under a blanket of stars, while a half moon kept watch over us. We wrapped ourselves in covers to keep warm from the chilling nights that had descended on Samaria. The next morning we made a quick breakfast of flatbread and dates then walked along a trail next to the Jordan River.

The Jordan was unusually high for this time of year. The waters lapped hungrily at the banks and rushed over the rocks and earthen fingers that stuck out from the shallows.

"Where are all the birds?" asked Jude. We craned our necks to search for life along the riverbank but saw none.

Father looked to the east and pointed to the dark clouds that veiled the morning sun. He looked worried.

"Is a storm coming?" Jude asked.

"It is certain," said Father. "We must try to reach Ephraim before the storm reaches us. I don't want to be on this dirt trail if it rains."

We pressed on, our little cart creaking under the weight of Mary and our provisions. After a few yards, Father stopped the cart. "James, how is the axle holding up?"

I stooped down to look at the axle. "There is a small crack in the middle."

Father walked over to look at the axle. When he stood up, he shook his head. "This cart is meant to carry tools and building supplies over short distances. I hope it can last at least to Jerusalem. Jude, help me move our food pouches over to the mule. If the cart breaks down, we'll at least have the means for carrying our food."

Jude pulled two leather blankets from the cart. Iron rings had been sewn into the side of one, approximately two feet apart. He placed this blanket over top of the mule. I helped Father carry the food pouches and water skins from the cart. He lifted each pouch and skin to determine its weight and, with long pieces of leather, tied them to the iron rings.

"The weight must be evenly balanced," he said. "We can't risk a sprained ankle or broken leg."

After he finished tying the last of the pouches and skins, I took the second leather blanket and laid it across the first to protect our supplies. With our food and water on the mule, Mary had more room in the cart. Jude rearranged the blankets and pillows to make her more comfortable. In doing so he uncovered the leather bag filled with coins.

"What is this?" Mary asked as she picked up the bag.

"Payment from one of our employers in Sepphoris," Jude replied.

"This is enough money to pay for three houses!" Mary exclaimed. "Joseph, where did this money come from, and why are we taking it with us?"

Father was busy tying a large strap that would keep the blankets from shifting on the back of the mule. He spoke as he worked. "The money came from Marcus of Sepphoris," he answered. "He was one of our employers." As Father recounted the story of Marcus and our unpleasant meeting with Herod Antipas, Mary's eyes widened in fear.

"Oh, Joseph, you shouldn't have taken that money," said Mary. "It's blood money, paid for by the sacrifices of our people."

"Which is precisely why I took it, Mary," Father said sternly. "The Lord will show us how to put it to use in ways that will help his people. It was once in our hands. Then it was in the hands of the Romans. Now it is in ours again."

Mary shook her head. "A son of David wouldn't accept money that was earned on the backs of Israel's own people," she pleaded.

Father walked from the mule to the cart. "And God's ways of providing for his people are often misunderstood. Our family has worked hard our whole lives. In a single day, Marcus almost ruined us with his arrogance. I agree that this money belongs to Israel, and it was returned to Israel by finding its way to us. It is a resource, Mary, like anything else a son of David would steward."

Father turned and walked back to the mule, leaving Mary without the means to respond. I looked away from her, as did Jude. At some point she would have to accept Father as her husband.

The winds from the coming storm kicked up much dust, and Father was forced to slow down, for we could hardly see. He stopped the mule again and looked up at the sky. "We're not going make it to Ephraim," he yelled over the winds.

He leaned over and pulled the mule along. Jude pushed on one side of the cart and I on the other. The wind blew into our faces, our cheeks stinging with the first droplets of rain. The air smelled musty. The clouds darkened, and daylight disappeared. Father leaned into the wind, staggering with each step. With the full force of heaven, the dark clouds dumped a waterfall of cold rain on our traveling family.

Father shouted back at us, "Away from the river! Away from the river!"

In the noise of the rain and wind, Jude and I forgot about the Jordan and its swirling brown muddy waters.

Jude was on the side of the trail next to the river. As he pushed the cart, he shouted, "Father, it's getting higher! The water is getting higher!"

With rising waters to our left and muddy slopes to our right, I didn't know where we would escape.

"There!" Mary shouted from the cart. Her hand pointed a small trail off the main trail that led to higher ground.

The cart was almost past the trail, so Father halted the mule and attempted to back up. Our tunics were soaked and muddy and sticking to our bodies. The blankets on which Mary sat were like sponges, soaking up the water in the cart. How Father managed to get our mule to walk backward I'll never know. It was as if the animal sensed the danger around us. Father yelled commands and, with a hand always on the mule, guided its every move. Jude and I walked along the side of the cart as it backed up the road.

While Father handled the mule, Jude and I angled the cart. "Watch the bank!" Father yelled.

The river had swollen to twice its size, and the rains continued to pour. Both Jude and I looked behind us, keeping an eye on our footing and the edge of the bank.

We heard Father's deep voice as he spoke to the mule. "Eeeaaasy."

The mule moved slowly and intentionally until both cart wheels sat on the edge of the bank. Mary crawled from the front of the cart to the back. She knelt and looked over the edge at the fast-moving waters of the River Jordan. Father straightened out the mule and looked up to see where the trail led before encouraging the beast forward.

Father was such a careful man. If he could have predicted what was to happen, I know he would have done things differently. When Mary moved from the front of the cart to the back, it shifted the weight and balance. What Father didn't know was that the Jordan's roaring waters were stealing the bank from underneath the trail. The mud and rock gave way to the powerful current, dumping Jude and me, and half of our cart, into the cold raging water.

I managed to maintain a hold on the left side of the submerged cart. "Jude!" I yelled. The winds howled; the rain poured; and the rushing sounds of the river swallowed up my cry. "Jude!"

I heard Father yell, "Mary!" I looked up to see a pair of long white legs dangling down the length of the cart. Mary managed to lunge forward and take hold of the front side of the cart. She had put the full weight of her body on her pregnant belly.

"James!" I heard from the other side of the cart. Jude poked his head above the water and whipped his head so that his water-soaked hair didn't cover his face.

"Are you all right?" I yelled.

"Yes," Jude yelled back. "Where's Mary?"

"I'm up here!" she yelled.

Jude pulled himself up, looked over the side of the cart, and saw Mary clinging to the front wall.

More mud gave way, jostling the cart. Jude and I watched hopelessly as Father's best woodworking tools slid into the water. We heard the jingling of coins too, as Marcus's treasure bag rolled down the center of the cart. Jude reached for the bag, but it slid past his fingers and plopped into the Jordan. Aunt Miriam's handmade pillows and blankets were also lost. Only Mary remained, still clinging to the front edge of the cart. The rush of the water dragged me under for a moment, but I pulled myself up, coughing a lungful of the Jordan into the empty cart.

"Give me your hand!" I looked up and saw Father's outstretched hand. I grasped his hand, dug my soggy sandals into the bank, and climbed toward the top of the riverbank.

I looked into the cart. "Where is Mary?" Father pointed across the road and hurried around the mule to the other side of the cart.

Then it occurred to me. Father rescued her first.

I followed behind him and reached the bank in time to see him reach out for Jude. When my brother made it up the side, the cart lurched backward, dragging the mule part of the way with it. The mule reared and whinnied, its white teeth clamped tightly around the bit. Father rushed to the cart and started untying the leather straps that kept the cart hitched to the mule.

"Jude!" I yelled. "We need to help Father!"

I rushed to Father while Jude ran around the mule to the other side. Everything we needed to complete our journey— food, water, dry clothing—was packed on that mule. If the angry waters continued to pull at the cart, the current would sweep away our mule as well. Father worked vigorously to untie the poles while Jude and I worked on the leather fasteners wrapped around the mule's chest.

"It's starting to slide!" Father shouted above the rain, and Jude and I rushed to either side of the cart to try to keep it from moving. Mary raced across the road and began to pull at the straps Jude and I had loosened.

"Loosen them at the same time, Mary," Father shouted. "A single tie can pull the mule in with the cart."

I imagined Mary's skillful seamstress hands working the leather. When Father had finished plucking the leather ties from both sides of the poles, he went to help her.

"Move away from the cart!" he shouted.

We looked at each other and at once released our grip.

"Up here!" Father motioned.

We ran up to where he stood with Mary. He had one hand on the mule's bit, and Mary held the leader.

As the cart began to edge slowly toward the river, Father scoured the cart's tether poles for a leather fastener he may have forgotten. He urged the mule to walk forward, and when he did, the poles dropped to the ground, the leather straps splashing in the muddy pools that had formed along the trail. As the cart rolled slowly backward, the rest of the bank caved in, consuming it. We heard a loud crash as a large tree, carried by the swift current, shattered the cart, swallowing it up in a watery grave.

Father's body heaved a deep sigh in despair. We had used that cart to farm our land and to haul our tools and building supplies. But more than that, the cart had been a wedding present from my grandfather. It was the cart he had used to move my mother, and my oldest brother, Simon, to Nazareth. When my grandfather passed some years later, the cart became a reminder of Bethlehem. And when my mother passed, Father used it to haul her body for burial.

I stared at Father, watching for expressions of grief.

"I am so sorry for your loss, Joseph," said Mary.

Father's serious face turned to Mary, and he reached out to hold her. She came to him and buried her face and belly into his wet clothes.

Father spoke between breaths. "Everything that matters is still here with me." He kept Mary in a tight embrace as he spoke to Jude and me. "We saved our provisions, but we must make it to Archelais before nightfall," he said. "I know we lost our treasure, but I buried a small purse of silver at the bottom of our bread pouch. Maybe I can procure a small cart from one of the town's artisans to help us complete the journey." He looked at Mary. "Can you walk?"

She nodded.

Jude stepped toward Father. "And you still have this." He reached into his tunic and pulled from his waist belt the purse he had tied there. It was full of the coins we had separated back in Nazareth.

"What is this?" Father asked.

"It is the other half of Marcus's treasure. James and I split it up in case we were robbed."

Father reached out for both of us and pulled us in close to him and Mary. The rains beat down; the fierce winds continued to blow; and we stood there for some time, the four of us holding on to one another.

Then the rains stopped. The sun's rays poked under the dark clouds, blinding our vision of the horizon. Our wet clothes stuck to our bodies, and the brisk winds chilled us. Father tugged the mule along while the rest of us followed behind him.

"It feels cooler," Jude remarked.

Mary kept her silence, her arms crossed around her body, just above her belly.

"It is," I replied. I waited for Mary to say something, but she was expressionless.

As we topped the hill, we saw the stone walls of a small fort.

"There is Archelais," said Father, pointing. "We should find rest there."

"It's a town of Roman rogues," Mary mumbled.

"We will be careful," said Father.

We passed a small stone slab with Greek letters. As Jude and I struggled to make out the symbols, Father said, "We've reached the town limits."

We trudged along a path that turned from dirt to stone, which made walking easier. Shops lined the main road. In the distance we saw a stone fort lined with Roman soldiers.

"This town belongs to Herod's son," Mary whispered. "Are we safe here?"

Father ignored Mary's comments. Just ahead of us stood a large mercantile with goods sitting in front of its stone walls.

"We'll stop here," said Father. "Jude and James, I want you to stay with Mary. Guard our provisions. I'll go see if we can find a place to stay."

When Father went into the shop, Jude spoke to Mary. "Why must you always question Father?"

Mary looked at Jude with miserable eyes. Her clothes were still damp, and I knew she hadn't eaten in hours. A woman this late in her pregnancy needed more food and water than we carried with us.

"I am more a daughter to him than a wife," Mary hissed. "I'm the reason he was asked to get married. I'm the reason we had to leave Nazareth. I'm the reason we have to make this horrible trip to Bethlehem. I should be at home resting, not journeying through all of Judea. You try and carry these burdens, Jude, knowing all the while that you're not wanted."

I interrupted. "That's not so, Mary." I nodded at Jude. "We accepted you. Jude was willing to die to protect you. Why can't you see what Father is willing to do for you, and for all of us? He will make you an official member of our family by claiming you and this child. You have to meet him halfway."

Mary bowed her head and sobbed, her head in her hands, the tears flowing down her face like the afternoon's rains. Jude made no move to comfort her, nor did I. We stood there, quite perplexed by her words and the emotion in her voice.

Jude looked at me and raised his eyebrow as if to say, "She's crazy."

I walked over and knelt before her. "I'm sorry to have upset you," I said, and reached out my hands. She grasped them tightly and pulled on them, signaling me to stand up. Jude walked over to us, and the two of us held her.

"What's going on?" we heard a voice ask.

We looked up to see Father in the doorway of the merchant's shop.

"Mary isn't feeling well," I said.

Father walked over to where we were standing. "Are you sick to your stomach?"

Mary nodded. Jude and I released her, and she fell against my father's chest.

"I have some good news," he said as he held her. "There is a man, a Pharisee, letting out a spare room on the next street. He will receive us immediately."

"And the cart?" asked Jude.

"There are none. Pilgrims traveling to Jerusalem for the Day of Atonement bought all the carts. We can rest our mule in a stable next to the home where we're staying. The merchant will supply us with provisions and spare clothing to last two days. We should reach Bethlehem by then."

Mary sniffled then pulled away from Father. She looked up at him and said, "I'm sorry, Joseph. I don't mean to add to your burden with my cares and complaints."

Father smiled and pulled her close. "Everything will be fine," he said, closing his eyes. "*Everything* will be fine."

Chapter Twenty-Seven

The next morning we woke early to begin our trek into Jerusalem. As we prepared our provision packs, Father told Mary she should ride on the mule, since we didn't have a cart to pull. With a little help from Jude and me, she swung a leg over and sat on the carefully arranged blankets. She fidgeted a bit, trying to get comfortable.

"Can you manage?" Father asked.

Mary nodded. "It's the only way."

We left Archelais just as the sun began to peek over the valley. To our surprise the Jordan had returned to its normal levels. The river was no longer the mighty creature that had tugged and pulled at our bodies, intending to swallow us whole.

"Father, why does God create moments so horrific yet ones so peaceful?" I asked.

"It took him six whole days to ask his first question?" Jude said.

Father laughed.

"Why does the wheat grow this way, Father?" Jude teased. "How do the stars stay in the heavens? What makes the rain fall? Why do some clouds rumble and others do not?"

Jude and Father's contagious laughter caught on with Mary and me.

When our chuckling subsided, Mary spoke. "It's a good question, Joseph. For all his questions, James asks intelligent ones."

Father nodded. "Yes, he does."

"And what do you say to this question?" Mary asked.

Father walked in silence, thinking about his answer. Then he stopped the mule and turned toward all of us.

"I don't think for a moment that God creates an angry river one moment and then a friendly creek the next. He already created the river, just like he created the heavens and the earth and the animals. He gave us—all of us—minds with which to think and hearts with which to decide. I chose to leave Nazareth. I chose a trail that all travelers take. I chose to travel during the storm. God didn't make the winds howl or the river rise. I put us near the river. God intervened by ensuring our safety."

I didn't have anything to add, but Father's words perplexed me. After a moment he said, "The choices I make in this life, small or large, are mine alone." He turned around to look at Mary. "I was asked to marry you, but I could have refused. Could I not, James?"

"I saw with my own eyes, Mary, and heard with my ears. Father could have refused and—"

"But I didn't refuse," Father interrupted. "I chose to marry you because I felt it was the right thing to do. I also chose to believe that our family and friends shouldn't hold you and Jude in contempt. And in choosing you, I also chose this child." Father stopped the mule and turned around. He took a deep breath. "I know this child isn't mine, but I believe the little life you are carrying is special, for reasons God has yet to reveal. After what happened to us yesterday, I firmly believe God is watching over us. If he wills me to protect you and this child, I will do what he expects of me. So many men don't know what God's will is for them, and that makes me blessed. I am among the few, like the prophets before us, who know with all my heart that this is what I must do for God."

As Jude and I looked at each other, a look of surprise and awe swept across our faces. I glanced at Mary, straddling an old mule, her face filled with love for my father. Father walked over to her and held out a hand, which she grasped. She laughed softly, and Father's yellow teeth showed as he returned a wide smile. He turned and walked to the front of the mule and, taking the leader, walked up a trail that led to the east entrance of Jerusalem.

I thought back to a year ago, when Father and I had come to Jerusalem to assume Mary into our family. We had approached the city from the north, passing the skull-like rocks and the fearsome groups of Roman soldiers. This trail wasn't much different. It was steep in places and littered with rocks. What differed now were the crowds of pilgrims making their way to Jerusalem for the Day of Atonement. The road was filled with warm, sweaty bodies and every kind of beast. The smell overwhelmed us, and at one point, Mary bent over and vomited.

Father slowed our pace. "The crowd thins out behind us," he said in a low voice. "We should take our time. If the crowd were to panic, we could all be crushed. If Mary is knocked off the mule, there will be no way for us to save her and the child from being trampled to death."

Jude and I walked on either side of the mule to keep it from being scared by a passersby and to protect Mary's legs from being crushed.

As the crowd thinned around us, Father walked over to the mule, just ahead of Jude. "Mary, do you remember the things we are required to do in order to celebrate this feast?"

Mary nodded. "I do." She smiled at Jude and me. "Do either of you know what is expected of our people at this time of the year?"

"To be forgiven our sins, we're supposed to sacrifice something of value, according to our means—either grain, doves, goats, or cattle," I said boldly.

"And the Temple practice of sacrifice?" Father asked.

"The priest sacrifices two beasts, usually goats, but occasionally sheep," said Jude. "One goat is killed and offered to God as a sacrifice for the sins of mankind. The other is freed into the wilderness or—"

"Or pushed off a cliff," I interjected. "Our sins for the year go with the scapegoat forever, never to return to us once God has acknowledged our repentance and forgiven us."

"What do you suppose the people in Jerusalem are doing today, James?" Father asked.

"They are eating, praying, washing, and doing charitable works. They might be purchasing doves or livestock to be sacrificed tomorrow. None of these things may be done once the sun has set and the Day of Atonement begins."

"You have taught them well, Joseph," Mary said.

Father paused before looking back at her. "I think their mother had just as much to do with their learning as I did. I can't take all the credit."

"You will tell me about her someday?" Mary asked.

Father nodded and grinned. "Yes. Yes, I will. And I would like that."

We walked another mile until the gates to Jerusalem were in plain sight. The sun cast afternoon shadows on the barren ground. We were all tired but glad to be near the Temple on such an important occasion.

Suddenly Mary cried out and leaned to my side of the mule. I lifted my arms to catch her, the weight of her and baby against my arms and hands. Father didn't have to stop the mule.

The creature halted immediately. He dropped the leader and ran back to me as I struggled to keep Mary from falling off the mule.

"Oh, it hurts, James," Mary called out. Her head bobbed to and fro, as if her neck were made out of dough. Once more she cried out in pain. Jude ran around to the other side of the mule, where Father and I stood. As people passed us, they stared.

"Where does it hurt, Mary?" Father asked.

She began to take deep breaths. "In the lower part of my belly," she said, grunting.

"Your baby may be ready to greet," Father said. There was a serious look on his face as his eyes scoured the road ahead. "Do you think you can make it to Jerusalem?"

Mary nodded and took two deep breaths. "It seems to have subsided. Let us continue on, but quickly."

Jude and I made sure she was secure in her place on the mule. Father grabbed the leader rope, but the mule began to walk without prodding from Father, as if knowing the urgency of the situation.

We made it through the gates of Jerusalem, and Father pressed against the crowd. He took a street that led to the left and stopped at the first storefront. A short skinny merchant with thinning hair and a long brown beard was sweeping the stone walkways in front of his store.

"You there," he called out to the merchant. "My wife is with child and about to give labor, where might we find a room?"

The man shook his head. "I can't allow a pregnant woman into my home," he said gruffly. "If she gives birth tonight, my family won't have time to purify ourselves before presenting our sacrifice at the Temple. I'm sorry." The merchant wagged his head in empathy, and Father grabbed the leader in disappointment.

Mary cried out once more. Father stopped the mule in the middle of the busy marketplace and walked back to her, still holding the leader. "Are you all right?" he asked.

"Yes," Mary said softly. "Please find us some place to rest."

Father looked at me. "Make sure she doesn't fall off the mule."

He led the mule across two streets and down a small road where a collection of stone houses stood. Father approached one of them and knocked on the door. A woman answered. "Dear mother," Father began, "can you spare a room for my wife and sons? She is about to give birth."

The old woman looked at Father and our mule with wide eyes. "She is too young to be your wife," she said in unnerving tone. "These men are too old to have her for their mother. Tell me. Is she really your wife? Are these really your sons? Or did you find them begging in the street and take pity on them?"

"She is my second wife. Good woman, I assure you, this is my wife, and these are sons from my first marriage."

The woman looked at me and at Jude then walked up to Mary. With her finger outstretched, she pointed at Mary's belly and jabbed it with her finger. "This child belongs to one of these sinful, sinful boys! This girl carries her sins in her belly! May God curse you and the sins of your sons!"

By this time the windows of several houses nearby had opened. At least a dozen faces stared at us as the old woman shouted her accusations. Father tried to plead with her, but she wouldn't listen.

"Away with you!" she cackled. "God has forgotten you!" The old woman opened the door then slammed it shut behind her.

Father looked at the faces staring down at us. "This woman speaks lies! Please, I beg you, won't someone help us?" he shouted.

One by one the shutters and doors closed, the wood hitting the stone with a thudding sound.

"No," he mumbled. "I won't have this child born on the ground. We must find the house of a priest."

We walked for what seemed like miles, pushing our way through the crowds, animals, and merchants. Jude tried to shout something at me, but I couldn't hear him over the noise. Jerusalem was not the gleaming city I remembered from a year ago. Pilgrims, merchants, and Roman soldiers now surrounded the Temple. Even if we wanted to get close to the Temple, we couldn't. The wait would have lasted a day, if not more.

We pushed our way past the temple and onto a street I recognized. This was the street that led to the high priest's home. We were filthy, tired, and put off by the lack of hospitality shown to us in the past two hours, but we pressed on. When we reached the end of the street, there were fewer people.

Father came back to check on Mary. "Any more pains?" he said, out of breath.

Mary shook her head. "Joseph, I don't know if I can last much longer."

Father nodded. "Boys, fetch the water skins and give Mary a drink. I'm going to knock on the door."

He walked up to the door and knocked on the olive wood with the whites of his knuckles. When no one answered, he pounded the door with his fist. "I call on the holy man of this house!" he shouted.

"Who's there?" bellowed a deep voice from behind the door.

"It is Joseph bar Jacob of Bethlehem! Husband to Mary! The child dedicated to God who once lived in this house!"

The heavy wooden door creaked on its hinges as the occupant opened cautiously. The man's head was covered in the blue scarf of a scribe, his glittering brown eyes peering at us from behind the safety of the massive door. He first stared at Mary, blinked twice, then looked at Father.

"Hitch your mule to the post and come in," the man said in a gruff voice.

Jude and I secured the mule, strapped our food pouches and coin purses to our backs, and followed Father and Mary inside. As the man unraveled his blue scarf, we gasped.

"Nicodemus!" exclaimed Father.

The scribe walked over, placed his hands on my shoulders, and smiled. "You are taller, James," he said. "I have always kept you in my thoughts and prayers."

"Thank you." I bowed my head. "I still wish to study at the Temple."

"One day, lad. One day," said Nicodemus. He walked over to Mary. "And you're a young woman now."

Mary didn't look up. She lifted her hands from her side and rested them on her belly. The scribe paid no attention to her gesture. He turned to Jude and said, "You have suffered much, I hear, attending to your father's demands."

Jude cocked his head in confusion.

"The news of Mary's pregnancy reached this house a week ago," the scribe said then turned to look at Father. "One of the villagers snuck out the day of the discovery to report Mary and Jude to the authorities in Sepphoris. Rabbi Boethus was absent that evening. I was the remaining authority."

"So you knew?" Father appeared both hurt and astonished. "I needed someone to vouch for Mary and Jude. You could have put this whole matter to rest, Nicodemus, and you didn't. You could have talked to Ezra, my brother, the elders... You could have made things right for Jude by talking to Leah's parents. We fled our own village out of fear! Why didn't you help us?"

"I'm afraid that I will fail you again, my friend."

"Friend?" cried Father. "We are not friends! You betrayed me from the moment you crafted the plans for this marriage! You risked the lives of my entire family, not to mention this girl!" Father pointed to Mary. "This innocent, beautiful, intelligent woman has more right to God's divine protection than anyone in this room! She carries a child, absent the peace of mind and body due any woman who is with child!"

Father's voice grew louder with every word. He motioned with his arms and hands, his body acting out the feelings behind each word. He spoke with such fire on his tongue that I was frightened. His appearance had taken on that of an angry bull. Had he been speaking to the high priest, he might have been suspected of being a Zealot.

"Hear then, O house of David!" the scribe shouted. He pointed his index finger into Father's chest and spoke with such force that it could have blown open the shutters of the house. "Is it too little for you to weary mortals that you weary God also?"

Father lifted his head as if expecting what was to come. But the scribe continued to raise his voice.

"The Lord himself will give you a sign."

Nicodemus walked over to Mary and placed both his hands on her belly. "Look! The young woman is with child!" He backed away, startled. Mary looked up at him and smiled.

"He kicks too," the scribe said, smiling. "And she shall bear a son and name him Immanuel." Father ran his hand over and over his dusty beard. Jude looked at me, and I looked at him. The words sounded familiar, but I couldn't place them.

Mary tugged at the scribe's tunic. "The angel told me to name him Jesus."

The scribe turned around and held her belly in his hands once more, his face cloaked in sheer joy. "Who was speaking to you, woman?" he asked firmly.

"An angel," said Mary.

He turned from Mary and looked at my father. "A son of Israel dedicated to God, so that—"

"Isaiah's prophecy may be fulfilled," interrupted Father. "Why, Nicodemus, didn't you tell me?"

"Oh, Joseph, you always knew somewhere in your heart that God destined you for something greater! You are blessed with such skill, intelligence, and fortitude!" The scribe looked around the room. "And you have a wonderful family."

"The messiah," Father said softly. "God has chosen Mary to be the vessel for the messiah."

"It would be an honor like no other ever bestowed on earth, Joseph," said the scribe. "Mary's child, the son of God! With the power to forgive us our sins and to restore Israel to its proper position in the kingdom of God!"

Father's eyes widened, and he took a deep breath.

"Nicodemus, I can't bear the thought of anything happening to Mary. She and Jude were within a stone's throw of mob justice. We almost lost our lives in the Jordan yesterday. In the last few hours, she's been experiencing birthing pains. We *must* find a place for her to have this child." He said his last words through gritted teeth. "You *must* help us, Nicodemus. God willing, somebody must!"

Nicodemus walked over to Mary, leaned forward as if to bow, and placed his hands, once more, on her belly. The look of joy, once upon his face, vanished like sand under the waves of the sea. He spoke in a low voice, with his head down, as if speaking to the unborn child. "If you stay here, I can't ensure your safety." He stood up and turned around to speak to Father. "Herod is here, in Jerusalem, to observe the Day of Atonement."

Our eyes must have widened, for Nicodemus raised his hands to calm us. "He is in the palace for now, but he will come here to join the high priest for the walk to the Temple."

"We have tried to find shelter," Father explained. "No one will take us."

"It is better if your family and the child aren't here," said the scribe. "Herod can sniff out a threat anywhere in Judea."

"And when the child is born?" Father asked. "Will Herod not try to find my family in Nazareth?"

"The king already knows those families who come from David's throne. Rabbi Boethus has spoken not only to Prince Antipas, but also the king himself. Once the child is born, you must find a way to live in hiding until the king passes."

"That could take years, Nicodemus!" Father protested. "How will I provide for this child and my family?"

"Has not God protected you thus far?" the scribe asked.

Father remained silent.

"Joseph, you can't control the will of God. You must put the fate of your entire family in his protection, as so many prophets before you."

"I am no prophet," Father replied. "I am a mere man, with a cold, hungry family to clothe and feed and shelter."

"There is nothing you can do, Joseph. Your trades, your preparedness, your savings, your shelter, all the things you have come to afford as safety and security no longer mean anything."

"I have a family to protect," insisted Father. "How am I to protect her," he said, pointing to Mary, "and this messiah?"

"The only way to protect them is God's way," said the scribe. "You need God's power now and nothing more."

Father looked beaten. He threw up his arms in disgust and stomped toward the door. He turned and growled, "Where am I to go, Nicodemus? Where would you take the mother of the unborn messiah?"

"To Bethlehem of course," said Nicodemus. "Claim this woman as your wife and this child as your own."

He smiled at Father then walked over to Jude and me. "Get Mary and your father out of the city as fast as possible," he said sternly. He looked into Mary's face, stared for a moment, then spoke. "God will not allow you to have this child in any way other than how he sees fit. Obey your husband. Do what he says."

Mary looked at Father. Father looked at us.

"James, Jude, get your provisions. We leave now."

CHAPTER TWENTY-EIGHT

Jude and I left the house and walked to where we had hitched the mule.

"Father is worried," remarked Jude.

"If Herod is here, it means Rabbi Boethus is here as well."

"James!" Father called out. "Is the mule ready?"

"Almost, Father," I said.

The scribe had followed Mary and Father out of the house. Jude placed the leather blanket over the pouches, and I worked fast to tie the straps together.

"Joseph, I'm sorry I can't help you," said Nicodemus. "You understand, do you not?"

Father turned to speak to him, but we were all startled by a gruff shout from across the street.

"Joseph bar Jacob!"

I turned to see two priests, one in a robe of purple, and the other in a robe of scarlet.

I walked over to Jude. "It is Rabbi Boethus and one of the Temple priests," I whispered.

As the two clerics walked up to Father, Rabbi Boethus immediately noticed Mary and the bulge that protruded from her cloak.

"Well, well, Joseph. I see you took your marriage proposal seriously," Rabbi Boethus said with a chuckle. "You didn't waste any time."

Father's blue eyes cast a stern look on the two priests. "That is my affair, is it not, Rabbi? A matter better left to a man and his wife, would you not agree?"

Rabbi Boethus slapped the priest on the back. "Are you not impressed by his piety, brother?"

The priest smiled nervously. "Joseph, I didn't know the marriage between you and Mary was formalized. I expected the local rabbi to inform Rabbi Boethus."

Mary looked at me then at Father. Father turned to speak to the priests when Nicodemus interjected. "Rabbis, Joseph stopped to inform me that he has traveled all this way to register the two of them in Bethlehem."

"And the child?" asked Rabbi Boethus.

Father nodded. "And the child," he replied.

Rabbi Boethus smiled. "Another son perhaps?"

"Perhaps," said Father. "Now if you will excuse us, we have a long way to travel, and Mary is late in her term. We need to find shelter."

"Then don't let us keep you," said the high priest. "It's a pleasure to see you and Mary together."

"Thank you, Rabbi," said Father. He helped Mary onto the mule then reached for the leader and tugged. The mule instinctively turned around, and Father waved to the two priests and the scribe.

"Good journey, Joseph," yelled Nicodemus. "May God be with you and your family."

Jude and I took our places on either side of the mule and walked down the street. Father didn't turn around to acknowledge the scribe. He moved at a quickened pace, avoiding the carts and animals and weaving his way into the crowd in an attempt to lose sight of the priests.

"James!" he yelled back to me. "We're going to leave Jerusalem through the south gate, but we won't be following the main road to Bethlehem."

I walked over to Father. "Are you afraid?"

"Yes. If Boethus needs a bargaining chip with the king, he can easily offer up a son of David and his pregnant wife in exchange for more power or favors."

"What are you going to do?"

Mary let out a groan. Father stopped the mule, handed me the leader, and walked back to Mary.

"The pains are coming back, Joseph, and they're so strong."

"How long can you manage?" Father asked. He placed a hand on hers and stared at her swollen belly.

"I don't know." She sighed. "How far are we from Bethlehem?"

"At least two hours. With all the pilgrims coming from the south, however, it could take longer."

Mary nodded. "Do what you must." She squeezed Father's hand and grunted. "I'll tell you when I can't go any farther."

Father nodded. He walked back to the mule and took the leader from me. "There is an old trail that leads to the east of Bethlehem, James. We'll travel to Simon's by way of this road."

"Isn't it out of the way, Father?"

"It is, but there will be less traffic."

"What if Mary is to have this baby? Will she have it on the road?"

Father shrugged. His eyes became tearful, and he wiped at them with the palm of his hand. "I wish I could provide more, James." He wrapped his arms around me. "I can't believe this is happening."

I pushed him away to look in his face. "This isn't your fault, Father. But you must keep your wits about you. Mary needs you. Jude and I need you. We have never been in this part of the land, and we need you to lead this family."

Father nodded. "Go back with your brother."

Jude saw the exchanges between Father, Mary, and me but had trouble hearing us, for the crowds were getting larger and louder.

"What was that all about?" he asked.

"Father is worried."

Father pulled the mule off the main road and onto a narrow dirt trail. We walked for what seemed like an entire afternoon. On occasion Jude handed Mary the water pouch. I tried to get her to eat something, but she wouldn't. The sun began to set, and Father quickened his pace. We walked until the shadows of the hills grew longer and the red hues of dusk had faded to gray.

Mary cried out, "Joseph!" She groaned and doubled over against the neck of the mule. The beast stopped. Mary groaned again then let out a scream. Her breathing grew heavy. A layer of sweat had formed across her forehead and glistened in the moonlight. She let out another scream and slumped against the neck of the mule, her head lying against its hair.

"Can you speak?" Father asked softly.

"It hurts so badly," Mary said in a weak voice. "I think this baby is coming, Joseph."

"We'd better find a place to camp," said Jude.

Mary let out another scream. "Will someone get me off this mule?" she groaned.

The waning moon began to shine brighter and the stars poked through the heavens. Father looked at the night sky, then walked up to the front of the mule, grabbed the leader rope, and pulled the mule along the trail.

"What is he doing?" Jude asked in a whisper. "Mary is about to give birth."

We walked several hundred paces. To our surprise Mary had stopped moaning.

"Are you all right?" I asked.

Mary leaned up, trying to sit up straight. "As long as these pains don't return, I'm all right."

"What does it feel like?" Jude asked.

Mary wrinkled her forehead. "Jude bar Joseph, is that all you can ask? It feels as if this mule is sitting on my belly!"

Father laughed.

Jude shrugged. "Sorry," he said. "I have only seen the birth of a lamb, not a child."

I smiled and looked up a Mary, who had managed a grin.

Father stopped the mule and pointed at a round tower made of stone blocks. In the moonlight it seemed as if it had grown up out of the earth. It was as tall as two houses stacked on top of each other. At its base, it was as wide as two barns but narrowed as it went up toward the sky.

"Migdal Eder," Father said in a loud voice. "The watchtower."

"What is Migdal Eder?" I asked him.

"A tower where the shepherd-priests can keep an eye on the Temple flocks."

We walked up to the door. It was made of solid oak, with iron hinges and a wooden latch that locked from the inside.

"This looks like the door you made for our neighbor's barn," Jude observed.

"It's very well made, Father," I said.

"Well, stop looking and knock on it!" yelled a voice. "This baby is coming!"

We turned to see Mary leaned over the neck of the mule once more. She called out, "Why is it that a man always stops to admire another man's work at the worst possible time?"

"Go stand with her," said Father to Jude.

Father banged his knuckles on the door, and a man in a cream-colored tunic answered. He had a blue sash that covered his shoulders and hung down past his hips. He rubbed the sleep from his eyes and squinted at Father. "Who stands here greeting me?" he asked in a squeaky voice.

"I am Joseph bar Jacob of Bethlehem," Father replied. "My wife is with child, and she is in labor."

The man propped the heavy door open and stumbled several steps into the moonlight. He looked at Mary, who was hunched over the neck of the mule, then stared curiously at Jude and me.

"Who are these lads?" he asked. His voice, now strong and clear, echoed in the valley.

"They are my sons, Jude and James," said Father. "Please," he pleaded, "give us a place to rest and room long enough for my wife to deliver this child."

"Of course, Joseph," said the man, smiling. "Do you not know who I am?"

Father looked closer. Our faces were covered in darkness, despite the moonlight. "I swear, man, I do not know you. How do you know me?"

The shepherd smiled, ignored Father and walked over to the mule. "Woman, give me your hand."

Mary lifted her hand and gave it to the shepherd. Jude ran up and helped Mary off the mule.

"All right," said the shepherd. "Let's get you inside."

As we began to walk, he announced, "I'm Levi. I will help your wife deliver the child."

Inside the tower another shepherd, dressed like the other, was lighting candles. He finished his task and walked over to greet us. "My name is Nemuel. I am at your service." The shepherd bowed and pointed to the row of stalls. "You may put your mule in a stall."

I heard his words, but I stood like the rest of my family, frozen in awe, staring up into the tower. None of us had ever seen the inside of such a structure.

"You should make your wife as comfortable as possible," said Levi. "The pains will come quickly. I'll check to see if she is ready."

The inside of the watchtower was the most peculiar thing I had ever seen. The room itself was round and lined with ladders. Several stone blocks were positioned along the inside walls. There were slits in the stones, intentional gaps, where shepherds could watch for wolves and poachers. The tallest of the ladders led to the top of the tower, where the shepherds could stand on a small stone pathway. A man could walk around the stone pathway and still be protected from the elements. Large wooden beams, the width of a man, lay across the top of the tower, notched into the stone, giving the shepherds not only a roof but also the means to see the entire countryside.

At the back of the tower were animal stalls, much like those in our barn, and a small fenced area. Toward the middle of the room, a stone floor had been laid that reached all the way to the door. There I saw beds, a fireplace, two tables, rugs of red and blue, more than a dozen cushions, and ten chairs.

Where we had entered stood a small altar and several stone shelves full of foodstuffs, candles, scrolls, blank papyrus, ink bowls, and wooden crafts. The room, filled with smell of burning candles and incense, lacked the strong scent of animals and dung. The stone floors were a brilliant white, and the entire tower appeared as if it had just been cleaned from top to bottom.

"Who lives here?" I asked.

"Why, we do, young man," said Nemuel, "and the rabbis in the fields."

Levi helped Mary settle onto one of the cushions. Her cries came more quickly. They were louder too.

Father turned to face Nemuel. "What do you mean? There are priests in this field?"

Nemuel stroked his white beard and smiled. "This is the watchtower of the sacrificial flock. The Day of Atonement is tomorrow, is it not?"

Father looked at Jude and me as if to say, "I don't believe him."

"Are you a rabbi then, Nemuel?" Father asked.

The old man nodded. "As is Levi," he assured us.

Father walked over to the nest of cushions Levi had prepared for Mary. She was propped up at the waist, her legs slightly spread, her arms wrapped around a pillow.

"You must give us privacy," Levi said.

Father walked over to where Jude and I stood near the entrance. Levi whispered to Mary. She nodded and pulled her tunic above her waist, exposing the lower half of her body. She spread her legs farther apart and nodded.

Father turned around. "James, Jude, turn around."

We both turned around, as did Nemuel.

"What's going on?" I asked.

"Levi is checking to see if the baby is ready," said the old priest. "The same is done when lambs are close are to birth. Levi helps the mothers deliver, to ease their pain and suffering. He will do the same for Mary."

"Joseph, Jude, and James," the shepherd called out. We turned around and saw Levi washing his hands in a stone bowl filled with water. "She is close," he said softly. "You may speak with her now, but soon you will have to leave the tower."

Father motioned for us to follow him across the room to the nest of cushions.

"Why do we have to leave?" Jude asked.

"Out of respect for her privacy and dignity," said Levi. "And should she become distressed, I'll need privacy so that I can work."

"Distressed?" I asked. "What do you mean?"

Father looked at me. His eyes were moist. "Some women don't survive childbirth, James. If a woman becomes distressed, a physician or midwife can help the woman deliver the child and save the mother's life and—"

Levi cut Father off. "Each of you must have your words now. Her time is near."

Chapter Twenty-Nine

Levi and Nemuel went outside. Father knelt next to Mary, leaned over her slowly, and kissed her forehead. "I don't know what to say." He paused then covered his eyes with a hand and began to weep. "All of my children were delivered at home. This is not the place for you."

Mary grunted as another pain coursed through her body. Her eyes became wide, and her face contorted. As the pain subsided, she took Father's hand.

Jude and I knelt opposite Father. Mary reached for my hand. "You will accept the child, will you not?"

I nodded. "Of course I will."

"I know you miss your mother. Will you accept me as your father's wife?"

I nodded again. "I'm grateful that God led you to us. I will love you like a son loves his mother."

Mary looked at Jude and reached for his hand. "You have been my protector since my arrival in Nazareth." Jude smiled and looked down. "You watched over me while your family worked in Tiberias. You taught me how to farm, how to care for animals, how to keep house, and how to keep Aunt Miriam's tongue in check."

We snickered when we heard this.

"You kept me safe during our travels to see my cousin. You knew what little there was to my life in Jerusalem, and you stood by me, even though you were wronged and shamed for things you didn't do. I shall always be grateful to you, Jude, for your care and companionship, and I shall love you as a mother loves her son."

"I love you too, Mary," said Jude. "My father is your protector now, and your child shall be my brother. Please don't worry anymore."

Mary lay back on the cushions, squeezed her eyes tightly, and cried out in a loud voice. The sound jostled my memory of the stoning of the young woman, and I realized Mary could have suffered a similar fate. If not for Mary's bravery, Jude's courage, and Father's wisdom, this occasion would have been marked with pain, suffering, and death.

Levi entered. "I have heard her cry. It is time for the child to enter the world."

Father, Jude, and I walked slowly out of the tower. As Father pushed on the door, he noticed two small initials just above the latch, "SJ."

"Those are craftsmen's initials," Father said, pointing to the letters.

"Ah. They are the initials of your son, Simon," Levi said, smiling. "He is as good a craftsman as his father. Now go and leave me with your wife."

I saw a small grin form on Father's face as we left the tower. Nemuel met us outside. His blue sash shone in the moonlight. He had a shepherd's crook and a small lantern. He made sure the door was shut before he led us away from the tower.

Father looked back. "Where are we going? Should I not stay closer to the tower?"

"It is a holy place, Joseph," said Nemuel. "She will be fine. And Levi is very skilled at delivering lambs."

"Where are we?" I asked.

"You are walking on holy ground," said Nemuel. "Migdal Eder has been here since before the time of our ancestor Jacob."

Nemuel turned around. His beard blew in the cool night air, and the blue sash dangled in the breeze next to his knees. He stood taller than most men, but the shepherd's crook was at least an arm's length taller than him.

"Over there, to the east, is Shepherd's Field. It is where the sacrificial flock is pastured for the Day of Atonement. There are three other shepherds in the fields watching over the sheep, goats, oxen, and lambs."

Father scratched his head. "I'm still puzzled. You said you and Levi are priests?"

Nemuel smiled. "We all are. Only Temple priests are allowed to keep the sacrificial flock. We ensure that the flocks are kept healthy and strong. Only unblemished stock may be used for Temple sacrifices, especially on the Day of Atonement, and—"

As we spoke, a strange glow appeared in the eastern sky, toward Shepherd's Field. I pointed at it, rudely interrupting the rabbi. "What is that?"

The glow became brighter. As the four of us stood under the sky, the band grew like white ribbon across the horizon, dividing the night sky. It was a band of brilliant white, brighter than the sun, streaking across the sky.

"Yes, what is that, Rabbi?" Father asked.

"I…I do not know," stuttered Nemuel.

A high-pitched sound accompanied the glow. It reminded me of the single note my mother used to sing as she sang the words in the Psalms. It was the most beautiful note I had ever heard, as if a thousand voices had collected together to sing.

"The air is warm," said Jude. "Warmer than it was a few minutes ago."

Father began to back away. He turned and ran toward the tower.

"Joseph, wait!" yelled Nemuel. "Levi will come for us when the child is here."

Father pulled at the handle on the door, but Levi, in his precaution, had locked it. Father banged on the door with his fist, shouting, "Mary! Mary!" When we had caught up to him, he looked back, and then beyond. "Look!"

The glowing ribbon of white could be seen all around us, between the earth and the night sky. The single note I had heard in my head grew louder.

"What...is...that?" Jude exclaimed.

He pointed to a thickening in the ribbon just beyond Shepherd's Field. A white shadow in the shape of a human figure filled the night sky. The figure had long hair but no eyes, nose, or mouth.

"Is it a spirit?" Jude asked quietly.

A rumbling, like the sound of thunder, filled the air, but the sweet sound of that single musical note continued to hum. We stared at the figure as it floated over the fields. I felt warm and at peace. My head was no longer filled with thoughts or worries but joy and comfort. After several minutes a hole opened in the sky, as if someone were poking a fist through a thin fabric. The ghostly figure dissipated, and the long ribbon of light was pulled through this hole. When the figure and the light were gone, the sky returned to black, the moon appeared, the land became dark, and the stars shone brightly.

We all looked at Nemuel. "I have never seen anything like it in my life," he said.

"What could it be?" Jude asked.

Nemuel stared at the sky. "Perhaps it was a *malach*."

I raised my eyebrows.

"A *malach* is a messenger from God," Nemuel explained. "Think of Isaiah or Jacob or Moses. God sent messengers to help them." He looked at the sky for another minute. "*Malachim* are spirits from God who have no free will. They only do what God commands them."

"So you think this light was from God?" Father asked.

A loud wailing sound came from the tower. The door flew open, and Levi stood at the entrance, drying his wet hands with a cloth.

"You must come and see your son, Joseph!" Levi's eyes were beaming. "And your wife... She is the most precious mother I have ever seen. It is as if she and this baby are one!"

We rushed through the door and saw Mary sitting on a new set of cushions, holding a baby.

"Joseph!" she said, smiling. "He's beautiful!"

Jude began to walk with Father, but I tugged on his tunic. "Give Father a moment alone with Mary."

Jude smiled and nodded.

We stood at a distance with the priests. Mary held the baby up for Father. Levi had wrapped him tightly in strips of cloth cut from a priest's tunic. Father reached out to hold the child. He looked down at tiny bundle then back at Mary.

"What a peaceful face," said Father. He turned around and motioned for us to join him. Then he sat down on one of the brown cushions; Jude and I each found our own. Father gave the child to Jude first. "Your brother, whom you protected," Father said proudly.

He helped Jude to hold the child in his arms. The baby yawned and turned his head to one side. Jude stared into his face. Finally he said, "He is beautiful." Jude turned to me. "It is your turn to hold him."

I sat with my arms crossed. "I'm doing just fine watching you. With my luck I'll drop him."

Mary giggled. "Oh, James, hold the boy," she said in a loud whisper.

Slowly I uncrossed my arms. Father took the baby from Jude and handed him to me.

"What will you name him?" Nemuel asked Mary.

"Jesus," Mary replied.

"Jesus?" Levi asked.

"Yes. Is it not a common name?"

The two priests glanced at each other and nodded. "It is."

Father looked at the priests with suspicion, the same way he looked at Rabbi Boethus the day we had met him at his synagogue more than a year ago.

"I'm sore," she said softly. "But these wrappings must be changed before I nurse him."

Father took the baby from Mary. "Where should we change him?"

Mary pointed to a stone feeding trough next to the stables. "We can't change him on our eating table, and I won't risk him catching a fever by laying him on the cold floor."

Father wrinkled his nose. "Over there?"

Mary sighed. "Levi did it earlier, Joseph. Levi, can you get me the blanket I used to cover the manger?"

Levi took a blanket from a pile stacked by the door and handed it to Mary. She placed it over the top of the feed trough, then took the baby from Father and laid him in it. He tore another tunic into strips while Mary removed the old swaddling cloths. She placed them in a bucket to be washed, and Levi handed the fresh linens to Mary. We stared at the baby for some time. His eyes were open; his nose and ears were perfect; and his little mouth yawned at least twice while we stood there. He looked up with dark-brown eyes that seemed to twinkle in the candlelight.

"He only cried the minute he was born," Levi whispered. "He's a very good baby, Mary."

Mary smiled as she wrapped him tightly in the fresh linens.

"How do you know how to do that?" Father asked her with a grin.

"I helped the priests' wives with their children. We had a lot of babies stay with us in those days." Mary smiled as she wrapped the last linen around the baby and tucked it in. "There," she said with a smile. "All snug." Mary looked at me. "Would you like to hold him again?"

She laid the baby in my arms. "Hello," I whispered. "Because of you we have had quite the adventure this past week."

Levi turned to Father. "Mary did very well. No problems or complications whatsoever."

Father's head began to nod as he tried to fight back his sleepiness.

"We saw something amazing, Levi," said Nemuel. "A light from the heavens shone down on Shepherd's Field while you were delivering Mary."

"I saw a light pass through the slits in the tower. I thought it was the moon," said Levi.

"We should discuss it tomorrow," said Nemuel. "It's very late, and our guests need their rest."

I found a cushion on which to lie, but before I closed my eyes, I arched my neck to take one more glimpse of the baby. Father had moved next to Mary. He had his arms wrapped around Mary and the infant. As the priests moved about the room putting out candles, I couldn't help think about how this perfect little child had upended our entire family.

CHAPTER THIRTY

Just before dawn, when the night sky was darkest and the mist settled over Judea, a violent knock rattled against the door of the watchtower. I leaned up, rubbed my eyes, and tried to see through the darkness. While the priests fumbled to light candles, Father stood. He scanned the room, took a knife from the shelf, and stood to the side of the entrance.

Levi was the first to the door. "Who dares knock at this time of hour?" he yelled.

"Levi, it is Jairus! Open the door!"

Levi fumbled with the latch and opened the door. It gave a creak that echoed throughout the room.

"Where is the flock?" Levi grumbled. "Are you not supposed to be tending the flock?"

"Yes, yes, we are. We moved the flock to a spot across the trail."

"Where are Kadmiel and Eliam?"

"We are here, Levi," said a voice from behind Jairus.

The three shepherds stumbled in, their crooks catching on the door. Their tunics, stained brown, reeked of sweat and dung.

"Where did you all sleep?" complained Levi. "Did you all lie in a cesspool?"

"We fell into a ravine," Eliam said quietly.

My eyes adjusted to the candlelight, and I saw that each man wore a frayed tunic with a worn-out blue sash. Their beards were covered in dust, and the hair on their legs was soiled with dirt. Through the open door, I heard the bleating of sheep.

"What was in the ravine?" Levi asked. He glared at the three of them. "Can I not trust you all with just one task? One night! One night! And you come back to me riddled in filth, smelling like a trough, and just when I had fallen asleep!"

"We had to round up the flock and come back to tell you what we saw," Kadmiel pleaded.

"It took much longer than we expected," added Jairus.

Levi put a hand up to cover his eyes and groaned. "This could not wait until morning?"

"Technically it is morning," noted Eliam, "though the sun isn't up yet."

"Yes, we know that!" growled Nemuel. "Now please tell us what is so important. I want to go back to sleep."

Kadmiel looked to where Jude and I stood. Just behind us sat Mary, nursing the baby.

"That's him!" Kadmiel whispered to Levi. "That is the boy!"

"That is a baby, yes," replied Levi. "But the matter is about your ignoring your duties as a priest and rabbi—"

Father interrupted Levi. "How did you know I had a son?"

In almost a whisper, Jairus said, "A *malach* told us."

Father looked at Levi as Nemuel pushed through to the front of our group. "*Who* told you?"

Jairus's eyes opened wide. "A messenger from God told us that a savior was born, that we should find him wrapped in cloths and lying in a manger."

I sensed confusion, but all I felt was fear.

Eliam pointed to Father's hand, which was by his side. "Why do you hold that knife?"

Father looked at the knife. "I sought to protect my wife and son. The knocking on the door sounded more like Romans than rabbis."

Father handed the knife to Levi and walked across the room to Mary.

"Who are you?" Jairus asked.

Father spoke with his back still turned. "Joseph bar Jacob."

"He is Simon the Carpenter's father," said Levi.

The three shepherds followed Father to where Mary sat. The baby was lying in the manger, sleeping.

"Would you like to hold him?" Mary asked.

They nodded excitedly. "Very much," they said together.

"Not until they wash!" exclaimed Levi.

The three men ran outside to the well. Nemuel collected fresh tunics and three blue sashes and went out to meet them. Father helped Mary settle in on the cushions.

She yawned. "The baby is tired."

Father laughed. "So is his mother."

He knelt next to Mary and held her hand.

"Father?" I asked.

"Yes, James?"

"Do you think Mary was dedicated to God so she could have this baby?"

Father looked at Levi, who was seated on a cushion on the far side of the room. "What did the rabbis mean when they said the messenger told them of a savior?"

Levi ran his fingers through his long, white, stringy hair. "It means this son of yours is special. Savior or not, God has a purpose for this boy."

"Is that why we saw that light?" Jude asked.

"It was no light!" Jairus exclaimed. "They were angels. More than the eyes could see and the brain could count! Each one gave off a bright light, and together they lit up the sky!"

As the other rabbis entered, the first rays of morning crept into the tower. Nemuel followed behind the others and shut the door quietly. "It is the Day of Atonement, brothers," he said softly. "Let us give thanks for this day and for the forgiveness of our sins."

When the rabbis began their chant, the baby startled. His tiny eyelids opened to the gentle voices of the singing priests. Mary handed the baby to Levi first, then to Jairus, then to Nemuel, Kadmiel, and Eliam. As they each held the child, their eyes became wet, and they were overcome with joy.

Father called Jude and me aside and spoke in a low whisper. "This place is no longer safe. We must travel to Simon's house today."

"What is wrong with this place?" Jude asked.

"The rabbis will drive the goats and sheep to Jerusalem for the Day of Atonement. If news of the angels, or the announcement of a savior, reaches Joazar or Herod, they will find us and kill us."

"Father, surely you don't believe this," I said confidently.

He turned to me and gritted his teeth. "I had a dream last night of a Roman soldier sticking a knife into that baby. I didn't dream it just once. I dreamed it over and over and over again. If that baby is even remotely connected to the bright light we saw in the skies last night, then he belongs to God."

As the rabbis continued to sing, Mary took the baby in her arms.

Father looked at Jude and me. "I fear this place. We *must* leave."

Chapter Thirty-One

Ten days had passed since the birth of my brother.

My brother Simon, his wife Adina, and their four children graciously received us into their home in Bethlehem. On the eighth day, the baby was circumcised in a nearby synagogue, in the presence of our family. Father assisted the rabbi in this sacred act and named him Jesus. Mary wiped away his tears with a small piece of blanket that Adina had sewn a few days before. The ceremony was simple, our prayers humble, and Father offered his gratitude to God by sacrificing two doves.

As we left the synagogue, I noticed a man with a short beard covered in bright-blue garments, standing by the door. In one hand he held a scroll and in the other a walking staff. There were rings on his fingers, and his sandals were thick, with straps made of soft leather. When he saw I had recognized him, he grinned slightly and put a finger to his lips. I walked over to Father, whispered to him, then pointed at Nicodemus.

Father looked up at him then down at me. "Ignore him until we reach Simon's home. I know he will follow us."

Two streets before we reached Simon's house, Mary approached Father. "You are troubled, Joseph. I have seen this look before."

"Where is Jesus?" Father asked.

"Adina is holding him. What is it, Joseph?"

Father kept walking. "Nicodemus is here."

Mary's eyes widened. "Where?"

"Don't look now, but he is following us."

"What do you suppose he wants?"

"I don't know."

"He's coming," I said. Father turned and faced the street.

"Why, Joseph," said Nicodemus in a booming voice, "I always seem to greet you at someone else's house!"

"I am sure God has his reasons," said Father.

"I have a message for you, from your brother." Nicodemus handed Father the scroll. "And I also would like to have a word with you."

"Mary, stay inside Simon's house." Father motioned for Jude and me to join him.

"Let's take a walk," Nicodemus suggested.

We followed him through the streets of Bethlehem until we reached a small courtyard that was adjacent to a bustling market filled with potters and metalworkers.

Nicodemus looked around us then asked, "Shall we sit?"

We sat close together, in a circle, under a large poplar tree. The scribe broke the seal on the scroll and handed it to Father. "Take a moment and read it," said Nicodemus.

We sat silently as Father read the words written by my uncle. Finally he rolled up the scroll and slipped it into the inner pocket of his tunic.

"Thank you, Nicodemus. Our family is relieved of our duties in Tiberias."

"You can thank Ezra. He gave Rabbi Boethus a handsome stipend."

A sick look came over Father. "Where did Ezra get the money?" he asked.

Nicodemus shifted. "He used a portion of his family inheritance."

Father swallowed hard. "What do you want from us?"

"What I tell you, Joseph, must never be repeated." The scribe looked at all of us. "Do you understand this?"

We nodded, and Nicodemus cleared his throat. "I feel responsible for your decision to take Mary as your wife. I also feel responsible to you and your family."

"This is about the child?" Father asked sternly. "He is registered in my name, along with Mary."

Nicodemus shook his head. "This is not about Jude, Clopas, or whatever rumors may be flying about in Nazareth. This is about Herod."

Father sat straight up. I felt a twinge in my stomach.

"On the Day of Atonement, a group of rabbis brought the sacrificial flock into Jerusalem to be sacrificed. They spoke to the Temple high priest about a *malach* that appeared to them in the fields. They said a savior had been born that night to a young woman who was staying with her family at the watchtower. Is this true, Joseph?"

Father sat motionless.

"You will not speak?" asked the scribe.

Father didn't respond.

"The high priest sent me to Migdal Eder that day," Nicodemus continued. "When I arrived it was empty. The room was clean, the watchtower locked. It was as if the rabbis had been lying."

Father shifted. "One can never know."

Nicodemus looked at me. I shrugged. "One can never know," I repeated.

The scribe cocked his head to one side to stretch out his neck and began to grind his teeth. "I had to report that no one was at Migdal Eder and that I couldn't confirm whether the rabbis' story was true."

"It must have been an embarrassment to you, Nicodemus. I'm sorry for your trouble," Father said softly. "Is this all you wish to tell us?"

"No, Joseph," the scribe said sternly. "Unfortunately both Rabbi Boethus and King Herod were in the company of the shepherd-priests that morning. The king was outraged."

Father looked around the courtyard nervously. He leaned over and spoke in a low voice to the scribe. "How much time do I have?"

"Two days, maybe three. The king will send a small group of advisors to Simon's house to inquire about the child." The scribe took a deep breath and exhaled. "When I worked as a messenger for the Temple high priest, I was at court often. At that time the king would send one or two advisors and a group of soldiers. An inquiry was made at the house of the suspected party, and if the advisors found evidence of treason, the soldiers were ordered to kill."

"Why would the suspect even allow them in the door?"

"Herod always sends gifts with his advisors, as a peace offering. The advisors promise a civil discussion, but once the conversation commences, and the advisors give the word, the accused and their family are killed. The soldiers keep whatever money was sent and whatever they can find in the home."

Father let his face fall in his hands as he rocked back and forth. "If we were to leave Bethlehem, would that save Simon and his family?"

The scribe nodded. "As long as Simon can say you aren't there, he and his family will be safe. The advisors are only allowed to act if the traitor is in the house."

"This child... It's a baby, Nicodemus! A helpless child born to a helpless mother! Herod is crazy!"

"Quiet!" said the scribe. "Those words alone are enough to get you killed." He looked around the courtyard for soldiers, and when he saw there were none, he leaned in to chastise Father. "Joseph, what has gotten into you?"

"I don't know. I'm so tired, I can't even weep. I've been scared for my family every single day for more than a year."

"You must hold your family together. If this child *is* the savior, he must be protected! You understand, do you not?"

Father nodded and gave a long sigh. He looked over at me and spoke. "You'll need to help me get our things together. We must pack for a long trip." Father looked at the scribe. "Thank you for warning us, Nicodemus."

"Don't thank me until you are safe," said the scribe.

"Where should we go?" Father asked.

"Where there are Roman roads and cities, far from the reach of Herod."

"And where is that?" Father asked sadly.

"Egypt."

CHAPTER THIRTY-TWO

Father broke the news to the rest of the family.

Mary wailed. Adina sniffled as she held her two girls. Simon held both sons, each on a knee. He pulled them in close, dropped his head, and shut his eyes. Jesus lay sleeping in fresh cloth wrappings on cushions next to Mary.

When Father finished speaking, I knelt beside him and put my arm around his shoulders. He leaned into me with all his weight and almost knocked me over. "We will never see our home again," he said softly. "James, I'm getting too old for this. I'll never see my brother or our fields."

"Father?" said Simon sternly. "You should send Jude back to Nazareth tomorrow."

Father looked up at him. "Why?"

"If Herod comes looking for you, and you're not here, he'll go to Nazareth. We can protect Uncle Clopas and Aunt Miriam if we send Jude back. Perhaps he can make up a story, saying that you all died while trying to cross the Jordan. It could stop Herod from pursuing things further, and it would help the Pharisees and Sadducees forget about you."

Jude stood up. "I like this plan. I can take care of our farm and help Clopas and Simeon carry on our business. And I can marry Leah, if she'll still have me."

Father put a hand on Jude's shoulder. "I'm sure she will, son."

"I'm sorry, Mary," Father said. The twinkle in his eyes had returned, but I could tell he worried about her.

"I'll miss Jude," she said.

"I know," Father said with a smile. "We all will—"

Father's tender words were interrupted by the sound of hoof beats.

"Nicodemus said we had two or three days," I said. "Who could that be?"

We stood still. Simon took his sons to his wife then went to answer the door. "Who calls on this house?" he said in a stern voice.

"We have come to see the newborn son of Joseph bar Jacob," said a scratchy voice.

Simon looked to Jude and me. "We're prepared to fight, Father," he whispered.

Father held up his hand. "Wait, Simon. Not yet."

Simon cleared his throat. "Who sends these visitors to this house?"

"We carry humble greetings from the king of Judea," said the voice from the other side. The words were broken but in our native language.

Why would the visitors identify themselves as messengers from Herod? This puzzled Father and Simon too. A messenger for the king typically would disguise the nature of his business and the master he served. Herod had so many enemies that his messengers were often executed and their bodies sent back to his palace.

Jude walked across the room to stand next to Mary and the baby. Father shook his head and tugged at his ear.

"What do we do?" Simon asked.

"I guess we let them in," said Father. "We have nowhere to go. The element of surprise is theirs."

Simon unlatched the door and opened it slowly. Three men stood there. Behind them were three servant boys about my age, dressed in plain tunics. The men wore magnificent fur robes, one dyed in a dark emerald green, another in a dark burgundy, and the last in dark purple. The stitching on the robes appeared to be gold, and the patterns that crisscrossed the front and back glittered in the sunlight. Such clothing was more splendid than anything I had ever seen, but the robes looked heavy and uncomfortable.

Three beasts also stood outside of Simon's home, drawing unwanted attention. They were enormous camels with humps along their backs. Each beast was fitted with leather reins, blankets that matched the riders' robes, and a leather seat. I gazed at these animals with such wonder that I forgot about my fear.

Finally Simon spoke. "Do you wish to come in?"

"We do," said the man in the emerald robe.

Before they crossed the threshold of Simon's house, the servants helped the men remove their outer robes and leather boots. A servant handed each of the men a yellow sash, which was worn like a belt across the middle of their plain tunics. The man who had worn the emerald robe approached first. His white hair was close shaven, but his white beard was thick and curly. He had a small growth on the side of his nose, and dark moles covered one side of his neck. He walked through the door and stood in the middle of the room.

"I am Anwar," said the man.

"Who are the rest of these people?" Father asked.

"They are my assistants. The man who wears the burgundy robe is Bashshar. The one who wears the violet robe is Mukhtar."

Anwar's assistants looked much older than him. Their bodies were thin, their hair and beards stringy, and the skin on their hands appeared worn and wrinkled from hard labor.

"I am an astrologer and a ruler," said Anwar. His words came slowly, for he didn't speak our language well. "My kingdom is far from Judea, hundreds of miles east of the Jordan."

"I am Joseph bar Jacob," said Father. "These are my sons, Simon, Jude, and James. This is Simon's wife, Adina, and my wife, Mary."

Mary held the baby close to her chest, his face hidden from view.

Anwar motioned for the servants to leave the house. "We're sorry for troubling you, Joseph bar Jacob. We only wish to see the child."

Father motioned for Mary to stand, but Anwar shook his head quickly. "No, no," said Anwar. "With your permission we shall go to the mother and the child. We don't wish for the child or mother to be uncomfortable."

Jude stared at me. I stared at Simon. We were looking for signs from the other, signaling the need for attack. Father looked only at our visitors and at Mary.

Simon whispered to me in a low voice, "I don't understand. Why did Father let these men into my home?"

"I don't know," I replied, "but he must have a good reason."

Father followed the three strange men back to where Mary sat reclined on cushions.

Jude walked over to me and whispered, "Their tunics are thin. I see no hidden knives or weapons."

"Stay here and keep watch over the servants," I said.

As I approached the cushioned area where Mary sat, the three men knelt on the floor in front of her.

"Mary, show them Jesus's face," Father said.

Mary glanced at me as if to say, "Be on guard." I slowly closed and opened my hands, ready to jump on any one of them. All three men appeared to inhale at the same time as Mary slowly pulled the child away from her chest. My baby brother's eyes were open, and they shone like stars. He lay perfectly still, staring at the old men kneeling before him.

"May I touch his hand?" asked Anwar.

Father looked at me then at Mary. We nodded. Mary loosened the cloth wrappings from around my brother's arms, exposing his arms, hands, and chest. As Anwar leaned in, he lifted his hand slowly, extending his index finger. Jesus arched his neck, looked at the old bony finger moving toward his hand, and reached out to grab it.

All three men gasped in delight. "Did you see that?" Soft giggling echoed between them, followed by pleasant smiles.

Mary cleared her throat and said in a gentle voice, "Would anyone like to hold him?"

One of the men held up his hand and nodded. "Me?" The man grinned from ear to ear and kept pointing to himself. "Me?"

It was Mukhtar. Of all the men, he looked the oldest, his brown wrinkly skin barely clinging to the form of his hand. His fingernails were dirty, and every so often, he opened his mouth and stuck out his tongue, as if gagging on a piece of food. He kept motioning to himself. "Me? Me?"

Whatever fear filled Mary's heart dried up like a single drop of water in the desert sand. She nodded at the old man as if he were a child asking for something sweet and then said, "Join your hands and make a circle with your arms."

Anwar showed the man what Mary meant, and when he had figured it out, she placed my brother there. The three men surrounded Mukhtar and looked at Jesus, who lay as still as could be. My brothers continued to stand vigilant, while the rest of us marveled at the curious travelers.

After a long moment of quiet, Father spoke. "What brings you to this house?"

With a smile still on his face, Anwar stood and walked over to Father. "The child," he said. "The shepherds told the priests of the bright light in the sky, the voices in the heavens, and the *malach* who announced that a savior had been born."

"How did you find us?" Father asked.

"We were with Herod when the priest told him about the child."

"Which priest?" Father asked.

"The high priest, Joazar."

Simon walked away from the door and stood in front of Anwar. "How did you know where to look?"

"I only had to inquire at the local synagogue. Your rabbi greeted me. We said we only wanted to come and worship the newborn savior."

Father ran his hand through his hair and looked over at the two astrologers who were still taking turns holding my brother. Then he looked at Anwar and smiled. "The baby will need to nurse and sleep soon. If you wish to hold him again, you must do so now."

Father walked over to Adina. The boys were playing with pieces of wood on the floor and stopped to watch while he spoke. "I need to speak with Simon, James, and Jude in private. Can you keep alert while we go outside?"

Adina nodded. "Father Joseph, will we be all right?"

He ignored her question and rubbed the back of his hand along her cheek. "You are such a good wife and mother." He stood and walked over to Mary and the astrologers. "My sons and I need to fill the water jars in preparation for our evening meal. Will you stay and have something to eat with us?"

"Most certainly," said Anwar. "Please, have my servants help you."

Father motioned for my brothers and me to step outside. Once the door closed behind us, he called out to the servants standing beside the beasts with humps.

Father pointed to a row of tall water jars along the side of Simon's house. "Servants of Anwar, please fill these jars with water from the city's well. The well is just down this street." The servants moved quickly, and when they had left, Father turned to speak with us. "Mary and I can't stay here any longer. Our entire family has been betrayed. Herod knows where to find us. It will only be a matter of time before his soldiers come."

"How long?" I asked.

"As soon as the astrologers return to Herod's palace in Jerusalem, they'll report on what they saw here today," said Father. "We must convince them to stay long into the evening or spend the night. We can entertain them, fill them up on wine, and let them sleep. That way you and I will have time to pack for our journey to Egypt, and Jude can prepare for his trip back to Nazareth."

"Why Egypt, Father?" asked Simon. "You could hide in the hills or go east."

Father shook his head. "Egypt is out of Herod's jurisdiction. Herod won't stop searching Judea until Mary, Jesus, and I are dead. The astrologers were sent as witnesses to the birth of Jesus. They now have positive proof that he exists."

"The roads to Egypt are long and treacherous, Father. The journey will take weeks," said Simon. "Herod will likely send his assassins after you."

"There is a place in Egypt where Jews are safe," Father explained. "It's also a place where Jesus can be schooled in reading, writing, and oration. I have to try, Simon. I can't stay here. The risk is too great. Everything we have suffered up to this point will be for nothing. I must try."

"How long will we be gone?" I asked softly.

"As long as Herod is king, James. It may be several years. That's why Jude must return to Nazareth to help Uncle Clopas."

We saw the servants walking slowly down the street, water splashing out of the jars.

"Have them hitch the mules and those other smelly beasts behind the house," said Simon. "If you're leaving tomorrow, be sure to feed and water your own mule first."

Father wrapped his arms around his sons and pulled us in together. He hugged us tightly and mumbled a prayer for our safety. As we headed back to the house, I spotted Nicodemus running toward us.

CHAPTER THIRTY-THREE

"This can't be good," Father mumbled.

The four of us waited for the scribe to reach the house.

"Nicodemus," Father began, "if this is about the strange astrologers in my son's home, you're a little late with your news."

The scribe held up his hand. He desperately wanted to say something but had trouble catching his breath.

"Jude, fetch Nicodemus some water." Father looked at the man who was now hunched over, struggling to breathe.

Jude returned with a cupful of water, and the scribe finished it all.

"You want to tell me what this is about?" Father asked.

"Herod," said the scribe, still out of breath. "Herod is coming to kill the child tonight."

"That can't be!" shouted Simon. "The astrologers are still here!"

"They're supposed to return tonight," Nicodemus said. "Once the astrologers confirm that they have seen your son, the soldiers will be dispatched on mounts. Joseph, you must get Mary and the baby out of Bethlehem—now."

"Jesus," Father said. "My son's name is Jesus. You can call him by his name, Nicodemus."

The scribe bent over once more to catch his breath then threw up his arms in disgust. "Jesus! There, are you happy?"

"You should leave," Father said. "I'm tired of your games."

"I can't go," Nicodemus said quietly. "I must warn the astrologers. They are guests of the king, but they will be killed once they report what have seen."

"Killed?" Father exclaimed.

"They are from lands far away, Joseph." Nicodemus, still out of breath, labored through his words. "Their armies are small. They invest their efforts in diplomacy rather than force. If Herod kills them, they'll send ambassadors. Herod will just keep killing them until they give up. These men mean nothing to him."

We heard a loud voice shouting from the house. "Anwar! Anwar!" We turned around to see Bashshar standing several feet away from us, close enough to hear our entire conversation. Both Anwar and Mukhtar appeared in the doorway.

Anwar held a finger to his lips. "The baby has finished nursing and is sleeping. We must be quiet."

Bashshar began to speak in a language foreign to all of us, except the scribe. From the man's body language, I assumed he was relaying the scribe's news. When he finished, Anwar stared at Nicodemus.

"Is this true, scribe?" Anwar asked in an angry voice.

Nicodemus nodded. "It is."

"We were tricked!" shouted Anwar. "All your king's talk of peace and trade—then to use us to decipher your Hebrew prophecies..."

"You are a traitor to us!" Bashshar shouted angrily.

Nicodemus's panicked face turned to Father. "Joseph, I'm only trying to help. I would be killed if they knew I gave you this information."

There was a long period of silence as eight men stood in fear. The shouting and the deception, the talk of murder—it reminded me once again of the day I had stood with my family at the top of the cliff to watch a young woman receive the ultimate punishment; the day of the long procession; the day my father had tossed a silver coin to a child beggar in the street. Less than a month had passed since I had spewed forth the word *rachamim* through bloody, swollen lips. I looked my father in the eyes, and as those seconds passed, so did the memories of this past year.

"Mercy," I mumbled.

Father nodded.

"Let's take this matter out of the street and into my home," said Simon. "It's getting dark."

Father relayed the news from Nicodemus to the servants and wives. "We must prepare to leave," he said. "Mary and Adina, it's a long trip to Egypt. Can you muster the strength to prepare our provisions?"

Both women appeared ready to collapse from the weight of the news. Neither said a word, but they nodded.

"Our lives depend on our having adequate food, water, and clothing," said Father. Then he repeated, "Can you do this?"

Mary stood. "Yes, Joseph. We will manage. How soon will we leave?"

"As soon as we are ready," replied Father. He looked at Simon and me. "Prepare the mules and cart. And pack all of Simon's tools. We will need to perform our trade if we are to survive."

"Yes, Father," I said.

"Prepare a mule for Jude as well, for his return trip."

"I can move faster on foot," Jude insisted. "Please, Father, take the extra mule. You may need it."

Father thought about this for a minute. "Very well, but you must take a sling bag so you can carry plenty of food and water." He looked over at Adina, who stood and nodded. Then he turned to Nicodemus. "Will you accompany my son back to Nazareth?"

"I can assure his safety," said Nicodemus. "I will travel with him."

After Father distributed the tasks, he turned to Anwar. "Is it possible that you and your assistants and servants would want to travel with us?"

Anwar shook his head. "No, Joseph. If we leave together, it will be easier for the Romans to find you. Our beasts leave very distinctive tracks. We always keep plenty of provisions packed on our camels. We will leave Bethlehem right away, but we won't follow your course. However, we would very much like to help you and your family. Please tell us what we can do."

Within minutes Father had the servants organizing and packing Simon and Adina's belongings, including our tableware, cups, plates, utensils, cushions, and other various items we would need to establish a home in Egypt.

"Leave the furniture for the soldiers to break and burn," Father ordered. Then he turned to me and said, "Make sure Jude takes the coins we received from Marcus. I don't want to spend Roman money in Egypt. The Romans aren't trusted there, and it might cause unwanted suspicion. I left Mary's dowry with Clopas. Between the gold coins from Marcus and the silver from the Temple, they'll have enough money to replace the cart and our masonry and carpentry tools, and pay their taxes."

I did what Father asked. As the food, water pouches, clothing, blankets, and towels were sorted, Father, Anwar, Bashshar, and Mukhtar organized the items by size and necessity. These were packed in Simon's cart and on our mules. Soon the house was nearly empty, and our voices echoed off the stone walls.

Once the cart and mules were loaded, father hitched the stronger of the two to the single-axle cart. Mary and Adina would need to take turns carrying the baby and Adina's small children, for there was no room for riders in the cart or on the mules. The men would each carry a sling bag filled with provisions.

By the time we finished preparations, the astrologers were ready to leave too. With heavy hearts, Simon, Adina, and their two boys walked through their house one last time. Father motioned for Mary and me to join him outside. After several minutes Simon and his family appeared with us.

"Nicodemus," said Father, "if for any reason you believe my family in Nazareth is in danger, send them to Egypt."

"Herod won't bother your extended family, Joseph," Nicodemus assured him. "And I'll make sure Jude reaches Nazareth safely."

Jude hugged each of us and said good-bye. With Mary he lingered a little longer.

"You will make a fine husband and father, Jude," Mary said tearfully. "When I see you next, I want to see a child hanging from each hand and foot."

Jude laughed. He hugged Mary one last time before walking over to me. "You saved my life," he said.

"It didn't need saving," I replied.

When Jude went to say good-bye to Father, Father wept. "I don't want to lose my son," he whispered to Jude.

"I don't want to lose my father," Jude whispered back.

They hugged for a second time and wiped their noses on the sleeves of their tunics.

"Take care of Leah first, and if God wills it, your children—then the farm and then your trade," Father said. "Lean on Ezra when you're lonely or afraid. He will be like a father to you when you need me."

Jude nodded then turned to Nicodemus. "We must go."

Nicodemus walked up to Father. "I'm so sorry for you and your family, Joseph."

Father looked into the scribe's face. "I remember the day you came to Marcus's house, the day you asked me to marry a young woman who had been dedicated to God."

"Yes," said the scribe. "I remember it too."

Father looked at Mary, who was holding my brother. "If my duty to God is to protect this child and this woman," he said, "I will perform that duty with all of my heart." Then he shook Nicodemus's hand.

"Come. We must go," said Jude.

Together with the astrologers, we watched as the shadows of Jude and the scribe faded into the cool air of a dark night.

Anwar approached Father. He and his assistants were wearing their robes again, but they also wore matching headdresses made with fine silks and gold thread. In the moonlight the men looked intimidating, and their robes made a swishing sound as they walked. Bashshar and Mukhtar approached each of us, gave us a hug, and bowed. When they reached Mary, they got down on one knee, paused for a moment, then stood. The servants helped Bashshar and Mukhtar mount the great beasts with humps, and once seated, the humble assistants appeared regal in their robes and headdresses.

Anwar turned to Father and hugged him. "Joseph bar Jacob, you are one of the bravest men I have ever known—"

His words were cut short by the sounds of clopping hooves and the squeaky cart axle, signaling that our family was ready to depart. I watched as my family, with their two mules and small cart, lined up before the astrologers, with their three magnificent beasts, long robes, two mules, and three servants.

Anwar called out to one of the servants in his own language. "Please excuse me for a minute, Joseph," he said.

He leaned in and whispered something to the servant, who then dashed off immediately. I heard him rustling through one of the packs. When the servant returned, he was carrying three bulging sacks made of silk. Each sack was in a color that matched the colors of the robes. The astrologers moved their beasts closer to where Father stood so they could watch Anwar.

"In our country," Anwar began, "it is customary that when a guest receives another person into their home, that guest must offer some sort of payment in return for the hospitality shown. However, our gifts could never repay you for the joy we experienced after meeting your family. Please accept our gifts not only as repayment for your hospitality but also to honor the birth of this child."

The emerald bag was presented to Simon. Anwar shook the bag, and it made a sound like pebbles crashing against one another.

When Simon opened it, he gasped. "Gemstones," he said. "Hundreds of them."

"You could trade them for tools or land or food," said Anwar.

"Thank you," Simon said softly. "I am honored."

"Yes, Simon, I know you are," Anwar said with a smile. Then he came to me. "You have a servant's heart, young man. You honor your father with your presence, and you honor those around you by serving them." From the burgundy bag came a beautiful glass jug, stopped with a thick cork and a metal chain. Anwar handed the jug to me and said, "Open it."

I took the jug from his hands and pulled the cork out of the top and let it hang from the chain.

"Smell it," Anwar said with a grin.

The top of the jug barely had passed my nose when it filled all my senses with a marvelous scent I can only describe as a field full of flowers. It was the most beautiful-smelling oil I had ever known.

"This is a very special oil, James," said Anwar. "Do you know what it is?"

I shook my head.

"It is a type of oil used by those who are wealthy, to scent their bodies. The plant used to make this oil is found only in my country. If you divide this into smaller jars, you could trade each one for a fortune in coins or goods."

Anwar approached Father with the last bag, the bag of royal purple. It was a bag twice the size of the bag Marcus had handed my father more than a year ago, and it too was filled with coins.

"Joseph, in order to evade Herod, you'll need to keep moving. To do so you may need to pay bribes, tolls, taxes, and provisions." Father acted as if the heavy bag wasn't even there. "I'm certain we can manage on our own," he said.

Anwar's smile turned into a slight frown. "You can accept the gift of this child as a gift from your God, but you can't accept my gift as a gift from your God? How will you buy food in a week? How will you afford lodging or tools for your trade? Think about this child. As he grows, will you not want the best teachers or the best physicians? If God truly has sent him as the savior, will you spare expense?"

Father shook his head. "I will give this boy and his mother everything I can provide."

"The journey to Egypt is long, Joseph. The need for build-ers and carpenters is not as strong there as it is in Judea. Fertile land is difficult for foreigners to come by. Your trade may not help you there, and you may not be able to farm. Please accept this gift as a gift from your God, for your family and this child. You have worked so hard to please God—now let God help you."

Father swallowed hard. He looked at the dark-purple bag in Anwar's outstretched hand and slowly reached out to take it. Anwar placed the bag in my father's hand and stepped away. He bowed once, turned around, and walked toward one of the humped beasts. After a servant helped him on his mount, Anwar turned the beast to face our family.

"To the family of Joseph bar Jacob," he called out. "May your God continue to go before you."

The beasts turned around to follow Anwar as he led the group east. We watched them until the dark night swallowed them up.

"That way is the desert," Simon said softly. "How do they know where they are going?"

"They're astrologers," Father said with a smile. "They rely on the stars in the night sky to tell them where to go."

I turned around and saw Mary to my right, standing by the cart, holding Jesus. He was wrapped in the cloth scraps from days ago, those cut from the old shepherd-priest's tunic at Migdal Eder.

Father motioned for us to follow. "Let us leave."

We moved swiftly but carefully, for it was night, placing each foot in front of the other with great care. Father walked ahead of me, leading the mule by the bit. The wooden cart creaked. We traveled several miles before we reached the top of the hill that overlooked the valley where Bethlehem stood. It had been one of Father's favorite places to visit when he was a child. As our family prepared to rest, I saw a small speck of light in the distance.

"Wait!" Father said sternly. He looked carefully at the dark valley and the light that shone brighter than any other part of the city. "Don't unpack anything else!"

"Do you hear that?" Mary asked quietly.

Simon asked his boys to stop talking while the rest of us listened. From the distance we heard awful sounds, like thousands of voices wailing in the night. Father stared at the bright speck for another minute then turned to face us.

"Herod's men have set fire to Bethlehem."

We stared in horror as we watched the city suffer, their screams echoing through the valley.

"Herod turned his rage on the people of Bethlehem," said Father. He took a breath and wiped the heel of his hand across his eyes. "Repack everything, and get ready to move. The soldiers won't be far behind."

Night wrapped its cloak of darkness around my family. In the distance, I saw Father leading the mule and cart. Simon carried provision packs and walked with his two sons. Adina kept both of her daughters close and Mary held Jesus. I turned around to look at Bethlehem one more time. The fire had grown larger. I lifted my eyes to the sky and gave thanks for my family's safety. When I turned back, I saw my baby brother lying in Mary's arms.

He was sleeping peacefully.

ACKNOWLEDGMENTS

After I'd spent years penning articles for pay, my wife had the foresight and wisdom to push me into writing fiction. I completed this project because of her help, love, and encouragement. She is my best friend, a patient wife, and a devoted mother. I am also grateful to my daughters for their inspiration, fantastic questions, and profound awe and wonder of the world. I am blessed in more ways than I can count.

My mother, Tippi Flerlage, and my aunt, Karen Wuenstel, comprised my first audience. They suffered through those first years, wrestling with some nasty drafts of my first works, long before this project ever started. I am indebted to them for their ongoing love, support, and constructive criticism.

The conversations Joseph has with James symbolize the thoughtful, painstaking conversations I have had with my own father, Jim Flerlage. And like Joseph, my father looks to the divine for guidance and support. He is a positive role model in so many ways, but as I look back, I realize what made the difference were three things: 1) he told me he was proud of me; 2) he told me he loved me; and 3) I knew I was unconditionally accepted for who I was as a human being. I can't think of greater gifts a father can bestow on a son.

The childhood relationship between James and Jude is reflective of the childhood relationship I had with my brother, Ryan Flerlage. Though miles separate us, I always know that I can count on him for anything and everything. Just as Jude was to James, my brother is a hero to me.

Professionally speaking, I would like to thank my editor, Stephen (Steve) Parolini, and author Erin Healy, for introducing me to Steve. I'm grateful for Steve's pragmatic approach to the writing craft and the publishing industry, but I'm also blessed to have him as a mentor and friend. I also would like to thank my cousin, author Irene Hannon, for sharing her knowledge and wisdom about the publishing industry. In addition I want to thank my first fiction editor, Tim McNeill, for his crash course in creative fiction and his relentless support of me and my craft. I am also indebted to my Amazon editor, Angela, and the publishing professionals at Amazon. They helped to make this book possible.

I was blessed with outstanding teachers and professors who happened to love teaching as well as writing. I'm grateful that they chose teaching as their profession.

My brother-in-law, Mike Theye, "happened upon" the first few chapters of this novel as I was messing around with the early stages of this book. At the time I didn't think of moving from writing commercial suspense to historical fiction. Mike championed this book for years; this novel would still be my personal research project if it hadn't been for his constant pestering and unwavering support. Consequently the experience also taught me never to leave my rough drafts in another person's car.

I spent more than five years researching *Before Bethlehem*. I purchased dozens of books and reviewed hundreds of publications. For me to wade through all this research and make sense of it all, I needed gallons of strong coffee and a patient, knowledgeable confidante. I am grateful to my friend and pastor, Fr. Darren Elin, for his spiritual direction, as well as his knowledge of biblical criticism, history, and anthropology. Fr. Elin not only helped me during my research but also served as a sounding board for all things biblical, spiritual, and theological. I am grateful for his friendship, spiritual leadership, and pastoral guidance.

Finally I would like to thank a small, handpicked group of readers who volunteered to serve as my first audience for this project: Judy Bowers, Kristin Crowley, Jim D'Wolf III, Rev. R.S. Darren Elin, Jim and Tippi Flerlage, Rev. Mary Laymon, Tom and Karen Long, Jay and Abby Messner, Tonia Miller, Patti Normile, Dee Sawyer, Michael Theye, Terry and Karen Theye, Vern Thomas, Rev. Marshall Wiseman, and Karen Wuenstel. I am grateful for the time you took out of your busy lives to help me hone my craft.

GROUP DISCUSSION GUIDE

The complimentary discussion guide included with *Before Bethlehem* is intended for all audiences, and should help readers foster meaningful conversations regardless of race, sex, age, ethnicity or religion. The questions are worded in a way that allows those who have not read the book to participate. The guide is divided into four separate parts, by chapter sections, to accommodate a four-session format. For a single session format, pick one or two questions from each section and continue with the others as time allows. Readers are encouraged to reflect on the characters' questions throughout the book, and when possible, come up with their own. (Christian readers may download a complimentary **Before Bethlehem Discussion Guide for Christian Audiences** by visiting www.beforebethlehem.com.) Share warmly, show respect and have fun.

SECTION 1: PROLOGUE – CHAPTER 9

1. Joseph recognizes and reacts to a group of impoverished children. How can we teach and/or demonstrate acts of charity and mercy to our children and loved ones?

2. Joseph explains to James the hardships that illegitimate children face in their society and the price they pay for being outcasts. Why is it important to have conversations about social concerns and injustices with our children and loved ones?

3. Joseph and Clopas disagree on the methods for teaching their older children about peace. What types of conversations would you have with your children about peace and how would you go about teaching them?

4. James remarks about the loss of his mother when he was young. In the temporary or extended absence of parents or family, who cared for you, and in what ways were they a positive impact to your life?

5. Prince Antipas demonstrates his authority over Joseph through fear and aggression. How do you respond to people who have authority over you? How do you respond to aggressive people? How do you handle fear? How would you teach your children to respond?

6. Marcus clearly seeks to right the wrongs he has committed against Joseph and his family. Think of a time when you were wronged by a friend, family member or coworker. Was the situation resolved

in positive way? Have you ever acted with good intentions, only to have them backfire? How did you resolve the situation?

7. Joseph goes out of his way to confront Nicodemus about the execution of the young woman. How do you confront a difficult problem with another person in a positive way? What can we teach our children about confrontation?

8. Nicodemus tries to sweep the matter of the young woman's execution "under the rug." What are the dangers of conflict avoidance? Why do we sometimes try to hide the truth? What are the repercussions to our relationships? In what ways can these behaviors hurt our children and loved ones?

9. Marcus offers Joseph and Clopas both an apology and restitution. How important is an apology? How do we say "I'm sorry" with humility? How do we accept an apology? How can we extend forgiveness with dignity? How do simple acts of restitution help to rebuild trust in a relationship?

10. Joseph, Clopas and James derive much peace and satisfaction from being in the fields. Do you have a place like this in your own life? Do you share it with loved ones? Why is it important to go to these places?

SECTION 2: CHAPTER 10 – CHAPTER 17

1. Joseph demonstrates radical inclusivity by including Miriam in their discussions, to the point that it makes Nicodemus uncomfortable. Where in your life have you witnessed radical inclusiveness? Have you ever included someone who made others uncomfortable? How can we teach our children and others to be inclusive?

2. Clopas is genuinely concerned for his brother, yet his advice tends to be ignored. Why do we sometimes ignore the advice of loved ones, even to our own detriment? How do we respond when our advice is ignored or rejected?

3. As Joseph and James travel along the Jordan, Joseph interacts with his son by doing and teaching. Do you feel that parents do enough to make time for their children? In what ways can parents be intentional about interacting with their children?

4. Joseph tells James that his work helps to keep him centered on what is important. Do you find tangible meaning in your work? Does your work life help to keep you centered on what is important? How can we improve the lives of others through the work we do? How can we add meaning to our work if little exists? Why is it important to do so?

5. Joseph takes James on a magnificent trip to Jerusalem. If cost were not an issue, where would you want to take your children (or loved ones) on a trip, and why? What other ways might we instill a sense of awe and wonder in our children?

6. Because he carried the seal of Prince Antipas, Joseph was judged "unclean" by Temple authorities. What things do we carry that may cause others to judge us unfairly? How should we deal with these situations when they happen to others?

7. Joseph takes great care to pass along pieces of family history to James. Which pieces of your family story will you pass along and why?

8. Joseph and James are clearly unwelcomed by the servants in the high priest's home. Think of situation when you didn't feel welcome. How did you handle yourself? What did you take away from the experience?

9. Joseph is upset by the way the servants are treating Mary. What can be done to ensure the fair and just treatment of women? What example should men set for their children, friends, and family?

10. Mary struggles with whether or not to trust Joseph. Think of a time when you found trust difficult? How did you overcome the situation? What do you

do, by your actions, to gain and sustain trust from others?

SECTION 3: CHAPTER 18 – CHAPTER 25

1. Jude risks his life for his family. Have you, or someone you know, risked their life or reputation for another human being? What insights from the experience would others find helpful? Share if you are able.

2. With his life at stake and his livelihood threatened, Joseph boldly faces a painful period in his family's life. Think of a painful situation where this happened with your immediate or extended family. How did you get through it? What lessons were learned? What would you want your children or loved ones to learn from the experience?

3. When James, Jude and Simeon are confronted by extreme violence, they have their fathers to turn to for guidance. After the terrorist attacks on 9/11, Fred Rogers delivered his famous "look for the helpers" monologue to help grownups discuss the tragedy with children. What else can parents and caregivers do to prepare for these conversations, should they be necessary?

4. After the unfair judgments against Jude and Mary, Joseph's entire family must reconcile with one another. How can families prepare themselves in

ways that will help them to avoid bitterness? What can families do to show mercy and forgiveness to one another during exceptionally difficult times?

5. Jude and Mary are subject to false accusations. Think of a situation where you, or someone you know, were falsely accused of something serious. How did you (or the other person) react? How does the experience of that situation guide your thoughts and actions today?

6. Clopas' unfounded conclusions about Jude and Mary eventually lead him to asking the entire village for forgiveness. Have you ever had to ask someone else for forgiveness? How would you teach your children or others how to do it?

7. Mary comes close to losing her life. Have you, or someone you loved, come close to death? How did the experience change you (or them)? What insights about the experience could you use to help others?

SECTION 4: CHAPTER 26 – CHAPTER 33

1. Mary is quite vocal about her fears and concerns. How do you cope with anxiety? Is it healthy? With whom can you share your fears and concerns? How would you teach your children how to cope?

2. Joseph explains his rationale for using the coins he received from Marcus. Why is it important to man-

age the financial, material and natural resources that are entrusted to us? How can we set an example for our children, families, friends, and neighbors?

3. Joseph loses his cherished cart in the Jordan River. When is it in our best interest to let go of things or memories? Why is "letting go" an important yet difficult process? What can we do to make it a healthy part of the human experience?

4. After the storm, Joseph, Jude, James and Mary find a moment of peace. Describe a "stormy" episode in your life journey and the moment you knew when things would be all right. How did you know? What did you learn?

5. Joseph declares his choice to accept Mary and her child. With all of the mundane choices we face each day, is it possible that humanity takes for granted its power to choose? When faced with a difficult decision, what methods do you employ to help you make the best choice? How do we teach our children responsible decision-making?

6. Both Joseph and Levi offer insights into their vocations. If you, or someone you know, works in a trusted vocation (e.g. paramedic, firefighter, police officer, soldier, clergy, etc.), describe how and why you/they chose this profession. How do you handle the trust and responsibility? What are the rewards and sacrifices?

7. Nicodemus is forced to break bad news to Joseph and his family. Have you ever had to deliver bad news? How did you find the strength to do it? What did the experience teach you? What could others learn from your experience?

8. The astrologers are essentially strangers to Joseph and his family. Think of a time when a stranger made a difference in your life. Describe why it was so meaningful. When have you been the stranger making a difference in someone else's life?

9. Discuss how *Before Bethlehem* may or may not have shaped your attitudes about friends, relationships, mercy and forgiveness. What parts of the story were the most meaningful? What parts did you struggle through? Explain.

About the Author

James Flerlage is an experienced writer, researcher and speaker. His articles have appeared in national and international magazines and in syndicated business and technology publications.

Among other credentials, he holds a master's in business administration, a graduate certificate in professional writing, and is a graduate of Sewanee University's Education for Ministry program.

Flerlage is happily married, the proud father of two daughters, and active in his church and community. In his spare time, he enjoys drumming, fishing and reading. He is currently working on his next novel.

He may be reached at jamesflerlage@beforebethlehem.com.

46814346R00177

Made in the USA
Lexington, KY
17 November 2015